Scared to

By Kerena

Also By Kerena Swan

Dying To See You

Chapter 1

The darkness outside has turned the window into a mirror, reflecting back the bright train carriage and the empty blue seats that surround me. Empty, that is, except for the older man with messy grey hair and unshaven chin. He might have started the day as a smartly dressed businessman, for all I know, but now he resembles a tramp. A drunk and volatile tramp. He's watching me. I avoid eye contact and sit with my legs tensed, ready to move away if I have to. He's quiet now but I heard him shouting and swearing earlier at a teenager squeezing past him to get off the train. The older guy had sat, uninvited, next to the young lad and drunkenly regaled him with stories, his agitation increasing as the young lad ignored him and looked out of the window. He's got a quick temper and he's not rational. The last passenger to alight had given me a pitying and almost apologetic look as he got off.

It's just me and the scary guy now.

He grabs the seat in front of him and my heartbeat quickens as he lurches unsteadily to his feet and moves nearer. Only one row nearer, thankfully, but perhaps he's making his way to me in fits and starts. I've made a mistake in choosing a seat with a table. It means there are spaces facing me and any moment now he might–

I jump as another train flashes past, making the windows bang and rattle. Spooked, I make another mistake by catching the man's eyes on me as I turn away from the noise.

'Hello beautiful,' he says, his words slurred by alcohol. He waves his can of lager, his middle finger lifted towards me. 'What's a lovely young girl like you doing all alone?'

I hardly think thirty-two is young but I suppose it might be from his perspective. He looks to be in his mid-sixties and has probably stayed too long at his office retirement party. He's wearing a crumpled, cheap suit jacket and half his dinner down the front of his shirt. The remains of a curry, judging by the yellow and brown hues.

He leans forward to peer more closely at me and I shrink back into my seat.

'Look at you with your shiny hair and big grey eyes. Gorgeous.' His wet tongue flicks over his lips, turning them into fat, shiny slugs.

I suppress a shudder and look away. I wish I was curled up on the sofa at home with Reuben, winding my finger into one of his blond curls, his soft lips kissing my cheek. I wish I was in my cosy pyjamas and slippers with a milky drink in my hand and a drama to watch on the television. Instead, I'm trapped in a draughty train carriage with a worrying stranger. I wind a single hair around my forefinger and pull on it – just hard enough to feel it through my scalp – but stop myself before I tug it out. Crikey, it's a long time since I've been anxious enough to pluck my hair out, a weird habit I'd started on my first day at school and one I've battled with ever since.

'Don't look so scared! I won't eat you.' The old guy is persistent, his eyes fixed on me. 'I'd just like to know you better.' His laugh exposes stained bottom teeth that have toppled sideways in his gums.

I turn to the window again, my heart hammering in my chest, and briefly cup my hands around my eyes to shut out the brightness of the carriage lights and the image of him. Outside, dark shapes rush past like spectres in the night. Am I nearing my stop? Maybe I should move along to the next carriage. He might follow me though, and I don't want to inflame him. Some men enjoy the chase.

The train slows and lights shine onto a deserted platform. I peer at the name of the station. Luton Airport Parkway. Just two more stops to go until Leagrave, thank God. It's only the end of August but I feel cold. I pull my cardigan tighter around me. The train moves off again and I lift my bag strap over my head and across my chest to keep it secure when I rush off the train. I see a loose hair on my blouse and brush it off. Did I pull it out after all? *Soon be home,* I tell myself. All I have to do is get through the station and over the footbridge to where Reuben will be patiently waiting to take me home. I can easily outrun this alcohol-sodden old fool.

I look at my watch. Gone midnight. No wonder the train is so deserted. Kirsty knows I don't like travelling from London at this time of night and I feel a flash of anger towards her for putting me in this situation.

'Let's go and see Becca and Rachel for a couple of drinks,' she'd said this afternoon. 'Becca's got a new job and I want to hear all about it.'

'I don't want to be late back,' I'd said. I know it never is just a couple of drinks.

'Come on. You haven't seen them in ages. They're meeting up at a new pub and it won't take us long to get there. It'll be fun and I promise we won't be late.'

It was fun to start with but I was conscious of the time. As the evening wore on and they all became more giggly and stupid, I became more sober. After two glasses of prosecco I'd had enough and wanted to go home but I didn't want to break up the party and even less to travel back across East London alone. I really should be more assertive. But if I'd spoken out they'd have teased me, calling me a fun sponge and tried to coax me to drink more. And if Kirsty and I had left earlier I know the others would have been moaning about me after we'd gone. They'd probably have asked Kirsty not to bring me again. That would have been preferable to this, though. I look at the man in the window and my chest tightens as his reflection catches my eye. He grins and moves a row nearer.

Next time.

Next time I'll stand up for myself. Maybe. The fact is that I'm no Kirsty. She lives a glamorous, fast-paced life as a casting director for the fashion catwalks and is used to the busy, challenging environment of London. She has an air of self-assurance around her that seems to protect her like a force field.

'Bugger off, will you?' she'd say to the man, and he'd back away. I know I should try to emulate her but somehow I can't find the confidence or the aggression. The good manners instilled in me from an early age win every time and I worry that something even worse might happen. Being brought up by loving, adoptive parents was great but they were very protective of me. It's difficult not to see danger everywhere when your childhood has been spent being told *'Don't climb to the top because you might fall'* or *'Don't stay out after dark, you don't know what bad people are out there'* and *'We prefer your friends to stay here rather than you sleeping there'*. I think this anxiety might have instigated the hair-pulling. I can't blame them though. I suppose their overcautious parenting is understandable given that they lost their first three babies to miscarriages.

The train slows and I sneak another look at the man, hoping he'll get off at Luton. He doesn't. Instead he starts crooning a love song about me being the only girl in the world. I rub my damp palms on the rough fabric of the seat.

'You need to get out more, socialise a bit,' Kirsty had said. 'You're becoming a recluse.'

I accept her invites once a month or so because I enjoy her company and value our friendship. I don't want to be one of those people who neglects her friends once she settles down with a man. I've known Kirsty since we were children. I'd much rather stay at home though, challenging Reuben to a game of Scrabble.

The train reduces speed as it nears Leagrave and I stand up. *At last!* My nerves are shattered sitting here on the slowest train in the world with only a filthy drunkard for company.

'Ah, we're getting off at the same stop, my precious,' he says. 'Fancy a little nightcap somewhere before you go home?'

My heart sinks. The man stands too close behind me and staggers, grabbing a handrail, as the train judders to a standstill.

4

I press the button to open the door then leap out like a startled animal breaking from the undergrowth. The platform is totally deserted, dark shadows skulking beyond the pools of light. I hurry over to the stairs and sprint up, only to pause near the top. The footbridge runs at right angles to the steps and its high sides mean it isn't possible to see if anyone is using it until the corner is turned, so I need to make sure there's no mugger waiting to snatch my bag as happened to Mrs Coleman at the dry cleaners. I glance behind me to check the drunken man isn't catching me up, then peep around the corner. A man is approaching from the other side. Young, athletic, dark-skinned, his walk loose and easy… Is he a threat? Should I go forward or back? Reaching into my pocket for my keys, I slot one between my clammy fingers to use as a weapon if necessary.

Before the guy draws nearer, there's a flash of movement behind him. I've barely had a moment to process the fact that it's another man – young and hooded – before he's grabbed the arm of the first man and swung him around.

'Give me your phone, watch and cash or you get this. Your choice.'

Oh God, not just a mugger but a mugger with a knife. He's waving it in the black guy's face, the long silver blade catching in the light. I scream at the black man in my head. 'Give him what he wants!'

Instead, his body bristles with anger as though the knife were no more than a plastic toy he could swat aside with ease.

'Fuck off and get a job, you wasteman, or you'll get this,' he says. He holds up a fist and yanks the mugger's hood down, exposing flaming ginger hair, a white face and, oddly, a mangled ear with the top half missing. There's a push and a grapple then the black guy doubles over, staggering, one hand clutching his chest, the other grabbing at the mugger's sweatshirt. *Jesus, he's been stabbed.* I want to run back down the steps but my legs won't respond to my brain. The black guy slumps to the ground and the mugger leans over him to pull the knife out with a wet, sucking sound, then grabs the man's jacket and rummages for his wallet, knife poised to attack again.

'Stop it!' The voice is mine even though I had no desire to speak. The mugger looks up, surprise tightening swiftly to menace. *Oh no! Oh no!* My stomach lurches as though I'm in a plummeting lift as he walks towards me with deadly intent. I turn and run back down the stairs, hearing fast, heavy footsteps behind me. My throat, choked with fear, strangles my scream. I jump the last few stairs and throw myself at the figure stumbling along the platform.

'Hello, my lovely!' The unsteady man beams with delight and grabs me around the waist, swinging me around and trying to pull me into a waltz. 'Changed your mind, eh? The ladies always did find me irresistible.' He chuckles, then pulls back abruptly as I shout in his ear.

'He's got a knife! He stabbed someone.' I look up the flight of steps.

The mugger has paused halfway down, to take in the scene. His eyes lock with mine then, slowly, he drags a thumb across his throat before turning around and running back up the steps. I hear his feet thud across the bridge, echoing in the silence, the sound fading as he leaves the station.

'Who's got a knife?' The drunken man sways and turns to look towards the empty steps.

Five minutes ago I didn't wish to be within ten feet of this old soak but now I almost want him to keep hold of me and protect me. 'We need to call the police. And an ambulance. We need to see if the man's still alive,' I say, trying to breathe evenly.

The drunken man seems to be sobering a little. 'Let me take a look,' he says.

He makes his slow way up the steps with me right behind him. At the top he narrows his eyes, thrusts his head forward and peers around the corner. 'Jesus!' He straightens up, sobering rapidly now. 'Where's my phone?' He pats his pockets.

'I've got one.' I draw my phone from my bag and, with shaking fingers, eventually manage to call 999. It's hard to get my words out – hard to think rationally to describe what has happened as my mind tries to spiral away to safer territory. We approach the prone form on the ground, glancing nervously towards the steps to make sure the mugger isn't coming back, and hear a groan. A dark pool of blood is spreading across the floor.

'He's alive but he's bleeding,' I tell the operator, trying to stop my voice from wobbling, then give our location. I put the phone on loudspeaker, place it on the floor near to me and tell the man to take his jacket off to make a pillow. *What to do? What to do?* The operator is still talking and I try to follow her instructions. *Stay calm. You can do this, Tasha.* I roll the injured man onto his back and lift his clothing to expose the wound. Blood wells and shines and I can hear a bubbling noise as air escapes his lung.

'Have you got a credit card?' The emergency operator asks.

'Yes, yes!' I grab my bag and rummage through my purse for my credit card, pull off my soft cardigan and bunch it up, then press the Visa card and cardigan over the wound, making sure I've left a small gap for air to escape. It's strange how my first aid training is all coming back to me. I hadn't wanted the responsibility of being the office first aider but I'm glad I did the course now. I relay what I've done and the operator tells me I'm doing well. The drunken man watches, then, swaying slightly, wanders towards the exit.

'Don't go!' I say.

He stops and looks at me in surprise. 'I'm not going anywhere,' he says.

I hear a groan. 'It's okay,' I say, trying to reassure the guy on the ground. 'Help will be here soon.'

The transport police arrive within minutes, which surprises me, and an officer takes over from me while another leads me down the steps to a bench. I sink into it, my legs beginning to tremble with shock.

'The ambulance will be here soon,' he tells me. 'You've done really well and probably saved his life. Did you see what happened? Would you recognise the attacker again?'

I lift a shaky hand to brush hair out of my eyes and am shocked to see my fingers are covered with blood. I think of the mugger's ginger hair, white face and mangled ear. 'Yes, I definitely would.' I describe him to the officer, who makes a few notes.

'We'll need you to come to the station to give a proper statement and we'll need your clothes to run forensic tests on them,' he tells me.

I look at him in alarm.

'We'll check for fibres: we need to eliminate your contact with the victim.'

I nod. If it means they'll catch him quickly then I want to help all I can. Poor Reuben will be even later to bed but he'll understand the seriousness of the situation.

'Will I get them back?' I ask. I'm wearing my best outfit.

'I'm afraid not,' the police officer says. 'Would you want them back after what's happened?' He looks at me with a small frown.

I look down at my blouse and realise how much blood I have on me. I shudder.

'No, I guess not,' I say, ashamed I'd even asked.

My phone rings and Reuben's face flashes onto the screen. 'Tasha! Thank God. What's happening? The police and ambulance are here and they've cordoned off the area.'

'A man was stabbed. I saw it.' My voice catches and wobbles and I have to swallow before I can speak again. 'I'm with the police. Can you go and fetch me some clothes and meet me at the station? They need mine for testing.'

'Are you hurt?' he asks.

'No. Just scared.' I feel tears prickle but take a deep breath which seems to help.

'I'll be there as soon as I can. Everything will be okay. I love you, Tash,' he says and hangs up.

The officer is watching me. 'The other witness doesn't look too reliable to me,' he says. He inclines his head to the grubby man sitting on a bench nearby, legs outstretched before him, his head tipped back and his eyes shut as though he's sinking back into drunkenness.

'He saved me,' I say, 'but he didn't see anything. He was still on the platform.' I think of him swinging me around. 'He didn't even see the man when he came after me.' As we walk towards the exit and the waiting police car I pause and look back to see a police officer standing guard on the opposite platform. An officer dressed from head to foot in white is putting crime scene tape around the bottom of the staircase where I'd last seen the ginger-haired mugger. A cold shower of dread drenches my insides.

Oh God. He'd stared at me and threatened me, hadn't he?

'Will I have to give evidence in court?'

'If we find him and he doesn't plead guilty, probably yes,' the policeman says. 'We'll have a much stronger chance of getting him sent down if you assist us.'

Oh no. I don't want to get involved in this. 'But the victim will be a much better witness than me. He got a good look at his face.'

'From what you've described you saw enough to convict him as well. Those features are distinctive.'

I look at him sharply, sensing that distinctive means familiar in this case. 'Do you know who he is?' I ask.

The police officer pinches his lips together and looks away. He gives a slight nod of his head then looks directly at me again. 'Let's just say you'll be doing society a huge favour if you get a Rigby put away. Between you and me, they're a family of scumbags.'

But I can't possibly give evidence, because if Rigby gets off he'll come after me. I'll never feel safe again.

Chapter 2

I hang my thick jacket over the back of the chair and switch on my computer then walk across the spacious, brightly-lit office to the small kitchen. My hands are chilled from the brisk October morning so I hold them over the radiator before filling the kettle.

'Hi Tasha, how was your weekend?' Amanda gives me a wide smile and her blue eyes crinkle with warmth. She passes me the jar of coffee.

'Good, thanks,' I mumble, and put a heaped spoonful of coffee into my mug with two sugars.

'Are you all right?' she asks, plucking a couple of stray hairs from my jacket. 'Oh God, it's today, isn't it?' She looks closely at my face.

I flash her a weak smile. 'Yes. I really hope he pleads guilty.' If I was religious I'd be praying to God now.

'Would that mean you don't have to be a witness?' Amanda asks. She flicks her thick caramel-coloured hair over her shoulder then picks up two brimming mugs of coffee. She always drinks two, straight up, first thing in the morning.

'Hopefully,' I say. 'I'm dreading them telling me I have to appear in court.' I slop some milk into my mug then put the container back in the fridge. A waft of stale yoghurt drifts out. 'The magistrates' court sent it straight to the crown court because they could only sentence him up to six months. I was told the severity of his crime is likely to incur a longer sentence if he's found guilty, so today is his first hearing in the crown court.'

'Good. He bloody well deserves more than six months. He might have killed that guy if you hadn't intervened. So if he pleads guilty, does that mean you don't have to appear as a witness?'

'Yes. If he's got any sense, he will. He'll get a lesser sentence if he does.'

I open the door for her and she walks steadily over to her desk, coffees in hands. Amanda had been horrified when I told her I'd witnessed a stabbing, as had the rest of the team. They've all been really supportive and I'm grateful for it but I think they're misguided when they say I was a true heroine. I don't consider myself to be brave and I'm sure if Reuben had been there, he'd have done more. Chased after the mugger perhaps and rugby-tackled him – like a woman had done on the news recently. Now that was brave.

I sit in front of my computer and respond to a couple of emails. I need to distract myself so I bring up my latest project. I'm designing a set of cards for Valentine's next year for a chain store, and I'm trying to find a unique angle. I think about Reuben and how I'd like to show how much I love him when an idea pops into my head and the 'I love you more than…' range begins to take shape. I start with a box of chocolates for those in new relationships then work my way up to 'I love you more than… my cat' and 'I love you more than… my car'. I design simple, fun pictures then decide to print them off and tack them to the white walls before I send them to Ian, my boss, for approval. We all do this in the office and comment on each other's work.

'Tasha, meet Laura. She's our new writer.' I swivel my chair and see a young woman with cropped black hair and Kohl eye make-up standing next to Ian. I'd been so caught up in my work I hadn't heard them approach. I glance at the huge clock behind them for the tenth time this morning. I'm surprised time has passed so quickly when I feel so nervous, but then designing and drawing always absorbs me.

'Hi, Laura.' I stand and offer my hand but my phone rings. I lurch forward to pick up my bag instead. 'Sorry! I really need to get this.'

Ian is frowning at me but Laura just shrugs and turns her attention to the walls where the new range of Valentine cards is on display. I put the phone to my ear then walk away towards a quiet corner.

'Natasha Hargreaves?'

'Speaking.' My insides twist. It's the call I've been waiting for. I recognise the voice.

'DC Phillips here. I promised to let you know the outcome of Rigby's court appearance.'

'Yes, yes,' I say, impatient for him to tell me.

'I'm afraid Mr Rigby pleaded not guilty so the case is adjourned for a full trial with witnesses and a jury. The framing of the charge is now attempted murder rather than grievous bodily harm. You'll probably be compelled to give evidence.'

'What about the victim? Surely he saw more than I did.'

'We'll be calling him too.'

'But what about forensics? They can find all sorts of evidence now, can't they?'

'There's very little to go on. A lot of people use that bridge.'

Should I or shouldn't I be a witness? Could I live with myself if he then went on to hurt someone else? Hang on. What was that word he used? Compelled? 'Can I refuse?' I ask.

'No, I'm afraid not. And if you do you'll be on the wrong side of the law.'

I've never broken the law before. My biggest offence was keeping fifty pence change from my mum's shopping and burying it in the garden to spend on sweets another day. I'd felt so guilty I'd dug it up an hour later and given it back to her.

'To be honest, with the severity of the crime it was never going to be dealt with by the magistrates,' DC Phillips says. 'He's committed grievous bodily harm with intent which is an indictable only offence. We're hopefully looking at March for the hearing so it may be a few weeks before you receive a witness summons.'

'March! But that's ages away.' I can't agonise over this for another five months – my sleep haunted by nightmares where I'm chased and stabbed, not feeling safe on the streets. It's already taken eight weeks to track him down and get this far. 'Has Dean Rigby been locked up now?'

'He's been released on bail.'

'You're joking! How can that be possible?'

'It's the judge's decision. We're not at all happy about it but there's nothing we can do. Please don't worry though. He won't come near you. He knows harassing the witnesses would increase his sentence and he doesn't know who you are or where you live.'

I don't feel reassured and as soon as he ends the call I ring Reuben.

'Dean Rigby is still out there. The judge gave him bail! I've got to go to court and it's not for four months.' My voice is getting higher and louder and I can see heads turning towards me in the office. I step through the double doors and make my way downstairs. My hands are shaking.

'It's okay, Tasha, calm down. You're a complete stranger to him.'

'That's what the police said. But what if he doesn't get convicted? He'll know who I am if I appear in court.'

'He'll get put away, I'm sure.'

I hear footsteps behind me. Ian puts his hand on my shoulder and squeezes it gently.

'I can see you're upset, Tasha. Why don't you take the afternoon off?'

Relief is swiftly followed by gratitude and I smile at him and thank him. I don't think I could focus on my work now.

'I heard Ian's suggestion,' Reuben says. 'Very generous of him. Shall I pick you up? We'll go home and snuggle up on the sofa. Watch a film or something. I'm owed some time off.'

The pressure in my chest lifts a little and I breathe deeply. 'That would be wonderful,' I say. I fetch my bag and coat, thanking Ian on my way past his desk, and wait in the office foyer. Reuben will be here soon – St Albans, where he works, being only a short drive from Harpenden. It's too cold to wait outside but even if it was a warm day I'd prefer the safety of the office building. While I'm waiting I check my phone for the local news. There's no mention of Dean Rigby so far. In fact, I haven't been able to find out anything about him, despite searching for hours.

Reuben arrives and pulls up alongside the building. I expect him to wait in the car but he runs over to me and gathers me into his arms.

'I know you're worried, Tash, but everything will be fine. I'm with you every step of the way.'

If only he could be with me all the time. The warmth of his body is reassuring and I lean into him and squeeze him tight. I don't close my eyes, though. Instead, I look along the street to make sure Dean Rigby isn't somewhere nearby, watching us.

Chapter 3

'Did you get the gift bag with Mum's necklace in it? The one hanging on the Christmas tree?' Reuben calls before he pulls the front door closed.

I glance down at the brightly-coloured carrier bags which sparkle with winter drizzle and see the small bag with a feathery angel on the side. 'I've got it,' I say. I step through our gate and cross the pavement to our car, walking around it to get into the passenger seat. I stop abruptly. 'Oh no!'

'What's up?' Reuben comes to see what I'm staring at. 'Little bastards!'

A five-foot long gouge scars the bodywork of our blue Ford Focus from front to back. Whoever keyed the car used a lot of pressure and it's going to cost a fortune to repair it. Money's tight and the excess on the insurance will eat into the small amount of disposable income we have each month. Who would do such a thing? My chest feels hollow. I know who. A bud of tension is growing in my stomach. I stare into Reuben's face.

'He's tracked me down, hasn't he?'

'I don't think so, Tash. My mate Dave had his car done the other day. It's probably local kids.'

I glance along the rows of 1970s semi-detached houses and the other cars parked on the road outside. They all look fine. Reuben follows my gaze.

'As I've said before, I really don't think you need to worry about Dean Rigby. He's a small-scale villain – hardly the mafia. Besides, the police are being careful to protect your identity and I'm sure they'll have warned him of the penalties of witness intimidation.'

As he speaks I remember a call I had a week ago from DC Phillips. 'Your evidence is vital to the prosecution, Natasha, as the victim has disappeared. You're now the only witness.'

An alarm had screamed in my head. Disappeared? 'What do you mean? Wasn't he in hospital?'

'He was discharged a couple of weeks ago.'

'Do you think Dean Rigby has done something to him?'

'We believe he's returned to Ghana. We're trying to find him,' the policeman had said.

I'm not convinced. I think something terrible has happened to him and I could be next.

'Come on, we'll be late for dinner. We don't want a scratch on the car to spoil our day,' Reuben says and climbs into the driver's seat.

I hesitate, my finger tracing the scratch across my door. Reuben starts the engine and pulls me out of my thoughts. I clamber into the car and place the bags of presents around my feet so I can fasten my seatbelt.

Reuben leans over to kiss me then starts the engine. 'Don't worry about it, Tash. I've got protected no claims on the insurance. At worst it'll cost us the excess.'

'But this could be a warning. The other witness has disappeared and it all rests on me now.'

'People disappear for all sorts of reasons and didn't the police say he was an illegal immigrant? I should imagine the thought of being caught up in the legal system was enough to frighten him back to wherever he came from.'

I know Reuben's doing his best to reassure me but his words offer no comfort. I have a bad feeling about Dean Rigby – the way he locked eyes with me and dragged his finger across his throat. That was definitely a threat. I sit brooding for the short journey to Reuben's parents' house.

* * *

'Uncle Reuben!' A small boy with blond curls, round cheeks and a wide smile hurtles down the front path to wait at the gate. A miniature replica of his uncle.

'Don't leave the front door wide open, Alfie, it's freezing.' Jessica appears, festive in her red dress and bauble earrings, and follows the boy down the path.

'Hi, Sis. Happy Christmas!' Reuben leans over to kiss Jessica's pale cheek then picks up Alfie and swings him around, his little feet just missing his mother who has stepped forward to help me with the bags of presents.

'Careful you two. Oh! What happened to your car?' She eyes the damage.

I open my mouth to answer then hesitate.

'It was probably local kids,' Reuben says. 'They're getting out of control on the estate.'

'What a shame.' She frowns and looks at me. *Does she suspect Dean Rigby too?*

Reuben lowers Alfie to his feet. 'How long until dinner? I'm starving.'

'Hardly,' Jessica laughs and pokes Reuben's soft stomach. 'I think Mum said she's almost ready to dish up. We've been waiting for you.'

'Can I look at the presents, Auntie Tasha?' Alfie looks up at me with the same cherubic smile Reuben uses when he wants me to do his ironing.

'Let's get in the warm first.' The semi-detached house is welcoming with its fairy lights around the porch and the smell of cooking drifting down the path. 'Don't we have to put them under the tree and wait until after dinner?' I ask Alfie as we step into the hallway. I find this a strange family tradition and I wonder how Reuben and his sister coped with waiting when they were children. Maybe this is why he doesn't like saving up for things now. My parents always allowed me to open presents as soon as they'd unstuck their bleary eyes and made their way to the lounge.

Alfie helps me to empty the bags and asks who each present is for. He lingers over his own, his small fingers prodding and shaking the parcels to guess what's inside. I begin to relax. Brutal violence and mindless damage seem a long way off now. I make my way to the steamy, fragrant kitchen and I'm immediately welcomed with a warm hug from Reuben's mum, Margaret, and a kiss on the cheek from his dad, Graham.

'I hope you're hungry, love. I seem to have over-catered again.' Margaret, a plastic apron sporting an orange and the slogan 'I'm juicy, squeeze me!' tied around her ample waist, carries a heaped platter of crispy roasted potatoes, stuffing balls and bacon-wrapped sausages to the table. 'Can you get the wine out of the fridge, Tasha? Reuben, I forgot the napkins and crackers. They're in the dresser.'

'The table looks stunning,' I say, admiring the red and silver napkins and crackers once Reuben has finished setting them out. I'd love to have everyone round for Christmas now we have our own place, to create a beautiful display of silver and gold, but we only have a small table and two chairs in our kitchen.

Everyone jokes and laughs while they bustle around preparing for the feast and I feel a glow of happiness. This is such a wonderful family and I'm lucky to be part of it. Christmas was always a quiet affair at home and as a teenager I'd screamed inside with boredom and frustration. I'd have cut my right arm off to have a brother or sister to play board games with or squabble over the sweets with. Being an only child put such expectations on me to be everything my parents hoped for. I couldn't understand why they hadn't adopted a second child as well.

'You're all we need,' they'd said, adding further to the pressure. They're good parents but they're set in their ways and have always preferred a quiet, uncomplicated life. So it had come as a shock when they told me they were flying to Australia at the beginning of December to stay with Mum's sister for three months before sailing back on a half-world cruise. Seven months in total. This is the first Christmas I haven't been with them and I feel a pang of guilt at all the seasons I'd wished I was elsewhere with a livelier family. Still, it's reassuring that they feel able to get on with their lives instead of constantly worrying about me. They like Reuben and feel confident he'll take good care of me.

'How's the job going, Reuben?' his dad asks.

'Good, thanks. I've managed to secure some great accounts recently which is great for my career prospects. We've just branched out to do the marketing and retail rights for food at festivals. I'm currently working on a four-week strategy.'

Graham looks bemused, as though his son is speaking a foreign language.

'I'm hoping to get more involved in the festivals actually,' Reuben continues. 'There's a lot of money to be made. Young people let it run through their hands like water.'

'You sound like an old man,' I laugh and the others join in.

'How's your job, Tasha?' Graham asks.

'It's good,' I say, 'although I don't enjoy the commute.' I'd love to be able to work from home where I can stay snugly within my own four walls. I used to enjoy the ten-minute walk to the station and going on the train, but now I hate it.

'We saw you in the local newspaper, presenting that cheque,' Graham says. 'You looked lovely as always. How much did your company raise again?' He pushes his glasses up the bridge of his nose and smiles warmly at me across the table.

I can see Reuben's brow furrowing and I pause before I speak – my fork halfway to my mouth. Reuben knows what I'm now thinking.

'In the paper?'

'You were on page five of the *Luton Today*.' Graham jumps up from the table and goes to the sideboard. He flicks through the newspaper and shows me the article. There's a picture of me holding a giant cheque out to the charity organiser, smiles all round and an easily recognisable face. I knew there was a photographer present but I'd thought he was taking photos for the company website.

'We haven't had the final figure yet,' I say, trying to keep my voice light. 'We've donated £500 to Age UK for the first batch of charity cards sold but there's more money to come. I think we're donating to Childline next.' *Has Dean Rigby recognised me in the paper? What if he's seen where I work?* I try to swallow a knot of anxiety with a mouthful of tender turkey. Crackers are pulled and I laugh as the jokes are read out even though inside my thoughts are whirling. The conversation ebbs and flows as everyone concentrates on their meals. I've lost my appetite.

'Have you set a date for the wedding yet?' Margaret asks.

I glance at Reuben. We've been engaged for six months now but as yet we haven't decided when the main event will be. He smiles warmly at me and reaches for my hand. Reuben is keen to settle down, get a bigger house, have kids. I want that too, but I worry I won't be a good mother. What if I have my birth mother's genes? What if I don't bond with my baby and reject it?

'Probably in a year or so, Mum. We need to save up first. Weddings don't come cheap these days and I know Tasha wants to do the whole white wedding in a church scenario.' Reuben looks from his mum and dad then back to me.

'So do you!' I say. 'We've talked it through and decided we'd like to do it properly. I don't think I'd feel married if it was just a few words and a handful of guests in a registry office.'

'Don't leave it too long to set the date,' Jessica says. 'My friend had to book her wedding reception venue eighteen months ahead.'

I've heard this mentioned before but it's difficult to plan when I don't have a budget to work with. Alfie pushes his vegetables to the edge of his plate and fidgets in his chair, clearly bored with the conversation. 'I need the toilet,' he says, and sidles from the room.

'Have you heard any more about the court case, Tasha?' Reuben's mum turns to look earnestly into my face. 'I didn't want to mention it in front of Alfie, he takes everything in. How have you been? It must be such an ordeal for you.'

'I was hoping Rigby would plead guilty to reduce his sentence but he denied the attack so it's going to a full trial. I've been called as a witness for the prosecution and told I can't refuse.' I look across at Reuben who gives me a small smile. 'I'm worried Rigby will come after me to stop me appearing.' I put down my fork, wind a single hair around my forefinger and tug it out. It falls into my lap.

Reuben's smile fades as he watches the hair drift downwards. 'Rigby doesn't know who she is,' he assures his mum. 'They'll probably withhold her address in court as well.'

I glance at the newspaper and Margaret takes my hand and gives it a squeeze. 'Don't worry, love. It'll soon be over and he'll probably go to prison for several years. Just think. You'll be helping to get a dangerous person off the streets.' She looks around at the faces watching her. 'Who wants pudding? And where's Alfie? Is that the rustle of wrapping paper I hear?'

* * *

As I leave the bathroom I see Reuben coming up the stairs. He pulls me into a warm hug and kisses the top of my head.

'I know you're worried about your face being in the paper but it was dark that night and he probably didn't get a proper look at you,' Reuben murmurs. 'He's hardly the sort to read an article about charity donations.'

He's probably right. I hadn't thought of it like that. After all, the paper is full of trivia such as the local library readathon and the six-year-old who won a ballet competition. Dean Rigby wouldn't read past the front page before he threw it away. I feel tension leave my shoulders and snuggle into him.

'Come on, you lovebirds. We're waiting for you.' Jessica is smiling at us from the bottom of the stairs.

The afternoon passes in a frenzy of gift exchanges, silly charades and standing for the Queen's speech. I laugh so much my cheeks ache and I squeeze Reuben's arm with gratitude. Alfie watches me as I pack our presents in bags and gather up belongings in readiness for leaving.

'Is that nasty man going to get you, Auntie Tasha?'

'What?' *How does Alfie know about him?*

'Alfie! Tasha doesn't want to talk about it,' Jessica says sharply.

'But Mummy, I heard you telling Uncle Reuben he was an evil bastard and she should be careful.'

The room tilts and I step sideways to gain my balance. I look at Jessica who is frowning at Alfie. Reuben folds his arms and clenches his jaw.

'Do you know Dean Rigby?' I ask Jessica.

She shifts her weight and looks at the floor instead of me. 'No. But what else can he be if he goes around knifing people?'

She's lying. She knows something and doesn't want to alarm me. As soon as I get home I'm going to scan the internet again to see if there's any information on him that I've missed.

Chapter 4

I put the book down and lean back in my chair. It's no good. I've read the same paragraph five times and I still haven't absorbed it. All this hanging about is torture. When are they going to call me in to court? I nearly choked on my tea when the police said progress had been swift with this crime; the whole process has taken six months so far. I jiggle my knee up and down and glance across the room at the witness care officer in the sensible suit and low heels who's checking her watch. There's still time for Dean Rigby to plead guilty so I don't have to go through with this.

'It won't be long now, Natasha. You'll soon be on your way home.'

I respond with a weak smile and wonder if I should ask the woman to call me Tasha. My full name feels so formal and alien and brings back memories of school or my mum telling me to tidy my room. She'd only called me Natasha when I'd done something wrong and now it jars when I hear it. I suddenly realise I've wound a hair around my finger and quickly release it. I must stop doing this. I look down and see to my dismay that there are several long hairs on my sleeve. I pick them off and drop them on the floor.

What had I said in my statement again? Even though I've re-read it several times my mind is suddenly blank. What if I contradict myself? The defence lawyer will probably pull me apart with his or her clever words and scornful looks. But worse than that, much worse, is what will happen if Dean Rigby gets let off? If only the victim hadn't run off back to Ghana.

I rub the tops of my arms then stand up to look out of the window. I can only see more windows opposite but I can hear voices in the street below and wonder if the press are out there, waiting to report on the growing epidemic of stabbings in urban areas. No, of course it won't be the press. It'll be at least a couple of days before the jury gives its verdict.

It's another forty minutes before I walk into the courtroom on trembling legs. It's a light, spacious room furnished with wood panelling and blue upholstered chairs. Men dressed in black robes and ridiculous wigs sit at desks covered with legal papers. An ornate crest is fixed to the wall above the red-gowned judge. I glance at his face. He looks quite scary and I'm glad to be on the right side of the law. He gives me a slight nod and I try to feel encouraged. I just want to get this over with now and get back to normal. Perhaps then my nightmares will stop.

I take my place in the witness box then scan the crowd watching me from the public gallery. A small group of people with bright ginger hair might be the Rigby family. I can see what Reuben means now. They hardly look the type to be interested in a charity article. They haven't bothered to dress up for court and are wearing grubby T-shirts and heavy gold chains. Their steroid inflated, tattooed arms are corded with veins and their large heads seem to have sunk into their puffy necks with the weight. Their posture and grim expressions speak aggression even though they're still and silent. My knees weaken again and I'm tempted to sit down. Was it one of them who slowed their car as they passed me in the street last week then speeded up again? I spot Reuben a few seats away and give him a tentative smile before summoning up the courage to look across the room at the people behind the glass screen. Where's Dean Rigby?

There he is.

I let out a breath I hadn't realised I'd been holding. The glass screen means he can't get to me. I've been told I don't have to reveal my name or address as the jurors have been given them. At least I have some measure of anonymity. I'd also been offered a screen but was told the prosecution feel their case is much stronger when the jurors can see the witness. The police reassured me that

Dean Rigby wouldn't be bothering me again so I've been brave and exposed my face.

I swear the oath then the prosecution lawyer begins asking questions. My memories of the event come flooding back and I answer clearly with a degree of confidence. When I describe how I'd administered first aid, the jury members give me slight nods or small smiles and I feel fortified by their approval and admiration.

'Did the accused have any identifying features?' the prosecution lawyer asks me, and I'm immediately back at the police station, staring at the row of men in the identity parade. Dean Rigby had been easy to identify.

'Yes, the top of his right ear was missing.'

'You've been told to say that, you lying bitch!'

I jump as the shout fills the court room and bounces off the white walls.

'Order!' the judge demands. 'Any more interruptions and you will be removed from court.'

I look at the woman with crackly ginger hair in the public gallery. Her round face is mottled red and her pale blue eyes bulge. She's probably used to shouting her opinions. I can feel the heat of the woman's anger emanating across the room towards me but it's nothing compared to the animosity from the large, red-headed young man next to her. His narrowed eyes don't waver from my face, the white around his lips and the pulsing vein in his temple a sign of his suppressed fury. This must be Dean Rigby's mother and brother. The family resemblance is indisputable. My internet search for Dean Rigby hadn't yielded anything except the electoral roll which showed there were several adult Rigbys at the same address. The brothers are most probably partners in crime.

I try to concentrate on the questions I'm asked but the raw hatred is disconcerting and I become flustered when the defence lawyer begins his cross-examination. Taking a deep breath and firmly holding the front of the witness box I take time to calm myself and think about my responses. I have to get through this. I answer clearly and concisely. The lawyer thanks me without smiling then abruptly shuffles his papers before sitting down. He doesn't look happy and I feel a bubble of optimism. The judge tells me I can step down.

A movement from the public gallery catches my attention as I leave the witness stand. Dean's brother is rubbing his knuckles over his jaw. Seeing me watching, he runs his thumbnail across his throat like Dean had done and a chill runs down my spine. I look quickly around at the other faces. No one else seems to have noticed but I'm sure I didn't imagine it.

I'm led from the court room then taken back upstairs. I sink into the chair, tip my head back against the wall and close my eyes. I never want to go through that again.

'Are you okay, Natasha?' The witness care officer gently touches my arm. 'Would you like a glass of water?'

What I really want is brandy and I don't even like the stuff. 'Yes please. Do you know how long it will be before the jury reach a verdict?'

'It could be tomorrow or it could be next week. Someone will call you as soon as we know.'

Chapter 5

The footbridge stretches out ahead of me but no matter how fast I run it grows longer and longer and the steps that lead down to safety stretch further away. I feel the stranger's presence close behind me. Hear his breath in my ear. Any second now he'll reach out and grab me. A scream curdles in my throat and squeezes out of my mouth in a strangled moan. A hand touches my head, gently smoothing my hair.

'Shhhhhh. It's all right. You're safe.' Warm arms wrap themselves around me and I feel my thumping heart slow a little. I'm at home. I'm in bed but I'm still scared. How would I cope with these recurring nightmares if Reuben wasn't here to bring me out of them? The darkness presses against my eyelids. Reuben has turned the landing light off again. How many times do I need to tell him to leave it on?

I will my body to relax and try to clear my mind. *Think of something nice.* My thoughts turn to planning the wedding. *Who to invite? What colour flowers to have?* Slowly, I sink into the rhythm of Reuben's even breathing and eventually drift off to sleep.

I sit up abruptly, my heart pounding in my chest and my eyes wide open. 'What was that?' I whisper. I'm certain I heard something. A sound like an object being dragged. Why is my sleep plagued night after night with strange noises?

Reuben groans and shifts his hips then reaches out to stroke my forearm. 'Go back to sleep,' he murmurs. 'It's nothing.'

'Someone's outside.' I try to work out what the object being moved is. I slip out of bed and cross to the window to peer between the curtains. The street seems to be quiet. The windows opposite are closed and shuttered by curtains and blinds. There's no one to witness what will happen if the Rigby family have finally found me.

If they're not here tonight, it's surely only a matter of time before they come. My picture was in the newspaper for Christ's sake. They'll know where I work. I'd never have agreed to present the cheque if I'd known it would be featured in the *Luton Today*.

Are the Rigbys watching me right now? Have they seen the curtains move? I draw back and slide under the duvet again then lie stiffly, waiting for further sounds.

Reuben has drifted back to sleep, his even breathing doing nothing to soothe my frayed nerves this time. I'm so damned tired. If only I could get a whole night's rest. Maybe I shouldn't have read the stuff on the internet and in the papers but there was so much coverage after Dean Rigby was sentenced last week to seven years.

'It's all over now,' Reuben had said. 'Let's put it behind us.'

Easy for him to say. Everything seems so much worse now I know Dean Rigby's cousin is in prison for murder and Dean's brother Lewis, the man who'd glowered at me in court, narrowly escaped prison because the witness to his crime disappeared. Dean might be in prison but his brother is still out there. I still see him dragging a thumbnail across his throat warning me he wants to slit mine. I pressed Jessica for more information but she just shrugged and said she knew of Dean from school and he and his family were notorious for getting into trouble but she was as shocked as me when she read the newspaper articles about the cousin.

'But they're locked up now, Tasha. Reuben's right. You worry too much. Don't let them take over your life,' she'd said.

I feel disappointed at the thought of Reuben discussing me with his sister. They think I'm over-dramatising the situation. At least Kirsty is more supportive when I phone her but I wonder how much of it is guilt at having kept me out so late in the first place. I plump up my pillow and turn over again, making the bed wobble, then pull a few hairs from my head to calm myself. Reuben groans and looks at his phone to check the time.

'For God's sake, Tasha. Just lie still and count sheep or something. We've got to get up for work in a couple of hours and we'll both be knackered.'

He doesn't understand how this fear is eating me up inside. How I have to look over my shoulder constantly, have to sleep with my ear uncovered, listen to the local news and check the doors and windows at least twice every night.

The sun leaks around the edge of the curtains, diffusing the room with soft light, before I'm finally able to sleep.

* * *

'Come on lazy bones, time to get up.' Reuben places a steaming mug of coffee next to me. I feel as if I'm emerging from the depths of the earth, tunnelling my way out of the warm cave of sleep to the bright light of day. I blink and groan.

'I can't face going to work today,' I say. 'I'm shattered.'

'You can't call in sick again.' Reuben sits on the side of the bed and takes my hand. 'I know you're tired, Tash. I'm knackered and I've slept more than you have. I get that you don't like the idea of pills, but maybe you should go to the doctor and get some help with sleeping. Just for a few weeks to tide you over until you're through this—'

'Paranoia?'

'No. Through this exhaustion. It'll give you some energy back.'

Some perspective is what he means. And perhaps he's right. But sleeping pills would dull my senses and I need them on high alert for when the Rigbys strike. As surely they will, even if they're biding their time to lull me into a false sense of security. Perhaps I should have fought to go into a witness protection scheme. But I didn't want to end my current identity to start a new second-rate life elsewhere without family and friends and maybe even my career. And what about Reuben? I couldn't have taken him away from his family. I wouldn't even broach the subject. Tears prick my eyes and I swallow. I cry so easily these days.

Reuben strokes the back of my hand. 'You've been stressed out for months Tash, and I've noticed you've started pulling your hair again. If you don't like the idea of sleeping pills, maybe counselling would help.'

'Counselling?'

'You've been through a traumatic experience. You could have PTSD.'

Is Reuben just being kind or is he getting fed up with me? I can't cope with this alone. I have to sort myself out or I might lose his support.

'I'm fine. But you're right about one thing. I won't let the Rigbys ruin my life.' I swing my legs out of bed, take a deep breath and sit upright. 'Okay. I'm up.' *Think positive.* I could survive a day in the office. Designing greeting cards doesn't feel like work as I'm doing something I love. A few strong coffees should cut through the fog in my brain and as long as the new writer, Laura, doesn't give me a hard time I'll be fine. Besides, if I don't go in Laura will do it all her way, even though she's only meant to write the text, and I'll have a tough time changing it again.

'That's my girl.' Reuben leans forward and kisses the tip of my nose then goes downstairs to prepare breakfast.

I'm ready in good time so sit for five minutes listening to the radio and sipping coffee while Reuben shaves upstairs. The reporter announces the local news headlines and my heart gives a jolt. A spate of burglaries has taken place and one householder has been stabbed not far from our street. Had one of the Rigbys done it? When Reuben and I had bought this small semi-detached house in Sandford Road, Luton, the Leagrave area had seemed okay. Not now though. Every day there are reports of drug raids, suicides, racial attacks and more. Maybe we should have paid a higher price, got a bigger mortgage, and moved to a better area.

I call farewell to Reuben then leave the house and go down the path. Despite what I said to him I still think I heard something last night so I check the ground for footprints and any other clues as to what the sounds might have been. As I pass through the gate I see our wheelie bin on its side on the pavement. The lid's open and packaging, soggy flowers and a chicken carcass are strewn across the path. I sigh then go back indoors for rubber gloves and a broom. As I lift a plastic chicken tray I uncover a newspaper and

I'm about to screw it up and throw it in the bin when I notice a small wooden handle poking from under the front page. I turn the page over and gasp. There's a photo of a young woman who bears a close resemblance to me. This isn't surprising in itself. Lots of young women have shoulder length brown hair and heart-shaped faces. What is shocking is that the point of the kitchen knife has been thrust through the woman's paper heart. Even worse – it's my own kitchen knife. My heart squeezes in fear and for a moment I go rigid with shock.

'Probably a fox looking for food,' Reuben says when I rush inside.

'But why was our knife in the bin?'

Reuben looks sheepish. 'I used it to scrape mud off my boots and must have thrown it away with the newspaper by mistake. I know it's unhygienic. Sorry.'

Sorry? Has he no idea what I've just been through? The sheer bloody terror of it? 'Don't use a kitchen knife!' I yell. 'We cut food with it. We–'

I work moisture into my mouth, trying to get a grip on myself because Reuben's staring at me as though I've turned into Godzilla and I'm supposed to be showing I can live without sleeping pills, counselling or anything else of that nature. 'Don't do it again,' I say, horribly aware that I sound like a schoolteacher now. 'I could have cut myself,' I point out, hoping the reasonableness of the argument will take that look from his face, but not stopping to see. Instead I hide behind a flurry of activity as I gather together rubber gloves and a new bin bag, and take them outside.

Could a fox really have tipped the bin over? Perhaps. But wouldn't a fox have taken the chicken carcass?

I take furtive glances up and down the street in case someone is watching me. Enjoying the moment, and planning the next which could be–

No! I'm not going to let the Rigbys ruin my life.

Chapter 6

I'm walking briskly and I'm almost home when my phone pings, telling me I have a message. I pull it out of my coat pocket.

Don't forget the milk R. xxx

Damn. I have forgotten. I turn abruptly and walk back towards the mini-supermarket in the next street, my senses on high alert for the Rigbys. I want to make lasagne tonight and Reuben used the last of the milk on his cereal this morning. My phone pings again.

And a bottle of wine? X

He adds a laughing face and a big red heart emoji at the end of the text. I smile and slip the phone back into my pocket. As I turn the corner into the next street I see a figure in a hoodie ahead of me and I freeze. He's strolling away from me but I don't want to get any nearer. What if it's Lewis Rigby? What if he's going to the shop? Maybe I'll cook something else for dinner and Reuben can have toast for breakfast. Black tea will taste all right. Or maybe Reuben can get some milk on his way home later. I hesitate a few seconds longer then see the figure get into a car. I let out a long breath as it drives away then I carry on walking. I'll get the items quickly and run home. I don't want to be out after dark.

I'm standing in front of the wine display when I overhear a conversation in the next aisle.

'Did they take much?'

'Only some of his wife's old jewellery. He didn't have any fancy electrical goods or money in the house.'

My pulse quickens. They must be talking about a burglary. The voices fade as they move along the aisle. I move too. I need to hear this.

'–another two days or so. He's had stitches to his shoulder but they said they want to monitor him. It's more the shock I think.'

It sounds like a stabbing. I feel the strength leaving my legs and I hold onto the shelf for support. *Where was this robbery? Near here?*

'Did they get a good description of him?' one woman asks.

Oh no. They're walking away. I hurry to the end of the aisle in time to see them approach the tills and rush to queue up behind them.

'Godfrey said it was difficult to see much. The man had one of those hoodie things on, hiding his face.'

The cashier is ringing the woman's goods through the till.

'Was it local?' I blurt out. The two older women look at me, surprised I'm butting in on their conversation.

'It was in Blackpool. My cousin lives there.' Her lips pinch together and she turns away from me. She's not happy I'm eavesdropping.

I don't care. I shake myself mentally, relieved the robbery wasn't near here, and pay for my shopping. When I leave I look up and down the street then begin to jog. I'm halfway home when I realise I forgot to buy the wine. Oh well. We'll just have to drink cocoa while we watch television tonight. At least we've got milk for it.

The daylight's fading as I approach our house, and the wheelie bins discarded along the street present new threats. What if someone is hiding behind one, poised to jump out on me? I run into the road to avoid a couple of bins then focus on my garden gate. My breath is ragged from lack of exercise. I've only run the length of two streets. *Wait.* Did I just see a shadow – a figure – walking down our path to the back garden? *No. Don't be silly. You're just hypersensitive at the moment.* I stall. I don't know whether to go forward or back.

I hold my key at the exact angle for the lock and rush to the front door. I let myself into the house, put the chain across, then hurry to the back window, checking the rear door is still bolted as I pass. It is. I don't turn the lights on. I need to stay hidden. Dusk steals the colour from everything and all I can see is the outline of the garden shed and the darkening sky above the fence. I stare intently at the shadows, waiting to detect movement, when the shed door opens and a man walks out carrying something long.

I gasp and put my hand over my mouth. *Oh God! Who is it? What's he got? Is it something to break the door down with?* I grab my phone. *Should I call Reuben or the police?* I run upstairs and lock myself in the bathroom. *Reuben. He'll tell me what to do.*

His phone rings and rings then goes to voicemail. I hang up and dial again. If he's in a meeting he'll know it's important if I call twice.

'What's the matter, Tash? Is everything okay?'

I'm crying and talking at the same time and he can't understand me.

'Are you at home?' he asks.

'Yes,' I manage to say.

'Do you need me to come back?'

'Yes. Quickly. There's someone about to break in. I'm locked in the bathroom.'

'I'm leaving now. I'm going to call the police and then I'll call you back. Don't leave the bathroom and stay quiet.'

He hangs up and I slump to the floor. Terror is flooding through me and I want to scream. Instead I grab a clean flannel and bite it. I switch my phone to silent but watch the screen for Reuben's call. I answer immediately.

'The police are on their way,' Reuben puffs as he talks and I hear the sound of his running feet. 'I'll stay on the phone until they get there.' He switches his phone to speaker and I hear his engine starting.

'Wait,' I say. I put the phone down and press my ear to the door but all is silent. No smashing glass, no thumps on the wood. The only sound is my racing heart pumping blood into my ears. Maybe the trespasser is working out the best point of entry. Time stops as I press the phone to my ear and wrap my other arm around my knees trying not to moan or make any sound. Reuben continues to talk gently to me but it seems an interminable wait before I hear a police siren. Relief washes over me like a warm shower after a walk in a storm. When I look at my watch it has only been five minutes. They're quick. Maybe they have it on record that I'm more vulnerable. After all, they know the Rigbys could be coming for me.

'They're here. I'll call you back.' I end the call with Reuben as the police bang on the front door and announce themselves. I run downstairs and let them in, resisting the urge to throw myself at the first sturdy officer to walk through the door. He sits at the table with me and writes down my details while his colleague checks around outside. He's soon back.

'No sign of anyone,' he says.

'I saw a man coming out of the shed,' I say.

'Did you recognise him?' the first policeman asks me.

'No.'

'Was he carrying anything?'

I try to recall exactly what I saw and nod my head. 'Yes, but I couldn't tell what it was. It was something long. He closed the door behind him then I ran and hid upstairs.' They look at each other.

'Is there anything of value in the shed?'

'No, only an old lawn mower and a bike. A few tools, pots of paint, the usual junk.'

We go outside and look in the shed to be sure nothing is missing then I give them a statement. They're about to leave when Reuben bursts through the front door, his hair sticking up and his face pale. The policemen fill him in and he looks wildly from them to me.

'But I told Pete next door he could borrow my spirit level. He's putting shelves up. It was probably him. I thought you said someone was breaking in?' Reuben looks incredulous and I begin to feel a little foolish.

'I... er, I thought someone was—'

'Rigby. You thought it was Rigby.' His voice is flat and his shoulders slump, then he sighs and gives an apologetic glance at the police officers.

'I'm so sorry. We seem to have wasted your time.'

The police murmur a few platitudes to me as they leave but I can't take in what they're saying. I feel totally humiliated by Reuben's apology.

Reuben runs his hands through his hair then sits on the sofa, his elbows on his knees. 'I can't believe you dragged them here and me out of an important meeting because you saw Pete coming out of the shed. Didn't you recognise him, for Christ's sake?'

'Clearly not!' Heat rises to my face and my stomach tightens. How can he be so uncaring after what I've just been through?

'You need help, Tasha. You're starting to affect my job as well as yours. I was late for an appointment the day we overslept and my company lost the deal. We both need sleep. Go to the doctor's and get some tablets or counselling. You're not well.'

I slump down next to him, hollowed out by the fear and shame, and let the tears slide down my cheeks. He puts his arms around me and holds me tight.

'Come on,' he says. 'Let's open that bottle of wine. You did buy some, didn't you?'

Chapter 7

I turn the corner into my street and marvel that it's still light at 7pm and I can see to the houses at the other end. I love it when the clocks go forward and offer the promise of long summer evenings in the garden and light mornings getting up for work. I crave daylight. I feel safer when I can see what's around me.

I'm glad I went to work this morning even though I had a disturbed night with terrible dreams. It's been a good day and my spirits are lighter than they have been for a long time. I'm getting through to Laura that we need to work together on the designs and our boss is pleased with the new range of birthday cards we've created. After the customary glance over my shoulder to reassure myself I'm not being followed, I hum my favourite tune and admire the bell of a daffodil and the bright colours of the tulips in a front garden. I frown at the rusty car on bricks in the next one. Such different lives divided by a small garden wall. Could there be a funny card design in there somewhere? I see card potential in every mundane thing but the perfection of nature entrances me most of all. Designers such as me can create beauty but we can never compete with Mother Nature.

As I walk, my mind wanders to the evening meal. Should I make a chilli con carne or a shepherd's pie? My phone rings and I stop to rummage in my bag. Why is it always so difficult to find a phone in a handbag? I answer just before it stops ringing.

'Hi cherub, fancy going out for dinner tonight?' Reuben sounds chirpy.

'Can we afford it? We've been out a few times lately.' I always worry we won't have enough money for the direct debits and I like a few pounds spare each month for emergencies but Reuben isn't bothered about having no savings in the bank. He pays more of the bills than I do as he earns more but he isn't great at budgeting and we ought to start saving for the wedding.

A noisy motorbike comes along the street behind me and I struggle to hear Reuben's response. As I turn to glare at the bike, the rider, clad in black leather and helmet, leans over and plucks the phone right out of my hand. I stare after him, momentarily stunned, and then begin to run.

'Hey! Give me back my phone, you thieving scumbag.' The bike disappears around the corner at the far end of the street. I look wildly about to see if anyone saw what just happened. An older man in a checked jacket, holding the taut lead of a straining Jack Russell, is picking up dog poo.

'Did you see that?' I call across the road.

'See what?'

'Never mind.' I start to run towards home, adrenaline giving me extra speed. I need to call the police again. I haven't heard of any other phone-snatching thefts around here. It's rife in London but surely it isn't reaching the towns? But maybe this was no random theft. I'm pretty sure I saw a flash of ginger hair.

I fumble with my keys and struggle to unlock the front door. I rush into the hall, skidding on letters scattered on the door mat and grab the landline phone in the lounge. Should I call Reuben first? Oh God, I can't remember his number. It's so easy to press a name on the mobile phone. No one remembers numbers anymore.

I ring the police instead, who take my details, give me a crime reference number and say an officer will call round at some point to take a statement.

'When?' I ask.

'Hopefully within the next twenty-four hours. Or you could come to the station.'

The police probably think I'm a drama queen now. I worry about all the information in my phone, about all the people of importance in my life, getting into the hands of a thief, or even worse – a Rigby. 'I'll come to the station,' I say. I'm prepared to give up my evening if it means they might catch the thief quicker. I'll tell them about the ginger hair.

I check the front door is securely fastened then pick up the letters and leaflets and drop them onto the hall table. They're probably bills and rubbish catalogues. I'll look at them later. I go to the kitchen to pour a glass of water, testing the back door is locked as well. My hands shake so much the water slops over the rim. Hopefully Reuben will be home soon. I don't want to be here alone when it gets dark. When Reuben and I bought this place we loved this house but now I'm beginning to hate it here. A flash of anger burns in my chest. Feeling safe is such a basic human need and I'm being denied it.

I walk through to the lounge and sit down heavily. What can we do? I could go to the doctor's as Reuben suggests but I don't think it will make any difference. I don't need medication to dull my senses. I need to be alert with so much crime everywhere. The adrenaline drains away and all my energy leaves me. I feel weak and vulnerable and my eyes throb and prickle with unshed tears. I put my hands in my hair and rest my elbows on my knees. I'm a good person, kind to people and animals, thoughtful and generous; so why are so many bad things happening to me? Have I done something evil in a previous life and now karma is repaying me? The sound of a key in the front door makes me sit up and rub my eyes.

'Did your phone go flat? You suddenly disappeared.' Reuben looks at me quizzically from the doorway, the pile of letters in his hand.

'I was robbed by a motorcyclist. He stole my phone as I was talking to you.'

'You're kidding.'

'Of course I'm not bloody kidding! Why would I do that?'

Reuben sits down and puts his arms around me. 'I'm so sorry. It was a stupid thing to say. Are you all right? Did he hurt you? Have you called the police?'

'I've called them and I'm not hurt – well not physically anyway. I think it might have been Lewis Rigby. He's after me. He's trying to intimidate me.'

Reuben pulls away. 'Hey, don't be silly. This could happen to anyone. Did you get a proper look at him?'

'No, but I'm convinced it was him.'

'I understand it must have been alarming but it doesn't sound as if you got a proper look at him. Are you sure you're not seeing things that are not really there?'

I suddenly feel overwhelmed and can't hold back the tears this time. They slide down my cheeks and drip off my chin. Reuben stares at me then holds me close as my chest begins to heave and my mouth widens with anguish. He strokes my hair until I calm down then kisses my forehead and pours me a glass of white wine.

'Everything will be okay soon. You'll see. Once this trauma fades in your memory you'll be able to move on and stop imagining the world and his brother are out to get you. I still think counselling will help. Loads of people are treated successfully for post-traumatic stress disorder.'

I'm on my feet and glaring at him with watery eyes. 'Why don't you ever believe me when I say I'm being targeted? I don't feel supported by you at all.'

Reuben rubs his face and sighs. He's running out of patience with me. 'Here, you've got a letter. It looks important.' He hands me an envelope made of thick cream paper and handwritten in ink.

I turn it over and see an embossed crest on the back with Jarvis and Walters Solicitors printed in small letters underneath. The name means nothing to me.

I pull the flap and poke my finger in. The paper's tough and difficult to tear. Is this to do with the court case? I don't think I can take any more stress in my life. I pull the sheet of paper out and press my fingers against my lips as I read the letter, my eyes widening with shock.

Chapter 8

'What is it?'

'Give me a minute, will you?'

'Tash?' There's a note of concern in his voice as I get up and go upstairs.

I need to be alone for a few minutes. Shutting myself in the bathroom I read the letter twice more. In all of my thirty-two years I have never asked my adoptive parents about my birth family. Mostly, I haven't wanted to rock the solid foundations of their world and hurt their feelings but I've also been afraid of what I might uncover – flaws and weaknesses that I might inherit. I'd preferred to close my mind to the first few weeks of my life and focus instead on the people who had chosen me – not those who had walked away from me. But now this letter has arrived from an unknown world and I feel like a delicate plant that has been ripped out of its soil bed.

A voice comes from outside the bathroom. 'Are you okay Tasha? Is it bad news?'

'I just need a minute.'

My birth father is dead, apparently, and now I'll never get the opportunity to look at his face, to see if I have eyes like him, cheekbones, jawline. Suddenly I find I need to know about him after all. Does my laugh sound like his did? Do my hands move with the same mannerisms? Had he walked with a long, easy stride or short, brisk footsteps? Had he turned grey, lost his hair, grown a paunch in his middle years? How old was he when he died? Why did he die? So many questions – like leaves falling from a tree so that only the bare outline remains with a wet pile of sludge underneath, hiding the answers. I'm too late. Now I'll never know. I should have looked for my father.

Even as I think of him I feel a pang of longing for Mum and Dad, the people who brought me up. I crave their comfort and security. More than that, I crave answers. How old was I when they adopted me? Where did they collect me from? Did they know who my real parents were? Was my birth mother still alive? My birth mother. My breath catches in my throat as the thought of her takes hold. Is she still alive?

'Tash, come out. I'm worried about you.'

I stand and unbolt the door then walk past Reuben towards the stairs. He pulls my arm gently towards him and wraps himself around me. I feel some of the tension dissipate and rest my head on his shoulder, his warmth seeping into my bones.

'I'm sorry if you think I don't believe you about the Rigbys, but you're such a worrier I feel you need me to ground you in some realism. All the things that have happened to you… us,' he corrects himself, 'are things that happen to other people every day.' He strokes my hair as he speaks. 'Don't shut me out. I want to help you. Please tell me what's in the letter.'

I inhale. 'My birth father has died and left me something in his will.' My jaw is pressed into Reuben's shoulder and my voice is muffled. I straighten up and look at his face. 'I've been asked to go to the solicitors to discuss it. I didn't realise he knew where to find me.'

'Aah. I forget you're adopted because you never talk about it. Do you know anything about your birth family?'

'Nothing. I've not asked about them.' A flicker of pain tugs at my mouth and I realise I've always assumed they'd be there if I ever chose to look for them. I'll have to look for my birth mother now. I can't bear to go through this emotional and almost physical pain again if I hear my mother has died. She might also be the only person who can tell me about my birth father.

'When's the appointment?' Reuben's voice pulls me out of my disjointed thoughts.

'It's on Monday.' I don't know if I can wait five days. The door to the secret room has been opened. I have a sudden desire to explore further. I want to know who the people are who created me but mostly I want to know why they gave me away like an unwanted kitten. Did they have other children? Have I got brothers and sisters, nieces and nephews? Had they ever thought about me? I don't know why I've blocked these questions all my life.

Reuben takes the letter gently from my hand and reads it through. 'Will you be able to get the time off?'

'I'm going whether they like it or not. I can't miss this, although it would be just my luck to inherit a box of old record albums and a Breville toaster!' I give a small laugh to try and anchor my feelings.

'A friend of mine inherited his grandad's Blue Peter badge.'

'No! What a let-down.'

'Do you want me to take a half day's leave and come with you?'

'Yes please.' I've never been left anything in a will before. Was my father wealthy? I'd always assumed my natural parents had been poor. The sort of people who had a lot of issues and lived chaotically but perhaps they were just very young and unable to cope with a baby for other reasons. They might have kept things for me. Old photos…

'What are you thinking?' Reuben is watching me carefully. 'Your face is a picture. You look sad one minute and delighted the next.'

'I don't know what to think!' I laugh. 'I'm getting hungry though, so I think I'll take you up on the offer of dinner. Shall we go for Italian, Indian or Chinese?' At least there are plenty of restaurants where we live.

'Indian, please. I thought we could go to The Engine.'

'You just want to watch the football. Let's go to the Red Chilli.' I pick up my letter and fold it then carefully put it back in the envelope.

'I want to go to the police station first, though, to give my statement.' And later I'm going to call Mum and Dad in Australia. Maybe they can answer some of my questions.

Chapter 9

'Thank you for coming, Miss Hargreaves, Mr Finch,' Mr Jarvis says.

I smile at the round, kindly face of the solicitor who is shuffling papers on his large oak desk, then glance at Reuben who is leaning forward in his chair, arms tensed and hands clasped in anticipation. I think he's worried I might hear something upsetting, but also curious, like me.

The solicitor places a pair of wire-rimmed glasses on his nose. His eyes suddenly look enormous. 'I'll read and explain key passages from the will then you're free to peruse it yourself, Miss Hargreaves. I'll be happy to answer any questions you may have.'

I have plenty of questions but they can wait. I listen carefully as Mr Jarvis explains that his firm of solicitors are executors of the last will and testament of Andrew Harrington. A small thrill shivers up my spine at the mention of my father's name. If he'd kept me I'd have been Natasha Harrington. I like it. Funny, I'd have had the same initials.

'Your father passed away six months ago so all probate and legal issues have been dealt with and a sum has been set aside for inheritance tax. His business has been sold, which has covered a lot of the costs.'

'Six months?' I sit back in my chair. 'Why wasn't I called in sooner?' Was someone contesting the will? An unknown brother or sister, maybe.

Mr Jarvis lowers his glasses and looks intently at me. 'I'm afraid it has taken that long to track you down, Miss Hargreaves.' He smiles and frowns in quick succession. 'If you had put yourself on the adoption contact register we'd have found you sooner. Your father was searching for you before he died.'

'I didn't know there was such a register.' I feel a pang of guilt.

'Tasha has had no desire to trace her birth family,' Reuben says, and squeezes my hand.

'Totally understandable,' Mr Jarvis says. 'Many people don't.' He puts his glasses back on and begins to read. 'I give, devise and bequeath all my real and personal estate of whatsoever nature and wheresoever situate…'

I stare at the typed document on the desk between us, trying to read it upside down. I can barely understand what he's droning on about. How weird that there's no punctuation in the paragraphs. Very few even have full stops. It makes it much more difficult to work out the meaning but I suppose there's probably a legal reason for it.

'…to my sole child, Natasha.'

Sole child? I feel a cold stone of disappointment settle in my stomach. I am an only child. I have no brothers or sisters, nephews or nieces. I take Reuben's hand and see understanding on his face. He knows how I've always longed for a sibling.

'You've still got me, cherub, and besides, at least you won't have to share the Breville toaster!'

'Toaster?' The solicitor lowers his glasses and looks at Reuben.

'Sorry. Just our joke. Please carry on.'

I'd called my parents via WhatsApp the other evening to tell them the news.

'Mum, Dad, I've had a letter from a solicitor to say my birth father has died and I'm in the will. I know I've never asked you before but can you tell me anything about my start in life?'

'We're sorry to hear about your father, Tasha,' my mother had said. 'I'm afraid we know very little about your background. We liaised with social services and the foster carers until we collected you but were told the birth parents would have no involvement whatsoever. Let us know what happens, love.'

I'd felt disappointed after the call and now I'm desperate to find out more. This man in front of me with the owl-like eyes and quiet manner should know something. He looks up and leans back in his chair, linking his fingers together and resting them on his rounded stomach. He can tell I haven't been absorbing the information.

'These documents can seem a little daunting when you're not used to legal language. In short, your father has left his entire estate to you with three exceptions. You have inherited a property in the Cotswolds called Black Hollow Hall. You own it and the ten acres surrounding it apart from the gatehouse which he has bequeathed to his oldest friend, William Summers. Your father's house in Cirencester has been sold and the proceeds given to Mr Summers.'

My brain screeches to a halt at the name 'Black Hollow Hall' and I can't absorb further information. It sounds like something out of a fairy story. I clutch Reuben's arm and give a small squeak of excitement. He turns to me.

'Bloody hell, Tash. A hall.' His eyes are wide with shock.

'Yes, and in the Cotswolds. It's beautiful there.' I've been there for a weekend with Mum and Dad years ago. As far as I can recall it's about 100 miles away and a two-hour drive. It's full of small towns and pretty villages. Definitely not the sort of place the Rigbys are ever likely to venture to.

The solicitor watches us closely and waits while we compose ourselves. He gives me a small smile and clears his throat. 'The other part of the will is a little more complicated. I've known your father for ten years. I was very saddened to hear of his sudden death but pleased we had met recently to rewrite the will. Your father told me it was his wish that you reside one day at Black Hollow Hall and so he began renovations. All work has ceased at present pending the outcome of today. The will states that if you move to the family home you will be granted the sum of £400,000 for the restoration.'

I gasp. I've never dreamed of having so much money. How much is this place worth?

'I understand the coach house has been converted to a self-contained unit and is habitable,' the solicitor continues. 'If you choose not to live there you can sell the property for its current value and keep the proceeds but the renovation funds will be donated to a group of environmental charities. Your father was conscious of the damage being done to our natural environments and wanted to help protect them. You have a month to decide.'

I don't need a month to decide. I want to live there and I hope Reuben will too. It's the perfect solution to all our problems. Well almost. I might have to find more local employment or do freelance work but I can bury myself away in the countryside and the Rigbys won't be able to find me. I'll feel safe for the first time in months and the absence of stress will improve things between Reuben and me. We'll have to sort out his job but maybe he could commute and stay in Luton for the odd night. Or work from home. Loads of people do that these days. I might also find out more about my birth mother. I look again at Reuben whose brow is furrowed. He's probably trying to take it all in.

'Here's the address and here are the keys. You need to view the estate before you make up your mind.' Mr Jarvis places a large, black metal ring on the desk in front of him.

Even the keys look exciting. They're mostly made of brass and are ornately decorated with moulded flowers and heart-shaped bows. I pick up a key with three roses at one end, and rounded brass pegs at the other, and stare at it. I wonder what door this opens. The keys are beautiful and so different from the functional but boring Yale keys to our own house.

'We can drive over this weekend and take a look.' Reuben's words are encouraging but he looks like a Man United fan at the Liverpool end of the stadium. Why is he so uncomfortable with this? Isn't he happy for me? For both of us?

'Do you know what the current value of the house is?' Reuben asks.

I wonder what sort of condition it's in. If there's £400,000 to do it up it must need a lot of work. Why would it be in such a sorry state?

'The property was built in 1764 and its value is approximately £1.6 million. The estate agent estimates that if the renovations are completed to a high standard it will be worth around £2.5 to £3 million.'

Reuben gives a low whistle. It's a good job I'm sitting down. I suddenly feel weightless and the room begins to spin. This is way beyond my vocabulary. We always count our money in tens and hundreds. The only time we've managed to save was for the deposit on the house and our parents helped with most of the costs. It's crazy. One minute I'm worrying about the council tax bill the next I'm rich beyond my wildest fantasies.

You mentioned something about a Mr er… Summers, wasn't it? Did you say he's inherited the gatehouse?' Reuben asks.

'He was seriously injured – paralysed from the waist down in fact – while working for Mr Harrington in his quad bike business. There was no question of negligence on Mr Harrington's part but they were friends and he wanted to help. He had the gatehouse fully adapted for William's needs and gave him a different sort of job. William maintains the grounds thanks to some specialist equipment your father purchased and he's been well provided for financially, including an ongoing allowance for maintaining the grounds. Andrew Harrington was a generous man, Miss Hargreaves.'

Yes. So generous he even gave his daughter away. No, I mustn't be bitter. I need to find out more before I judge him. 'Before we go do you know my mother as well?' I hold my breath.

'I'm sorry,' Mr Jarvis says in a soft voice, 'I don't.'

* * *

We sit in the car and look out of the front windscreen in stunned silence.

'I can't take it in,' I say eventually. 'All that money. Our lives are going to change completely.'

'I know. It's beyond belief.' Reuben sounds as amazed as I feel. 'I can't get my head around it either but I'm happy for you, Tash, I really am.'

He sounds as though he's trying to convince himself. Is he dismayed that I'm so wealthy now? He's always been the main earner in our relationship. Perhaps this new shift in power is difficult for him to accept.

'I'm just a bit worried because I like my life as it is. You hear about people winning the lottery and their lives change so much they become miserable. I like being near my family and friends. I don't think I want to move to the back of beyond, holed up in a ramshackle old house with only the bats and spiders for company.'

I don't know what to say to reassure him. I know how close he is to his family.

'Maybe it would be better to sell it now,' he says. He turns to me and takes my hands, a gleam of excitement in his eyes. 'We could buy somewhere stunning just outside Luton for that amount of money and be nearer to civilisation. We could move a few miles out so you stop worrying about the Rigbys and we'd have some over to pay for the wedding.'

'How do you know this place isn't near civilisation?' I pull my hands away. I'm disappointed he won't even consider living there.

'Anywhere with a gatehouse and a name like Black Hollow Hall has to be remote.'

'I would love to live in a big old country house. It's the stuff of dreams. And your family could come and stay for extended visits. Can you get more time off this week? We need to go and see it before we decide anything.'

Reuben frowns. 'I doubt it. I've got a big project on. I've been asked to look at a drinks marketing package for a festival and I'm quite excited about it. We'll have to go at the weekend.'

The weekend! I can't wait that long. I want to jump behind the wheel and drive over there straight away.

'We could go now?'

'Don't be ridiculous. It would be dark as soon as we got there and there's probably no electricity. Derelict old houses can be death traps.'

He's right but I can't bring myself to acknowledge that. Well, if he doesn't want to go until the weekend maybe I'll hire a car tomorrow and go on my own. We can't really discuss this further until we know what we'd be letting ourselves in for.

Chapter 10

I programme the address into the sat nav, having followed the instructions from the man at the hire place, and pull out of the car park. My stomach fizzes with anticipation and I can't stop grinning. I've studied Google Maps and chosen the country route so that I can get a better feel for the area. There's never much to see from a motorway. The journey will take about two-and-a-half hours but I don't mind. It'll give me time to mull things over and prepare myself mentally for what's to come. Mr Jarvis has told us the house is in need of extensive repairs and modernisation so I'm expecting it to look dilapidated and forlorn.

'Your father left it empty for almost twenty years and the neglect shows,' he'd said. 'It had a hole in the roof which caused considerable damage. From one of the chimneys collapsing, I believe.'

'Why did he abandon the house?'

'He didn't say but he did tell me his diagnosis of prostate cancer changed his whole perspective on life. He decided he wanted to get the place fixed up and habitable again and he wanted to find you. He was paying someone to track you down.'

'Did he die of cancer?' I'd felt a twist of remorse that I hadn't been with him at the end.

'He was mugged. In Kensington of all places – a fatal blow to the head.'

Reuben and I had gone silent, shocked that an act of violence had ended my father's life. But then London was even worse for violence than Luton. It seemed to come with being a big city.

As I leave Bicester and Oxford behind and drive towards Burford, the landscape changes to wide vistas of gently sloping hills patched with early April sunshine and cloud shadows.

Massive horse chestnut trees, lace-trimmed with bright green leaf buds, promise spectacular summer displays of their new finery. Birds swoop and chase each other in the warm spring air.

Passing through one pretty stone village after another, I marvel at the quaintness of the Cotswolds and feel my heart sing. Nature and beauty nourish my soul and I'm at my happiest when surrounded by it. I slow the car as I pass unspoilt cottages, their gardens bursting with spring flowers. For a fleeting moment I recall the rusty car up on bricks in the front garden near my home then push the thought away. I admire instead the picturesque churches with lychgates and yew trees, and traditional pubs with pretty beer gardens. And there are even old red phone boxes. It's like stepping back in time. What a wonderful place to live. What joy to look at trees and countryside instead of buildings, roads and traffic jams. I could happily stay here for the rest of my life. Reuben loves the buzz of being close to the centre of things in Luton, as well as being close to his family, but surely once he sees the Cotswolds he'll fall in love with the place too.

I can't wait to see Black Hollow Hall. It seems strange to think it's mine. Reuben paid most of the deposit on our house and because he earns more he pays the bigger part of the mortgage too so it will be good to feel I'm contributing more to our finances.

He's been very quiet since the reading of the will and I've found it difficult to understand why. In the end I had to tackle it head on when we were preparing the evening meal.

'What's worrying you, Reuben? You've not been yourself since we got back from the solicitors.'

He'd shrugged and carried on chopping onions. 'Everything's fine. We'll visit the house at the weekend and see what sort of state it's in.'

'You don't seem fine. Please tell me what you're thinking.'

Reuben put the knife down and faced me. 'Okay. I'm worried you'll fall in love with the place and want to live there. I don't want to move to the countryside and I certainly don't want to be over two hours away from my work and family.'

I'd opened my mouth to speak but suddenly didn't know what to say. It was asking a lot of him to consider moving away from everything he knew, but on the other hand wasn't it asking a lot of me to stay where I didn't even feel safe? Last night my sleep had been fractured again by noises outside – my pounding heart and tense limbs had kept me awake until dawn.

I take a sharp bend to the right then draw in a breath of wonder as I enter a long village street. To my left is a wide stream with arched stone bridges leading to a meadow and on the other side is a long row of ancient cottages. A coach disgorges Japanese tourists who move en masse to peer over the garden walls and take photographs. Bibury is rather too pretty for its own good. The people who live here must get fed up with visitors gawping at them all day.

I'm tempted to stop at the ice cream man but the sat nav says I still have twenty miles to go. I need to push on as I want to be home before Reuben gets back from work. I haven't told him I planned to hire a car and view the property. His cautious attitude is dulling the shine of my wonderful inheritance and I want to see my house on my own. I still haven't decided when to tell him. Maybe I'll wait until we come again at the weekend.

Finding Lower Bramcote proves to be more difficult than I anticipated. The computerised voice in the car takes me along single-track lanes with hedges and trees so high it's like driving through tunnels. The tarmac ends and is replaced by a dirt track. I can't risk taking the hire car through these potholes. After a wide detour I'm beginning to give up hope when a sign for the village appears on the grassy verge. I try to visualise the Google image I'd looked at before leaving home but I'm not sure which road into the village I've taken. Still, if I've struggled to locate the place, the Rigbys won't find it.

The lane opens up to a quintessential English village green with a pub, amusingly called The Dog House, and a general store. There's also the requisite pond complete with ducks. I park the car and enter the shop. I select a bottle of water and a dubious-looking pasty from the fridge then take them to the till. A late middle-aged woman in a flowery dress and cardigan is watching me closely and running her finger to and fro on her gold chain.

'Could you possibly tell me where Black Hollow Hall is?' I ask.

The woman's eyes widen and her thick eyebrows lift.

'Are you an estate agent? I heard tell that place was going to be sold – turned into flats or something.'

Not if I can help it. 'It's my house. I've just inherited it.'

The woman's jaw goes slack and she takes a step back.

'No, really? Do you have time for a cup of tea?' She looks at me with hope in her eyes. 'I can tell you a thing or two about that place.'

Chapter 11

I quickly weigh up my options. It's tempting to stay for a cup of tea. I want to befriend the locals but I'm pushed for time. I'm not sure, either, how accurate the woman's information would be. Selling for flats! Where has she heard that from? I can imagine being a shopkeeper in a small village would give a person a unique position from which to hear and repeat the local gossip. No doubt everyone will soon find out that a young woman has inherited the Hall and any morsels of information I feed this woman will be chewed over then regurgitated with the addition of her own seasoning.

'I'd love a cup of tea but I have a tight schedule today.' God, I sound stuffy and superior. 'Can we get together for a chat another time?'

The woman sucks in her breath and her hands grasp the edge of the counter. 'You're not going to live there, are you? Have you been there before?'

'No, I er…' What's wrong with the place? I'm starting to wonder what I might be taking on.

'It's not habitable.'

'It can be restored. I've been left some money to fix it up.'

'Even so…' The woman shudders. 'It's very isolated, away from the village. Will you be living there alone?' The woman's eyebrows jiggle up and down and I'm transfixed by them.

I haven't said I'm going to live there but I don't contradict her. 'No. My fiancé will be with me. We're not sure when we're moving in yet. There's a lot to sort out.' Persuading Reuben for starters if I want to live there.

'There most certainly is. I hear William is living at the gatehouse now. He'll look after you. Such a shame for him. Damaged his spine in an accident and he was a lovely boy. When he was a lad he used to run errands for the old folk and fix stuff for them. We don't see much of him now though. The accident changed him. We all went to visit him in hospital but he didn't really want us there, seeing him like that. We thought he'd come round to wanting company but he never did. Made it crystal clear he wanted to be left alone. It's not healthy in my book, but we're all different, I suppose.'

I open my mouth to speak but the shopkeeper barely draws breath before she continues. 'I see William occasionally when he drives through the village in that adapted car of his but it's as much as I can do to get a wave from him. It wouldn't surprise me if he drove round the back roads to avoid us and he does his shopping *online.*' The woman makes inverted commas in the air with her forefingers. 'As though I haven't got a living to earn. Anyway, you shouldn't rely on him for company up at the Hall.' She shakes her head slowly from side to side. 'I don't know how he can bear being up there all on his own, especially at night.'

I pay for my lunch items and open the door. 'I hope you bring some happiness and light to that place,' she calls after me. 'It's seen some very dark times.'

What does she mean by that? No, I don't want the ramblings of the village gossip spoiling my mood. I get into the car and drive away but her words come back to me. What happened at the Hall?

I follow the single-track lane for a mile or so until I see the pitched roof of a stone gatehouse through the trees then stop the car. It's delightful and my glad mood rushes back. Small leaded light windows sparkle with sunlight and the garden sings with wildlife. Should I go and introduce myself to this William? Perhaps not right now as I can't leave my car blocking the lane. I turn into the driveway and through two huge, ornate stone gateposts. The gate on the left hangs at an odd angle and ivy weaves its way through the wrought iron. Just past the gates on an apron of paving is a large, black 4x4 vehicle. Is this William's car or does he have a visitor?

A hundred yards ahead, the driveway rises in a small hump and the stone walls of a bridge are visible on either side. There must be a stream running through the grounds. There's no sign of the house beyond – just an avenue of trees meandering into the distance and woodland to the right.

I pull onto the grass verge and get out of the car, peering between the trees. I'm struck by how much shadow the canopies of the trees cast and a sudden movement startles me. It must be a bird launching from a branch, of course. Those damned Rigbys have left my nerves in shreds and that woman in the shop hasn't helped, but this place is beautiful. The perfect antidote to my stress.

I breathe deeply. The air is deliciously fresh and fragrant. It's like drinking prosecco after breathing in the traffic fumes of Luton. Perhaps I will call on William.

I walk to the small porch at the front of the gatehouse and knock on the thick wooden door. I look around while I wait, admiring the delicate wooden fretwork above my head and the quarry tiles beneath my feet. If the gatehouse is so pretty what must the hall be like?

There's no sound from within. Maybe William can't easily get to the door. It doesn't look wide enough for a wheelchair. Walking around the path to the back of the property I suddenly realise it's been widened. A ramp and rail lead to an electronically controlled door. I knock again but there's still no answer. I'm tempted to peer inside but good manners prevent me. Maybe he's out working. I'm intrigued by the idea of this man managing the grounds from a wheelchair. What's the specialist equipment Mr Jarvis had mentioned?

I return to my car and drive on. The driveway is rutted with a strip of grass down the middle so I drive slowly. It doesn't look as though it has been used very much in recent years. I can barely contain my excitement. Any second now I'll get a glimpse of my house. I follow a bend in the road and gasp.

There it is.

The mellow Cotswold stone walls sit contentedly beneath a complicated roof line of three gables at the front and one to each side. A huge window, with honey-coloured stone mullions, rises two storeys high to the left of the massive front door. Smaller leaded windows reflect a patchwork of glorious trees in the grounds. It's massive by my Luton house standards but not so huge it wouldn't be homely. It's absolutely breath-taking. I can't believe such a stunning building belongs to me.

I climb out of the car and gaze up in awe. I forgot to ask the solicitor how many bedrooms it has. It must be at least six. There's a cluster of chimneys in the middle of the roof that look as though they've recently been rebuilt. Patches of lighter mortar between some of the stones give evidence of repointing and a large area of roof tiles have been replaced – probably where the chimneys had fallen through. Clearly some work has already been done.

A faint rattling sound comes up behind me and I spin round. A muscular, broad-chested man, probably in his late forties, is seated high up in a chair with massive caterpillar wheels. His mouth is almost hidden by his dark beard, and blue eyes observe me with curiosity, then he looks away briefly as though my appraisal of him is too intrusive. I smile at him.

'Hi, I'm Natasha. I guess you must be William.'

'Hello. Yes, I've been waiting for you.'

'Have you? I didn't tell anyone I was coming today.' Had the village bugle announced my imminent arrival? Surely the woman in the shop hadn't called ahead.

'I've been expecting you for the last couple of weeks or so. Did Mr Jarvis explain who I am?' He's very serious. Maybe he prefers having the place to himself.

'He said you were my father's oldest friend and that you live in the gatehouse. He also said you maintain the grounds.'

'That's the intros over with, then. Would you like me to show you around the gardens? I'd give you a tour inside the house but the steps are a bit tricky.' William smiles for the first time and gives a small shrug. 'Sorry.'

I feel instant warmth for the man; it must be so frustrating not being able to access places. 'I'd love to see the grounds,' I say. I look around, noticing the neatly cut lawns and pruned shrubbery. 'You're doing a great job here.'

'Thanks. Your father was a good friend. He and I were at the village school together. I spent a lot of my childhood here.' He looks over my shoulder at the trees and his smile falters. 'I miss him.' He shakes himself slightly. 'This way.' William points to the left side of the house. 'I'll show you the coach house first. Will you be moving in here?'

I feel as though I'm shedding winter clothes for my skin to be kissed by the sun. The stresses of the last months lift off my shoulders and leave me free to breathe in the beauty and peace of this place. All along I've wondered if moving here might be exactly what I need to release me from the Rigbys, to bring me closer to my birth family and to give a better quality of life all round to Reuben and me. To help our relationship get back on track.

'Maybe,' I say, thinking my next step is to persuade Reuben to agree.

Chapter 12

'That's an amazing vehicle you've got.' I'm almost running to keep up.

William slows down. 'It's a tank chair – designed by a man in America. I can go through sand, snow, woodland and mud. I love it.' He pulls up in front of a stone outbuilding with small windows. 'Here we are. The coach house. Have you got the keys?'

I rummage in my handbag and pull out the large metal ring. I consider the lock and select a key with a heart-shaped bow. It doesn't fit.

William studies them. 'I'm not sure which one it is. I've never used them.'

I try a key with a four-leaf clover and the lock clicks.

'I'll wait here for you.' He tilts his face to the sun and closes his eyes.

The coach house is small but neatly fitted out with a good quality kitchen and bathroom. The bedroom and lounge diner are furnished in pale oak with cream and duck egg blue bedding and curtains. Clearly my father had good taste. I'll have to show Reuben this building first so he doesn't think the entire place needs work and we'd be living in a building site.

'Did my father stay in here?' I ask from the doorway. I want to ask William about my mother but I should wait before I bombard him with questions. After all, he's probably being friendly to me because I never knew him in the days before his accident so I don't want to remind him of the past more than necessary just now.

'Only occasionally, if he was expecting an early appointment with someone about the house – you know, architect, building control etc. He had a new-build house in Cirencester. He left that one to me so I could sell it and have financial security. I'll call it wages and carry on maintaining the grounds for you. If you want me to,' he adds, looking directly at me.

'Of course! You're doing a fantastic job.'

'Great.' He rubs his hands together. 'I'd hate to be idle all day. Come on. Let's look at the main house. We'll use the grand entrance, I think.' William shoots forward, his huge triangular treads easily crossing the deep gravel.

Selecting the biggest key and getting it right first time, I place my hand on the warm wood and give it a push. I look back at William who nods.

'I'll be over by those trees when you've finished,' he says and trundles off.

I step over the threshold to a worn, stone-flagged hall and inhale sharply, scarcely registering the smell of damp and dust. It's cool in here after the warmth of the sun. A magnificent staircase sweeps to the right in a graceful curve to the second floor. The wide treads and red patterned runner draw me towards it but I drag my eyes away to look around. The whole of the ground floor of our Sandford Road house would fit in this hallway. The walls are panelled in oak and ornate carvings of leaves and flowers decorate the wide doorways. I cross the hall, pieces of plaster crunching under my feet, and enter a room with a lofty ceiling. Sunlight stripes the floor from the ten-foot-high mullioned window and lights up the myriad of dust motes that float in the air. Furniture draped with white sheets hints at hidden antiques and plush sofas.

I hadn't considered the place might have belongings in it. Portraits in ornate frames line the walls and I wonder if any of the eyes that seem to follow me are my relatives. I walk through to another room and see a table and what must be twelve chairs, again covered over. What lavish dinner parties we could host for all our family and friends. It would be a whole new way of life for us. I could try out elaborate recipes and we could invite the neighbours and get to know people. *What neighbours though?* I look out of the French doors at the acres of parkland and woodland in the distance. I've never lived anywhere without other people a few feet away. Even Mum and Dad's detached house in Dunstable is on a densely-populated housing estate.

But I feel safer here than in Luton. Moving on, I find a door at the back of the dining room that takes me to a corridor with numerous rooms leading off it. I peek into one. It's a small office with an old desk and chair, and shelves crammed with box files and home management books. The next two are store rooms – ornate old tins and boxes line the walls. The third door, on the right this time, leads into a wide kitchen complete with a huge black fireplace housing a double-oven range cooker that looks like something I might see in a National Trust house. Pots and pans, thick with dust, hang from a large square rack suspended from the ceiling. I run my hand along the stove front imagining a red-faced cook basting a side of beef. I pause to look out of the window and see the coach house, stables and what was probably the dairy across a paved yard.

Adjoining the kitchen is a scullery, where a poor maid had probably been up to her elbows in caustic soda suds most of the day, and finally, a small room with an old pine table and a wall covered in shelves that still hold footwear. A boot room. Wow. No more tripping over Reuben's numerous pairs of shoes by the back door.

Retracing my steps I explore the other downstairs rooms, taking care to avoid piles of masonry and broken roof tiles. A sitting room with an elaborate fireplace and oak floors has high French doors at the far end leading to a terrace. I peer out and see that it runs along the back and right-hand side of the house. The last room is clearly a library; its shelves crammed with old leather-bound books. I cross to the double doors that overlook the side terrace. Huge stone urns with tangles of ivy stand either side of crumbling stone steps that lead to neatly cut lawns sweeping downhill to a small lake. A lake! I can't believe I own a lake. What will Kirsty say to that? I return my gaze to the room. Did my father sit and read in that chair? This place is a piece of history. My family history. I long to pull the dusty tomes from their resting places to see what people read about all those years ago but William is waiting for me outside. There's plenty of time for that later.

Upstairs is almost as enchanting as the ground floor with its views of the grounds and generously proportioned rooms, four-poster beds and large armoires. For a moment I wonder if anyone has died in these beds but quickly dismiss the thought. I forget to count the number of bedrooms but it's soon evident there is only one bathroom. That will have to be rectified and the place will need replastering and painting. Maybe we could build partitions and add en suites. I look around the wide landing at the doorways. Six bedrooms. I was right. I feel a small sense of victory at guessing correctly.

A tiny box room at the end of the landing to the left contains nothing but a huge old wardrobe. I open it and see dusty old suits and coats. The floor of the wardrobe is littered with old footwear. The musty smell is quite unpleasant. Finally, I climb a small winding staircase to a set of beamed attic rooms laden with boxes, an old rocking horse and a fort complete with miniature soldiers and cobwebs. I shiver at the thought of all the spiders lurking in the corners. I've tried to overcome my irrational fear but I still shudder even when I see pictures of them. I step over piles of children's books to pick up an old teddy – was this my father's? – when the door behind me slams shut. My heart leaps into my mouth and I whirl around. A remnant of flowery curtain flutters. *Just a draught from the broken window.* But this attic is a bit creepy. Maybe I'll wait until Reuben is with me to explore it further.

Stepping outside again, I'm struck by the warmth of the sunshine. I hadn't realised it was so cold in the house. Sorting out central heating will have to be the priority. Reuben feels the cold and would hate being uncomfortable. How much would it cost to run though? The will didn't provide for any running costs and I'm beginning to wonder what we could do to generate some income. William sees me and crosses the lawn.

'Sorry I took so long,' I say.

'No problem. Did you have a proper look around? What do you think of the place?' He looks up at the house. 'Andrew said it needed a lot of work but I imagine it's still charming.'

'It is! It's beautiful.' I hadn't really noticed how much work was needed. I'd been too captivated by the elaborate coving, ceiling roses and panelling. I can focus on the renovation issues later and worry whether the £400,000 is going to cover it.

'Would you like a cup of tea? If we're going to be neighbours maybe we should find out a bit more about each other. I've got some of my favourite malt loaf or, if you prefer, some chocolate digestives.'

'Can I take a look at the terrace and grounds at the side first? I was surprised to see water.'

'We have a small lake fed by a stream. There are some very old goldfish in there, and carp, too, if your fiancé likes fishing.'

'I don't think Reuben's ever tried it. He's more into the gym or watching Arsenal at the pub with his mates.' I wonder if there are any gyms in the area. The nearest town of Tetbury is about twenty minutes away. But hey! Maybe we could build a gym in one of the outhouses or at least install a bench press and weights. I need to think up a few sweeteners to help him see the move as positive.

The lake is as smooth as polished granite and surprisingly dark. It's framed by clumps of reeds and overhanging willow and the small stream I'd crossed earlier trickles musically over stones and into the main body of water. A small boat house leans precariously, its rotting timbers giving up the fight to stay upright. It reminds me of the old man at the train station on the night of the stabbing. I suppress a shudder. I never want to go to Leagrave Station again but thankfully it seems a million miles from here. Instead, I envisage myself sitting by the lake with my easel and paints. Who would have thought there could be so many shades of green?

'This lake is where the house gets its name from. It was a stone quarry centuries ago so it's very deep and was probably the source of the stones the house is built from.'

I look at the dark depths and feel a sudden chill. What might be at the bottom of the quarry?

'Did you ever swim in it as boys?'

'Only once and it was so cold we ran straight out again! Your father slipped over and got so muddy he couldn't put his clothes back on.' William giggles like a school boy, his shoulders wobbling with mirth.

I feel a flash of gratitude towards this man. 'I'm so pleased you're here, William. I hope we can be friends. I've so many questions I want to ask about my father and the history of the house. If you wouldn't mind answering them.'

'Of course. I'll do whatever I can to help. Come on, let's get a drink.' He set off across the rough ground towards the long driveway and I jog back happily to my car. I'm relieved to have a friendly, although somewhat reserved, close neighbour and at least Reuben will have some male company.

Chapter 13

I take a bend too fast and feel the car pull towards the grass verge. *Whoa, that was scary.* I ease my foot off the accelerator. *'Better to be late in this world than early in the next!'* I can hear my nan's high-pitched voice in my mind. 'Okay, okay,' I mutter.

The return journey seems further somehow, and I've stayed too long. Reuben will be worried if I'm not home when he gets in and I want to tell him face to face where I've been. I glance at the screen of the cheap pay-as-you-go phone I bought at the weekend. Phew, he hasn't called. The phone is on silent because I have no intention of answering it and don't want to be distracted when I'm driving. At first I decided to wait until the weekend to reveal I'd already visited the house but now I'm so excited by the day's events I won't be able to contain myself.

I'm glad I viewed the place on my own. It's given me time to think about how best to persuade him that moving there is the right step for both of us. Reuben is so practical and realistic at times, it's exhausting trying to counterbalance him with my own creative ideas and positivity. I'm a racing car going at 100 miles an hour and he's the parachute on the back, preventing me from crashing. We make a good team but it takes a lot of work and compromise. Not on this occasion though. I'm determined to move to Black Hollow Hall. When I was there it was the first time since I witnessed the Luton stabbing that I truly felt at ease and free from the threat of harm.

William is a huge asset to the place. Not only does he manage the grounds beautifully but he knows so much about the house and my father's history. I'd been tempted to bombard him with questions while we drank tea but I knew they could wait. I had to ask one though. 'The woman in the village shop said dark things had happened here. Do you know what she meant?'

'Did she wiggle her eyebrows a lot?'

I laughed. 'Yes.'

'That's Muriel. She loves a drama so if there isn't one, she'll invent one.'

'So nothing bad has happened here?'

'No more than any other old house. Don't take any notice of her. She's just an old busybody.'

'She said you don't go in there because you shop on the internet.'

'To be honest I prefer to stay away from the village. I can't stand all those pitying looks they give me. I'd rather drive into Stroud or Tetbury.'

'Don't you go to the pub either?'

He hesitated, then said, 'Those people knew me before. I can't bear them comparing me with the man I used to be. Don't go telling me they mean well. I know that. But pity…' He shook his head and I sensed him cringing inside. 'The village isn't well equipped for wheelchairs and I hate asking for help. Anyway, I have everything I need here. I can live an almost normal life.'

I can understand that. I'd been impressed when he'd lifted himself from his tank chair to a normal wheelchair using only his arms. He's incredibly strong and fiercely independent. I'd offered to bring his wheelchair closer before he transferred himself but he'd told me firmly he was quite capable and I'd backed away. For all his assurances that he was fine by himself, William's isolation strikes me as sad. Lonely. Perhaps Reuben and I can help him to see past the pity so he can enjoy a social life again.

* * *

The nearer I get to home the more I yearn for the lush green landscapes I've left behind. Luton looks plain and functional with its warehouses, cheap outlet shops and estates of mostly characterless houses. I notice a big man with flame-red hair walking along the pavement in my direction. My heart lurches in my chest and my hands grow damp on the steering wheel. I fight the urge to brake sharply and turn down a side street. I'm being stupid, though, because it isn't him. Even so, I'm conscious of how anxious I've become now I'm back in the town. Home should be a haven but Luton feels hostile. Alien. I don't like it here anymore. In fact, I hate it. I drop the car back at the hire centre then walk to the bus stop, constantly looking around me, my nerves as taut as guitar strings, ready to snap with one more turn of the screw. At least in the Cotswolds I wouldn't keep seeing people that look like Lewis Rigby.

The bus takes ages to arrive and I spend the time checking my watch and working out what to say to Reuben. If I'm lucky I'll be home before him so I'll be able to choose my moment to tell him where I've been.

I open the gate and walk up the short path, looking at the small plain house with its plastic windows, tatty front door and scrubby patch of lawn. It's hard to believe I own a period property with ten acres of land. When we purchased this house I'd been delighted it even had a tiny front garden. I approach the porch then freeze with horror. Lined up on the doormat are three mice with the heads missing. Each corpse has a mess of blood and gristle pierced by a white neck bone. The grey-brown fur on the bodies looks untouched. I recall how both Dean and Lewis drew fingers across their throats to let me know they'd like nothing better than to slice my head off. Is this another message from Lewis Rigby?

I unlock the door and step over the mice and into the hall with a grimace. I'll leave them there for Reuben to find and clear up. Perhaps now he'll believe the Rigbys have got it in for me.

* * *

'I see next door's cat has left us a present or two,' he announces as he enters the hallway.

'In a neat row like that?' I look at Reuben in disbelief. I should have known he'd say something dismissive.

'Don't tell me you think this is the Rigbys again! You're being ridiculous, Tash. You're not helping either of us if you keep seeing bogeymen round every corner.'

I clamp my teeth together and clench my fists as I walk away. I won't react. I need to stay calm so that we can have a meaningful discussion later. I'll cook a nice meal and open a bottle of wine then broach the subject of moving. Once we're away from here, we won't need to argue about the Rigbys.

* * *

'I can't believe you went behind my back and viewed the place on your own.' Reuben stabs at a piece of meat with his fork and I wince as his cutlery squeals across the plate.

'It wasn't like that. I did it on impulse. I was too excited to wait until the weekend and…' My voice trails off.

'What?' he asks. 'You thought I'd try to talk you out of it?'

I can't deny it.

'That's because I'm such a controlling bastard, I suppose.'

'Don't be daft.' I'm itching to tell him about Black Hollow Hall but need him to be in a more receptive frame of mind. I pick up the wine bottle and refill his glass.

'I know what you're doing, Tash.' He raises his eyebrows at me. 'Getting me drunk so I'll be in a happy mood, while you regale me with stories of your amazing house.'

'You've sussed me!' I laugh and raise my glass to my lips.

Reuben sighs. 'I understand it gives you an emotional connection to your family home and I understand you're interested in your history but I don't think you should lock us in the past when we should be looking to the future. Houses are just bricks and mortar when all's said and done. It's the people inside it who matter.'

I can't stop my face falling with disappointment. It's not just a house to me.

'Oh, go on then. Let it all out. Tell me all about the place. You'll burst a blood vessel if you hold it in much longer.'

'Oh Reuben, it's beautiful. I can't believe it's mine... ours,' I say hurriedly.

'You were right the first time.'

'A technicality.' I shrug. 'What's mine is yours.'

I can't contain my excitement as I describe the house and the grounds. My words tumble out and I'm waving my hands about. I paint a visual picture then I start my practised sales pitch.

'We can convert one of the outbuildings to a gym. I'll show you what I mean when we go there on Saturday.'

'Oh yes?' Reuben chews his steak slowly.

'And there's a lake with carp so you could take up fishing.'

'Really?'

'And you could ride around the estate on a quad bike.'

Reuben nods slowly as though giving it serious consideration. I'm fizzing with exhilaration. At last I'm getting through to him. When I've finished enthusing over the elegance of the house, my intrigue over its contents and the potential of the place, he sits back and looks at me.

'I still don't want to live there,' he says.

Chapter 14

A strong gust of wind spatters rain against my side window and my chest sinks with disappointment. I sit motionless, staring at the windscreen wipers as they try valiantly to clear the deluge. Even at the highest speed setting they're struggling. Reuben leans forward, fingers white from gripping the wheel as he overtakes a lorry throwing up a cloud of spray.

'Bloody weather. I told you we should come next weekend.'

'The forecast said it would brighten up by eleven.' *Please let it be sunny soon.*

Reuben says nothing. After his declaration that he won't be moving to Black Hollow Hall I've been wracking my brains to make the idea appeal to him. Seeing the place in a deluge of rain won't help and the journey's already stressing him out.

Maybe the country route would have been better, I want to say, but I bite my tongue. I mustn't upset him further even though I know I'm right. He'd insisted the motorway would be quicker.

It isn't. The heavy traffic and bad weather cause congestion and delays so by the time we leave the M4 and enter Tetbury, Reuben is in no mood to appreciate the beautiful sixteenth and seventeenth century houses almost untouched by time. The rain has eased to a fine drizzle but the sky is still the colour of old porridge.

I can't wait to show Mum and Dad Black Hollow Hall. They'd be more enthusiastic. They'd surprised me when I'd called them after I'd visited on Tuesday.

'I've had some amazing news, Mum,' I'd said when I finally managed to get through on Skype. I could hear Mum relaying the message in a loud voice to Dad in the background.

'My birth father…' It had sounded strange calling another man 'birth father' but I thought saying 'real father' sounded worse as my dad has been the only real father to me. '…has left me–,' That moment my dad had appeared in the background then sat next to Mum. 'Hi Dad! You look well.'

His eyes crinkled in his tanned face. 'Hello love, what's this amazing news?'

'I've been left a place called Black Hollow Hall in my father's will. It's in the Cotswolds.'

'Good grief! Is that what the solicitor needed to see you for? It sounds rather grand. What's it like?'

'I went to see it today. I can't wait to show you.' I recall telling my parents every detail and how excited they seemed.

'We're glad you've finally made a link with your past,' Mum had said. 'We're just sorry you won't meet your real father now.'

I'd been astounded. 'I never searched for my birth parents because I didn't want to hurt you.'

'Really? What a shame! We thought because you never mentioned them you didn't want to track them down.' Mum had laughed but it was tinged with sadness. 'We wouldn't be so selfish as to keep you all to ourselves. Have you heard anything about your natural mother?'

'No. I don't know anything about her.'

'If you want any help to track her down, just ask. We really don't mind, Tash.'

I'd ended the call with a lump in my throat. My parents were such good people. I wasn't sure I'd be as open-minded if I were in their position.

* * *

'Don't follow the sat nav. It took me the wrong way last time,' I say to Reuben as we get nearer to the hall.

'Direct me then.'

Panic darts through me and I wind a hair around my finger. I'd studied Google Maps again before we left but it all looks different in reality. I hate giving him directions. I know we'll end up arguing. He's already grumpy.

Fifteen minutes and several pulled hairs later we make another U-turn and Reuben curses under his breath as he accelerates again. Flustered, I look wildly from left to right for anything familiar.

'Wait! It was there on the right. We've just driven past it.'

'But you said it was on the left!' Reuben sighs dramatically and reverses the car.

'Isn't the gatehouse pretty,' I say, desperately.

'Very.' Reuben's voice is wooden.

This isn't going well at all. As we pass through the gates I'm disappointed to see William's driveway is empty. For some reason I'd expected him to be here to greet us. When the house appears through the gloom of the day I look at Reuben and wait for his reaction.

He stays silent.

'What do you think?' I ask.

'It's bigger than I expected. It would cost a sodding fortune to heat.'

He's right – it will take a lot of heating. 'If we use the money to renovate the house it will be worth a great deal more than if we just sell it now. It's a no-brainer really.' If I can keep the Hall for the time it would take to restore then maybe he'll change his mind about the place and we'll end up staying here.

'Hmm… the will says you have to live here to restore it, though.'

'I've also got some ideas for generating income from it. I'll tell you later. I want to show you around first.' I'm out of the car and waiting by the front door before Reuben even leaves his seat. He walks slowly towards me then points his key fob at the car to lock it.

'I don't think you need to lock stuff up around here,' I laugh.

'Suppose not,' Reuben concedes, looking around. 'There's no bugger around to nick anything. Okay, let's have a look inside.'

I open the door but have to give it a hard shove. The wood must have swollen up with the rain. The house smells strongly of damp this time and the huge hall is gloomy and layered with deep shadows.

'It's bloody creepy in here! Wouldn't you be scared living in a place like this?' Reuben looks at me incredulously.

'I'm only scared living in Luton. Constantly scared. At least here I feel safe. Do you seriously think the Rigbys will find me in the middle of the countryside when even we have difficulty finding the place?'

Reuben sighs deeply. 'I suppose not. But can you honestly say you wouldn't be even a little bit scared living here? It's in the middle of nowhere, and at night… you wouldn't be able to see a thing.'

For a moment a sense of unease prickles over me as I picture myself alone here when Reuben's working away. But I'd get used to it. I love this place. It's my family home and it's a world away from Luton. 'I'd be fine,' I insist.

I'm not sure Reuben believes me but he looks towards the staircase. 'Didn't Mr Jarvis say the chimney had come through the roof? Maybe that's why there's so much plaster on the floor and half the ceiling is missing. Is there much damage upstairs?'

'I didn't notice. I think it's all been fixed. Maybe it didn't go right through the roof although I haven't looked over that side of the attic. Would the aftershocks have made the plaster fall off down here?'

'Maybe.' He sighs again. 'It needs a lot of work, Tash.'

I look up at the ornate plaster ceiling marred by bare patches exposing wooden laths and see, for the first time, the paint peeling off the walls like the bark of a silver birch. Strange I didn't notice this before. 'We've got the money to pay people to fix it and we've got somewhere to live in the meantime. Oh!' I put my hand over my mouth. 'Damn. I meant to show you the coach house first.'

'We're here now. Where next?'

I lead him from room to room, appalled at the extent of the damp patches – like continents on a wall map – and rotting timbers everywhere. I'd been so caught up in excitement on my first visit that I'm recognising the extent of the damage and decay for the first time. It's as though I'm looking at a completely different house. The rooms are dark and musty and the white sheets on the furniture loom like spectres in the half-light. It's incredible how sunshine can transform the place. But even now I feel its potential. The rightness of it as our home.

'It'll need completely replumbing and rewiring and it would probably be wise to reconfigure the layout upstairs to adapt it to more modern day living,' Reuben says. 'En suites and such like. Do you know if your father had any plans drawn up?'

'No, but William might know. Maybe he'll be back soon. He's probably gone to the shops in Tetbury. Come and see the coach house.'

* * *

'Nice,' Reuben grudgingly admits when he sees the neat and functional accommodation. 'Bit on the small side though.'

'It'd only be temporary. We could get the basics done in the Hall then make a couple of rooms habitable and move in there.'

'With all the noise, dust and mess? You do realise the house would probably take the best part of a year to restore?'

'I expect it would.'

'And we'd need to sort out our employment.'

'We can do that.' I've already made tentative enquiries about working from home. 'Shall we look at the grounds?' The drizzle has stopped and a weak sun is showing its face occasionally before hiding behind white clouds again.

'I'd rather not get muddy, thanks. I've seen enough from the windows. I'd prefer to see what the nearest pub looks like. Maybe some of the locals can tell us something about the place.'

I hope they're more positive than the woman with the jiggling eyebrows. She'd have no trouble discouraging Reuben from moving here.

Chapter 15

Reuben pulls into the car park of The Dog House and gets out without saying a word. I know from experience it's better to remain silent, allow him time to mull over things then give his opinion. If I try too hard or too soon to persuade him about moving, he'll dig his heels in and refuse to listen to my viewpoint. Instead, I give all my attention to my surroundings and look around the cosy snug. Antique oak pews with red velvet cushions are set against the walls. A cheerful fire crackles in the old stone fireplace and reflects off the copper companion set and coal bucket. Tables and chairs are dotted about the room in small clusters and the bar area gleams with polished glasses and bottles filled with colourful spirits.

There are only a couple of old men seated near the fire playing dominoes. Their cloth caps rest next to pints of bitter and a curly red poodle lies at their feet licking and nibbling its paws. Or is it a poodle? It looks too shaggy-haired. Maybe it's a cross-breed. The men and dog look up with curiosity as we walk in. Reuben nods politely and heads straight for the bar.

'Just visiting the area?' the landlord asks politely, his florid face open with curiosity.

Reuben parts his lips to reply then pauses and looks at me.

'We've been to view Black Hollow Hall. I've just inherited it.' I enjoy the momentary look of surprise. Maybe I shouldn't have revealed us as the new owners so soon but the locals will find out before long anyway.

'Muriel said she'd met you.'

'She'd heard the Hall was going to be converted into flats but I don't know where that idea came from,' I say, hoping he'll supply an answer.

He doesn't. 'Nice to meet you,' he says, then moves on to serve someone else.

We carry our drinks and a sandwich menu to a table.

'Flats?' Reuben tilts his head on one side as though this idea is worthy of consideration.

'It would be criminal to desecrate the place like that,' I tell him, and I'm glad when he doesn't pursue it.

'Who's Muriel?' Reuben asks after he's made figure-of-eight patterns on the table top with the base of his glass.

'The village shopkeeper and fount of all local knowledge. Don't pay too much attention to what you hear though. Her stories are as reliable as a red-top tabloid.'

'There's nothing in the will to say you can't divide it up and sell it after the renovation. I'm sure it would be worth a lot more that way.'

'I'm not dividing it into flats!' My voice is louder than intended and the domino players look up. I lower my voice. 'It would be sacrilege to do that to the old place and it's been home to my family for decades. Remember the solicitor said my father was conscious of the damage being done to our natural environments and wanted to help protect them.'

Reuben is about to say more when the pub door opens and two men stride in, their voices brash and loud in the quiet atmosphere of the lounge bar. The second man has a black Labrador on a short lead.

'So I said to him… "You show me the money; I'll show you the dream!"' They both laugh uproariously.

I watch them approach the bar, their dog straining to greet the poodle who now stands, wagging its tail in welcome. The men are both built like rugby players and have clean-shaven faces and designer-labelled clothes.

'Roger, Julian – usual is it?' The landlord reaches for a pint glass.

Reuben leans nearer to me. 'Bit bloody Jilly Cooper territory around here isn't it?'

'How would you know? Have you read her books?'

Reuben flushes. 'I might have read a few pages when you left it on the table. Anyway, I've been thinking about your comment earlier. The will doesn't prevent you selling the property after the work's been done so maybe it does make sense to restore it to its former splendour then reap the rewards. As Mr Jarvis said, it'll be worth a lot more when it's finished, almost a million quid more, in fact.'

My heart beats faster. It sounds like he might be prepared to move to the Cotswolds while we renovate the house. It'll give him time to fall in love with the old place and decide to stay. I'll have to make sure he gets involved in decisions over designs and fittings. Maybe a snooker or cinema room will help.

'If we decide not to sell though, the house could generate an income,' I say. 'I've been looking into it and there are loads of options. We could let a few rooms out occasionally – maybe have murder mystery weekends or such like; we could advertise it for photo shoots or filming too; or we could hire it out as a wedding venue.' I sit back and look at him. Surely this will tempt him. 'Wouldn't it be wonderful to work for ourselves and run our own business?' I pause. The man at the bar is staring at me intently. When I return his direct gaze his mouth widens into a smile and he steps forward.

'Aah. So you're the new owner of Black Hollow Hall. Marvellous place. You're a lucky woman. I'm Julian, by the way.'

He offers his fleshy hand and I shake it warily. Julian is all charm. He has wide cheekbones, broody eyes and dark wavy hair, and it's obvious he thinks he could tempt the fish from the sea. He turns to Reuben.

'Congratulations, old boy. You must be delighted.' His white teeth flash.

'It's Tasha's house, not mine.'

There's an edge to Reuben's voice I haven't noticed before. Is he feeling jealous or sidelined? Perhaps it's important to him to play the alpha male. The balance of our partnership is shifting and he's clearly unhappy about it.

'Listen Tasha… I hope you don't mind me calling you Tasha,' Julian continues, 'if you decide to sell, please, please come and talk to me first. I'll make you a very generous offer.' He hands me a business card, 'Julian Masters – Property Developer,' and his fingers touch mine.

I resist the urge to snatch my hand away. 'Would you consider turning it into flats, by any chance?'

Julian purses his lips and tilts his head to one side as though weighing me up. He's probably trying to work out if I would reject the idea outright or be interested in a quick sale.

'The house has great potential,' he says cautiously, 'though it needs considerable work. It's too big for most families these days and maybe multiple-occupancy would be best as it's so isolated. Few people would want to live so cut off from everyone else.' He looks from me to Reuben. 'That sort of isolation wouldn't suit me and it certainly wouldn't suit my wife to be there alone when I'm away. She'd get the shivers at the thought of it.'

Chapter 16

'What a tosser,' Reuben says as he opens the car door. 'I wouldn't want you to sell to him.'

I hadn't warmed to Julian either. It's clear to me he's the man who intended converting Black Hollow to flats and I wonder how far he got with his plans for it. He seems like a man who won't take no for an answer, judging by his confident manner and appearance of wealth. I'm relieved the house is only in my name and I'm not married to Reuben yet. I think Julian might be quick to capitalise on Reuben's reluctance to be here.

'Can we go back to the gatehouse to see if William's there now? I'd like you to meet him. He knows so much about the place. He used to live in the village but practically grew up at the Hall as he was my father's closest friend.'

Reuben looks at his watch. 'I was hoping to get back for the 4pm kick-off.' He sees my expression. 'Okay,' he sighs.

William's car is on the drive this time. The sun's out now and the hedges sparkle like a jeweller's shop window. We go round the back of the cottage and knock politely. William answers almost straight away.

'Tasha! Good to see you… and this must be Reuben.' He leans forward in his chair to shake Reuben's hand. 'Come in,' he says, expertly manoeuvring his wheelchair so we can get through the doorway and into a cosy lounge. He gestures to a small two-seater sofa. 'Would you like tea? I've bought a toffee pecan cheesecake if you fancy some.' He smiles his wonky smile again. 'I have a sweet tooth,' he confesses with a shrug.

William's enthusiasm at seeing us makes me think he must be starved of company due to his self-imposed exile. I hope Reuben and I can help him develop a social life again. Reuben's grinning. Clearly his opinion of William is higher than his opinion of Julian.

'Cheers mate. That'd be great. We had a sandwich at The Dog House but you know what women are like. There's always room for cake.' He winks at me and I tut at his blatantly sexist comment.

'You eat more cake than I do,' I say, giving his arm a little shove.

William grins at the pair of us then wheels himself away to make tea at the lowered kitchen worktop. Reuben looks about the room. 'Nice place,' he says.

The room is simple and elegant with light grey furniture and the occasional navy cushion and lamp. Every diamond-paned window looks out onto trees and grass

'Did you meet any of the locals in the pub?' William asks.

'Yes. Julian,' I say. 'He wants to buy Black Hollow Hall and turn it into flats.' I can't stop the indignation creeping into my voice.

'That doesn't surprise me. He's done similar conversions with other large houses around here then gone on to build small housing estates in the grounds. When we were growing up together he always said he was going to be rich one day. I think he needed to compete with Andrew.'

Housing estates? I think of the beautiful lawns and trees being decimated to make way for brick boxes and driveways. It would be a tragedy and I won't let it happen. I want to see Black Hollow restored to its former glory. 'Do you know if my father had any plans drawn up for the house?' I ask.

'He did. I think they'll be in the coach house somewhere. He kept everything in there because the Hall can get quite damp.' William places cake and plates on the small coffee table. 'I'm going to put the Arsenal game on at four if you fancy watching it with me.' He looks up at Reuben. 'I doubt you'd be back in time for it.'

'How did you know I'm an Arsenal fan?' Reuben's brow is furrowed.

'Saw your keyring.' William laughs and Reuben joins in, clearly delighted at meeting another Arsenal fan.

'What do you think, Tasha?' Reuben turns to me. 'Can you occupy yourself for a few hours? You could have another look around the place and maybe find the architect's plans.'

As I walk along the drive, giving a little skip occasionally, I think about the slight change in Reuben's attitude. Was he trying to get rid of me so he could watch the game without me sighing with boredom, or is he really interested in the plans? If I find them I'm going to take them home to study but first I want to look around again, especially in the attic where the chimney has caused damage. It had been quite dark up there when I'd looked with Reuben but the sun is shining now.

I enter the grand hall and shiver. It's chilly in here after the warm sun outside. This time, I vow to myself, I will look at the house as it really is – not with rose-tinted spectacles and not with Reuben's disparaging eye. There's such a lot to be done: restoring the ornate cornicing where chunks are missing, walls to be replastered with a lime and horsehair mix and damaged floorboards to repair, beside the basic utilities. We'll need to find specialist builders and craftsmen. Thankfully, the stone mullions and thin oak window frames are in good condition but they wouldn't keep the winter heating in. We might need to install removable secondary glazing frames for the cold season. No doubt the Grade II listing will prevent us fitting any permanent secondary glazing. But oh, won't it be wonderful with blazing log fires. I walk from room to room thinking how my father walked these floors, turned this door handle and saw this view from the window. Did he ever think about me and regret my adoption? And had my mother been here too?

Up in the attic room on the right I linger momentarily over a box of old toys that might have belonged to my father – a metal spinning top, wooden bricks with the alphabet on and a bristly old bear with straw erupting from bald patches – before going across the landing to the room on the other side. The water damage is obvious in here. The walls are black and green with mould and the plaster sags in places like damp sheets on a washing line. I'll need to make sure I don't touch it because the whole lot might fall down. There must have been a hole in the roof for a while before it was discovered. I step carefully around rotting timbers, testing the soundness of the wood with the ball of my foot before putting my full weight on them, and peer out of a tiny window in the eaves. I can see a grassy meadow from here and the edge of the lake. Wait. Is that a figure walking near the edge? I squint to see more clearly now the sun has disappeared again. Yes, it is. A man, I think, and my mind leaps straight to Julian, though it could be anyone out for a stroll. Whoever it is, it won't hurt for me to put in an appearance. It'll reinforce the idea that this place is mine now and liberties can no longer be taken.

I rush downstairs and quickly lock the door. It's drizzling again and my hair and cheeks are soon coated with a fine mist. I trot across the gravelled driveway towards the lake to get a better look at the man. He's still there, a dark outline in the distant gloom. Looking at him means I'm not looking where I'm treading and I gasp as my foot twists sideways, a burning pain shooting up my ankle. I've trodden on something. I look down and see an alphabet brick, like the ones in the attic, lying in the grass. What's it doing down here? I pick it up. It doesn't appear to have been exposed to the elements for long as the painted letter B is still bright. Architects, builders, surveyors… all sorts of people have been in the house but a child's brick seems an odd sort of thing to have taken. Maybe it struck a nostalgic chord momentarily only to be tossed aside as the taker realised he had no real use for it.

I look back at the man but he's gone. Perhaps he saw me and hastened away to avoid a tricky conversation about trespassing. Good. I'd rather avoid that sort of conversation too. I push the brick into my pocket to return it to the house. It still feels an odd thing for someone to have taken but I don't suppose it matters.

* * *

'What do you think of William?' I ask as we drive home.

'He seems nice enough,' Reuben says. 'Anyone who supports Arsenal must be okay.' He looks at me and grins then nods at the envelope on my lap. 'Is that the plans for the Hall?'

'Yes. I thought we could study them when we get home, see what's involved and work out some timescales.' I hold my breath, waiting for him to say whether we can move to the coach house or not while we renovate the place. He's already acknowledged there's a lot more money to be made if we do. It would be crazy not to.

'I'd have to stay part of the week in Luton,' he says, as though he can read my mind. 'I wouldn't be able to commute to work every day from the Cotswolds.'

A flurry of excitement tickles my insides. 'That wouldn't be a problem,' I say. 'I'm sure I'd be fine and I'd have William nearby.'

Reuben's brow creases. 'What about your job though? The will didn't say anything about living expenses. We'd still both have to work.'

'I can ask to work from home one day a week and maybe I could drop a day or two. If we rent out the Luton house for a year we won't have so many outgoings and the mortgage will be paid.'

'But where would I stay when I need to be in the area?'

'Your mum's? Maybe you could work from home sometimes too.'

Reuben gives a small shake of his head. 'I'm not sure. I need to think about it and I'd have to ask Mum and Dad about staying. Working from home occasionally shouldn't be a problem. Lots of people do it these days. You need to understand though, Tash. I'm only considering living there while we do the place up. I don't want to live there long-term.' He looks at me to emphasise his point then turns his attention back to the road again.

I want to yell with joy and throw my arms around him but I tuck my hands under my legs and press my lips together. I know he says he doesn't want to live there long-term but he's practically agreed to move there short-term. I'm sure I'll be able to win him round. I have the time it takes to renovate the house to change his mind.

Chapter 17

'Is that everything?' Reuben carries the last box and slides it into the boot then leans against the bumper. 'Have you had a final look around? Got your handbag?'

I'm suddenly reminded of Christmas. Crikey, so much had happened in five months. After Reuben reluctantly agreed to move to the Cotswolds four weeks ago I've been busy packing up essentials to take with us and the time has raced by. It's difficult to know what to leave behind. I hope the new tenants, when we find some, will look after our furniture. Maybe it would be better placed in storage.

'Let's wait and see who's moving in first,' Reuben had said. 'It might be a young couple who'd appreciate it.'

I wonder if Reuben is disinclined to dismantle our old home because he wants a bolthole in case things don't work out. I won't say it out loud though. He might admit it's true and I want this move to be as positive as possible.

'I think I've got everything and if I haven't, your mum and dad can bring it when they visit us.'

I'm pleased Reuben's family were excited at the news of my inheritance but I felt guilty when his mum had looked upset.

'That's such a long way, Reuben, and won't you both be a bit isolated?'

'It's only temporary and just a couple of hours away. Besides, I'll be staying at yours when we find tenants,' Reuben had tried to reassure them.

His boss has agreed to him working Mondays and Fridays from home but he'll need to be in the office the other three days. I hope it won't be long before we find tenants so he can work less and help with the restoration. He hasn't agreed to give up his job but I'm confident I can persuade him eventually. After all, I've got him to move, even if he's only accepted it in the short-term. I honestly believe this lifestyle change will be good for him too; real exercise in the fresh air instead of a gym, new challenges and the potential to build our own business one day.

We climb into the heavily-laden car and set off. I take one last look at the front door of our little house. The varnish still needs redoing where eggs were thrown at it. Reuben had insisted it was local kids on Halloween but I don't think so. No one else in the street was targeted. A clear image of the terrifying Rigbys in court grips my mind but this time I manage to shake it off. They can't frighten me now. My spirit lifts as we leave Luton and I want to hug Reuben and kiss him. It's too dangerous while he's driving so I'll have to wait. I put my hand on his leg and squeeze it instead.

'I bet you're looking forward to semi-retirement,' Reuben teases.

'I'll still be working two days at home and Fridays at the office. I'll be focusing on the restoration project on the other days. I'd hardly call that retirement.'

I'm lucky my employers are being so flexible. I just hope Laura won't take advantage of my absence to do everything her own way with the designs. She can be a bit awkward at times. Still, I don't want to think about work anymore. I have a week's leave and I'm going to enjoy it. The only worry I have is that money will be tight so we'll have to spend wisely. It's ludicrous that I've inherited a property of such value but no funds to live on. My father must have overlooked that reality in the equation.

'Are you sure you'll be all right on your own when I'm away?' Reuben asks yet again. He's only managed to book a couple of days off and is back to work next Tuesday.

I roll my eyes. 'Yes, like I said before, I've nothing to fear at Black Hollow. But I'm definitely not staying in Luton on my own. If you're not there I'll stay at your parents' on Thursday nights.' All in all, we're both happy with the arrangements and they're a comfortable compromise until we can evaluate our finances better.

'We'll need to sort out our desk and computer as a priority,' Reuben says, 'I booked the internet installation for Monday.'

'That's quick.'

'Forward planning, cherub, forward planning,' Reuben taps the side of his head.

'I was thinking… maybe we could convert the dairy to an office later on,' I say.

'Hmm. We'll see.' Reuben refuses to be drawn on any long-term plans that might be for our personal benefit in case I interpret it as his agreement to live there permanently.

I look out of the car window at the rolling green countryside. The April rain has given way to brighter days in May and this time I've managed to persuade Reuben to take the country route. The trees are stunning. Horse chestnuts display candles of red and cream flowers like festive Christmas trees and the hawthorns in the hedgerows are a marshmallow confection of pink and white blossom.

Pure happiness bubbles up inside me. I open my window and shout, 'I love the Cotswolds!' at the top of my voice. A group of crows lifts from the trees, admonishing me for my outburst. Reuben looks at me with eyebrows raised and a small grin on his face.

'Excited are we?'

'Yes. Sorry, I couldn't keep it in any longer.' I wriggle in my seat then lean across to kiss him on the cheek.

'Steady on! You'll have us off the road. Or is that your intention? Do you want me to find somewhere off the beaten track for a while?' He's grinning widely now.

'Where we're going is off the beaten track, remember? I'm sure you can wait another hour.'

Reuben sniffs. 'I might not be interested then,' he teases.

'You're always interested.' I give Reuben's leg a playful squeeze then look out of the window again. These views are too spectacular to miss.

'Let's get married,' Reuben says suddenly.

'We are getting married. You proposed last year, remember?' I laugh but I know what Reuben is saying. I don't want to get married yet. I have fantasies of a big wedding at Black Hollow Hall when it's restored and beautiful and I still need to persuade him to stay there first.

'You know what I mean. Let's bring it forward.'

'Why? Are you worried I might dump you now I'm a wealthy woman?' I try to make him smile but he frowns.

'I love you and want us to be a proper couple. And yes, to be honest it would make me feel more secure with the whole situation, and like I'm a legitimate part of it.'

'But then you could bump me off and inherit the house.' I should stop teasing Reuben but I can't resist it. Anything to distract him from the real issue. I don't want a wedding to plan with everything else going on and next he'd be talking about starting a family. I do want kids but not quite yet.

'We could get married quietly. You know… sneak off and not tell anyone. We could have a ceremony next year as a double celebration when we've finished the house.'

'We could…' I say slowly. 'It wouldn't be the same though. I want to plan it properly and for it to be a real wedding on the day.' I bite my lip. 'Let me think about it. Have you heard any more from the estate agents?'

'They said the photographs are sorted and it's going on the market today. They had someone in the office who was interested but they wanted it at a much reduced price so I said no.'

'I agree. We need to see how much interest there is before we offer a discount.' *Is he trying to keep it empty in case he wants to go back?*

It's late afternoon by the time we arrive at Black Hollow Hall. Reuben parks as near to the coach house as he can and we unload our belongings. I make the bed up with clean linen and Reuben carries clothes up the stairs.

'Let's go to the pub for something to eat then finish unpacking later,' Reuben suggests. 'We can go to the village shop for a few basic supplies until we find a proper supermarket tomorrow.'

'Good idea, I'm getting hungry.'

* * *

The pub menu is reassuringly wholesome and varied. Reuben chooses steak pie while I opt for sea bass. The pub's fairly quiet but the landlord remembers us and is chatty and helpful. He gives us directions to the nearest supermarket and petrol station, and tells us what we can expect to find in each of the nearby towns.

It's dark by the time we get back to the Hall. It looms up almost menacingly in the headlights and when Reuben turns the engine off we're plunged into total darkness.

'Damn. I meant to bring a torch. I'll have to use my phone.' Reuben flicks his phone on then walks to my side of the car to light my path.

We reach the cottage and step inside. I run my hand across the wall near the door trying to locate the light switch.

'Here.' Reuben shines his phone at the wall. The switch is further down. He flicks it on but nothing happens. 'Maybe this one is faulty.' He flashes the phone light around the room looking for another switch then walks over to a table lamp and clicks the button on the base. Nothing. 'We've got no power.'

'But I'm sure there was electricity earlier. I looked in the fridge and the light came on.' Didn't it? I'm not so sure now. Reuben's light flickers then goes out.

'Fuck. My phone's gone flat. Has yours got a torch on it?' Reuben's voice floats across the dark room. There's a loud thud. 'Ouch! Bloody coffee table. We don't even know where the fuse box is. Why didn't I check this before we went out?'

'You weren't to know. My phone doesn't have a torch.' I'm glad Reuben is here. I feel a twinge of unease. Will I be able to cope on my own? I'm not so sure now. 'Let's go to bed. It's all ready and we can't see to do anything else.' I don't want our first night here to be spoiled and I'm determined to make this move work. I feel a pair of arms grab me and I squeal in surprise.

'An excellent plan. I don't need light for what I've got in mind.'

Chapter 18

'Ah, here's the fuse board.' Reuben has his head inside a cupboard. 'It doesn't look as though any of the circuits have tripped out though.' Puzzled, he leans against the sink and peers across the yard. 'The supply must come from the main house. If we can find the meter we'll be able to work out if there's an isolator switch.'

'Blimey, that could take us ages and I'm dying for coffee. Shall we go out for breakfast?'

'We need to get this sorted. The fridge-freezer has to be working and cold for the food shopping. I also want to charge my phone. I need to keep in contact with work.'

I follow Reuben across the flagged yard to the back door. He sorts through the big bunch of old keys and opens the lock with the first key he selects.

'Huh, how did you manage to find the right one so easily?'

'Lucky guess,' he says, with a shrug.

We enter through the scullery and, after a cursory look around, move on to the boot room then into the large kitchen.

Reuben opens a floor-to-ceiling cupboard then bangs the door shut. 'Not here,' he says.

The next room is the store cupboard with shelves full of decorative old tins and jars. I'm looking forward to going through everything. Who knows what treasures I might find? That task will have to wait, though. Right now we need electricity.

'Ta da!' Reuben's voice drifts from the office next door.

I go to see what the source of power looks like in case there's a problem in the future.

'That's odd!' he says. 'Didn't you say there was electricity when we arrived? You said the fridge light was on.'

'I think it was.'

'Well, see this big lever here? It's been pushed up so it's cut off the electricity to the coach house.'

He pulls it down to restore the power.

'Maybe the fridge was lit up because the sun was so bright,' I say, and feel pleased with myself for being so practical. I'm not in Luton with the threat of the Rigbys hanging over me anymore. I don't need to see bogeymen behind every little mishap.

'I suppose someone stopped the power to the coach house after my father died,' I say, wanting Reuben to see that, now I'm living here, I'm back to my level-headed self, or almost. No paranoia in sight.

'I suppose.'

I slide my arm through his. 'Let's get that kettle on, shall we?'

The power in the coach house works perfectly now. 'Thank God,' Reuben says. 'I didn't fancy our chances of getting an electrician out today. Talking of workmen, we could ask William if he knows who your father was using. The standard of craftsmanship in this coach house is pretty high.'

'Good idea. We can go there first. Give the freezer time to chill before we shop and put the food away.'

* * *

We don't need to stop at William's place because as we walk to the car we spot him on his adapted sit-on mower cutting the lawns at the front of the house.

'Hmm,' he says when we ask about the contractors my father had used. 'I'd look elsewhere if I were you. Andrew had quite a few problems with the local firms.'

'The quality of the work looks great,' Reuben points out.

'But they took forever to do it. Kept buggering off to other jobs. Whoever you get, you might like to make it a condition of the contract that they only work on this project. If you like, you could let me know who you find and run their names past me before you book them in. I can tell you if any of them are the ones he used.'

I'm glad to see William appearing relaxed in Reuben's company as well as mine.

'Thanks mate. We'll do that,' Reuben says. 'We're going into Cirencester today to sort out a new phone for Tasha. Do you know which networks have the strongest signal around here? Mine's Vodaphone and it keeps dropping out.'

'Mine's the same,' William says. 'There's a lack of phone masts locally and we're in a dip. It might be worth you contacting one of the network companies and offering to have a mast on the edge of your land where the ground's higher. They'll pay you for the privilege and you'll get a better reception so it's a win–win situation.'

'Is it worth waiting until we have good reception to get a decent phone on a new network package?' I ask Reuben. 'There's a landline in the coach house and I'll be able to use the internet for emails and Skype so won't need a phone much. Seems a pointless expense if there's no signal.'

'What about using apps? Don't you want to read books on your phone?'

'I can use my e-reader.' I think for a moment. 'I do miss my camera though and this phone doesn't have a torch.'

'We can buy a torch and our old camera still works. I brought it with us to take better pictures of the house. Come on. Let's get the supermarket shop over with.' He nods to William then walks to the car.

I'm about to follow when I pause and turn to William. 'Are there any public footpaths through here?'

'Not that I'm aware of. Why? Have you seen someone?'

'There was a man by the lake.'

'Probably just a local out for a stroll.'

'Have you ever approached them and told them it's private property?'

'To be honest, I just want a quiet life and I'd rather avoid any confrontation. Sorry. I'm sure they'll soon get the message once it's known that you've moved in.'

'Not to worry,' I say, pleased with myself for discussing trespassers so calmly and rationally. And if the local had been Julian I hope he'll also get the message the Hall isn't for sale and turn his money-making interests to other projects.

Chapter 19

'Are you sure you'll be okay?' Reuben asks as he puts his breakfast plate on the kitchen worktop. 'I don't like leaving you on your own.'

'Of course I will.' I'm getting fed up with him asking me. 'Don't worry. I'm going to sort through the stuff in the kitchen cupboards and work my way through the house. The time will fly by and you'll be back before I have chance to miss you. Besides, you're only going for two nights.'

Reuben picks up his holdall and kisses me gently on the mouth. 'Don't cope too well without me. You might not want me back. I'll call you tonight, say around nine, so can you make sure you're by the phone?'

'I won't be anywhere else at that time of night.'

The cottage feels strange after he's gone. Somehow the rooms seem double the size. I make the bed and wash the breakfast things then look at my watch. It's only 7am. Sod it. I'll go back to bed for an hour. There's nothing to rush for.

I awake to knocking. I groan and swing my legs out of bed. Crikey, it's 10am. I hadn't meant to sleep that long. A glance in the mirror is a mistake. My hair's tangled and I still have smudges of mascara under my eyes where I didn't clean it off properly last night. I feel totally disadvantaged. I could ignore the knocking. Perhaps they'll think I'm out and they'll go away. No, wait. It must be William. I can't think of anyone else who might come to my door.

I go downstairs and peer through a narrow gap, hiding behind the door so he can't see my dressing gown and pyjama outfit. William is halfway across the yard in his tank chair. He turns as I call to him and he heads back towards me.

'Sorry, I didn't mean to wake you.' He looks worried.

'I'm glad you did. I shouldn't have slept that long.' I could win a "sleeping for England contest" since we moved here five days ago. A result of all the fresh air and exercise, I suppose, or more likely the lack of fear.

'Shall I come back later?'

'No, it's okay. Can you give me five minutes? I'll throw some clothes on.'

I run upstairs, drag a brush through my hair and rub my face with a flannel. I pull on a pair of jeans and a T-shirt then run back downstairs.

'I feel bad not inviting you in. Would you like me to bring a coffee out to you?'

'You wouldn't want track marks all over your carpet and anyway, your doorway isn't wide enough. A coffee would be great though, thanks. I'll wait here.' He gives me his wonky smile and I smile back. I bet he was quite a catch a few years ago.

I carry a dining chair outside and sit next to William in the warm May sunshine.

'I've been through the list of tradesmen Reuben brought over to me the other evening.' He hands me a folded piece of paper. 'I've put a line through the ones who let your father down and I've added some new ones you might like to try. I suggest you get at least two quotes for each job. Have you worked out what has to be done first?'

'We need to get a structural engineer out to check the joists, lintels and load-bearing walls are doing their job, especially after the chimneys fell in. We also need to ensure they're secure now.'

'Your father had all that done. The chimneys and roof were repaired and the structure checked. The paperwork for it should be around somewhere.'

'I think we need to get the architect back to explain his design for the new layout upstairs.'

William frowns. 'I'm sorry if I'm speaking out of turn but that would be wasting money. The drawings are done and approved by the council and if you're happy with them you just need a builder to put up partition walls for en suites and knock through a doorway here and there.'

'You make it sound so easy,' I laugh. 'What would be next on the list?' He clearly knows more about building work than I do.

'Plumbing and wiring would need doing around the same time because you'll be running cables and pipes in or through the walls and under the floors. It's best if you can get a team that has worked together before. There's nothing worse than workman wars. I've found a couple of companies who do all that. They're on your list.' William nods at the piece of paper.

I unfold it and read the names. One's from Cirencester and the other from Cheltenham. 'Aren't they a bit far away?' I ask.

'People are used to travelling distances to work around here. Give them a call. They'll soon tell you if it's too far. Anyway, thanks for the coffee. I've got shrubs to prune.'

I look at the list of names again and go indoors to phone them.

* * *

A couple of hours later I'm feeling hungry and in need of company so decide to go to the pub for a light lunch. I walk to the front of the house where I've parked the little Renault we've bought so I won't be stranded here when Reuben's away with the Ford Focus. I loved this little car from the first moment I saw it on a garage forecourt in Cirencester. It's the first one I've owned myself and even though it only cost a few hundred pounds and doesn't have much power I still feel pleasure every time I get in it. I might not have bought a new phone that day but I bought a taste of freedom.

The Dog House is surprisingly busy but it seems a large group of American tourists has descended, clearly delighted at finding a quaint, traditional pub serving typically English food. Their voices rise against each other's in their enthusiasm for their surroundings. They must have recently arrived in the area. I squeeze past their chairs and reach the bar.

'I was hoping to get some lunch,' I tell the barman, 'but I'm not sure if you have any room.'

The barman leans across the counter. 'Helen, can this lovely lady share with you?'

I turn around and see a petite woman with short dark hair look up from her menu and smile.

'Of course! Come and join me.' She pulls a chair away from the small table and waves her hand at it.

As I approach, she half stands and thrusts out a small, fine-boned hand, adorned with tasteful jewellery. She's wearing a simple shift dress of cream linen and a short navy jacket, making me feel scruffy in comparison in my jeans and T-shirt.

'My husband isn't coming now so I'm glad of the company,' the woman explains. She has a voice like a newsreader, all her vowels and consonants precisely pronounced.

I sit down awkwardly and introduce myself. I need to make friends but I'm not sure if this sophisticated woman is my sort. I can't imagine her watching old Disney films and stuffing her face with popcorn and Maltesers as Kirsty and I do sometimes.

'You're the new owner of Black Hollow, aren't you?'

'Yes.' I'm probably a hot topic in the village.

'It's a beautiful house with a lot of potential. What are your plans for it?'

'To repair and restore it, mainly.'

'It's very isolated, don't you think?'

'Yes, but I don't mind and William is nearby.'

'How are you getting on with him? I imagine he can be a bit serious at times. Such a shame for the poor man.'

No wonder he gets hacked off with people around here. Helen is probably being sincere but her sympathy comes across as sickly sweet and false.

'He's been very friendly and helpful so far,' I say.

'We rarely see him these days,' Helen says. 'I think he goes to Tetbury for everything. We saw him in a pub there one day last year but he wasn't at all happy when it started to rain and we rushed over to help him indoors. He actually swore at us for interfering and said he was going home. It was a pitiful sight, watching him get soaked as he got his wheelchair and himself into that car of his, but what can you do if someone refuses help?'

Poor William. It must have been horrible to have people watching his struggles.

'It's all the more tragic when you think of what he used to be,' Helen goes on, 'Julian told me William was the highest achiever in sports at school – the fastest runner, the best footballer – and always picked first for the teams.'

'Julian?'

'My husband.'

I should have guessed. The same aura of prosperity surrounds Helen as surrounds him. At least she doesn't resent me for spoiling Julian's plans. Unless she's hiding her feelings, of course. I realise she's speaking again.

'Your father was very good to William after the accident.'

'What happened?'

'William worked for your father in the quad bike business. They were larking about racing a new design of quad bike up at the Hall when William came off and landed badly. Broke his back, I believe. He was in hospital for ages.'

'Did you know my father?'

'I only met him a couple of times. Lovely man. Always polite and considerate. Have you met old Bob over there?' She nods towards a man with rheumy eyes who's nursing a pint and chewing on the end of an unlit pipe. 'He worked at Black Hollow years ago as the gardener and his father was the chauffeur before that. Bob knew your father when he was a boy and could tell you a story or two. A lot has happened there over the years.'

I wonder if Bob knew my mother too. 'Do you know what sort of things happened at the Hall? Muriel in the shop hinted at bad things but I wasn't sure how much to believe.'

'I know people have died there but I suppose that's only to be expected with an old house,' Helen says cautiously. 'Maybe you should talk to Bob and get it straight from the horse's mouth, so to speak. I'm sure he'd love to see the place again. You could invite him for tea.'

'Perhaps I will. At least he doesn't look like the sort of man who'd make things up. The woman at the shop offered to tell me stories but she struck me as the sort of woman who'd invent anything for a bit of drama.'

'Muriel? She's Julian's mother.'

Shit. 'I didn't mean—'

'No matter. Have you tried the quiche? It's very good.'

She smiles at me but I can't tell whether I've offended her or not. She's a hard woman to read.

I realise Julian's a hard man to read too. Everything about him had shrieked public school wealth when I'd seen him here in the pub. The image he'd projected hadn't fitted at all with a gossipy mother who eked out a living in the village shop. I suppose he's set on 'bettering' himself and perhaps his plans for the Hall had been part of that process.

Oh, dear. I've thwarted his plans and now I've insulted his mother too.

Chapter 20

Weaving my way through the loud tourists to the front door, I notice the old man again. I pause then sit in the chair opposite him. He looks up from his pint of bitter, his face opening like a flower at the pleasure of finding someone to talk to.

'Bob, isn't it? I'm Tasha, the new owner of Black Hollow Hall. Can I chat with you for a few minutes?'

Bob leans back in his chair and looks me up and down. 'Well, well, well. You must be Andrew's daughter. I heard you'd inherited the place. Mrs Harrington told me about you years ago. She used to visit the rose garden while I was pruning. She enjoyed a chat.' He taps the side of his nose and barely pauses for breath. I open my mouth to speak but he's off again. 'I think she used that place to sort out her head once she discovered I was all ears and no mouth. Told me all sorts, she did. You look a bit like her.'

'Was this Andrew's mother or wife?' I finally get a word in.

'He never married – well, not that I know of. Not after all that happened. Your grandmother never forgave herself, you know.'

'For what?' I notice a few people nearby have stopped talking. One has paused with her glass halfway to her lips.

'Forcing Sally and Andrew to put you up for adoption and sending Andrew away to college in London. He was sixteen at the time. He accused his mother of ruining his life and didn't speak to her again. She was always fragile after that.'

I'm stunned. My father was only sixteen when I was born? 'How old was my mother?'

'She was sixteen too.'

A thousand questions crowd into my head and I don't know which one to ask first. This is my opportunity to find out the history of my natural family but the tourists are giving us their full attention now. 'Bob, would you like to come to the Hall and have tea with me? There's so much I want to ask you.'

'I'd love to, Miss Tasha. Not today, though. I've got a doctor's appointment.' He rubs his knee and sighs.

'Please, just call me Tasha. How about tomorrow?' Reuben will still be away but it will give me time to digest everything and privacy to mourn the loss of my father. I also want to mull over the whereabouts of my mother. Sixteen! They were still children.

'Tomorrow would be lovely but I can't walk there I'm afraid.'

'I'll come and fetch you. I can pick you up from here at three.' Thank goodness I have my little car now.

Old Bob leans forward and pats my arm with his bony, blue-veined hand. 'I'm looking forward to it.' He gives me a smile, revealing gaps in his haphazard teeth.

'Just one more question.' I have to ask it because I can't bear not knowing the answer... 'Do you know where my mother is?'

'Sorry.' His wrinkled old face is full of compassion. 'She ran away after you were taken from her. If anyone has heard from her since then it's news to me.'

* * *

I'm disappointed to find William isn't home because I want to talk to him about what Bob told me. William would probably have known my mother and might have more information. I decide to walk around the grounds to think about the news I've been given. Where is she? Where did she run away to? London possibly. Kids always think London is the city of opportunity. Or maybe she went looking for my father?

Skirting around the lake I marvel at the reflection of sky and trees. The water is so still. A pair of swans emerges from the rushes and I watch them glide elegantly to the middle of the lake leaving an arrow of ripples behind them. This place is serene and beautiful and I feel my spirits calming. I promise myself I'll bring my paints and easel out here soon. The Luton house and the Rigbys are a million miles away. I can't wait to show this place to my parents and Reuben's family. It's a shame Mum and Dad are not home until mid-June and Margaret and Graham haven't been able to visit yet but they promise they'll come over soon.

Finding myself back at the stream I decide to follow its grassy banks to the start of the driveway. The clear water trickles merrily over stones, reflecting sunlight onto the iridescent blue bodies of dragonflies dipping in and out of the water. Large clumps of ferns splay like fireworks under the shadowed pines at the edge of the wood. The stream meanders through the trees and I walk alongside it, the shade cooling my hot skin. When I reach the small bridge and look towards the gatehouse there's still no sign of William so I decide to return to the coach house and do some work for a while. I open my laptop and click on my latest project – a set of birthday cards depicting a married couple in humorous exchanges. I'm soon immersed in getting the characters right and the message conveyed in their expressions.

* * *

I feel a sudden pang of hunger and look at my watch. Three hours have passed and the sun's fading outside. I open the fridge, reassured to see the light working, and pull out ham and salad items. It's nice not having to think about cooking proper dinners while Reuben's away. He helps with the preparation but it's always a chore wondering what to cook. Life is much easier when I can graze on bits and pieces from the fridge. It's also easy when I can nip to The Dog House for a snack at lunchtimes and it gives me a chance to meet people. I'd never have gone into a pub on my own in Luton.

With the simple salad consumed and the plate washed I switch the television on while I wait for Reuben to call. I'm so caught up in a house renovation programme, trying to learn a few tips, that the trill of the phone makes me jump.

'Hi cherub, everything okay? Do you miss me?'

'Everything's great here. Of course I miss you. How was your journey this morning?'

'Terrible. I tried the Oxford route as it's shorter than the M4 but the tailbacks went on for miles. I was late for my meeting.'

My heart sinks. I was hoping he'd miss the heavy traffic by setting off so early.

'I'm bloody knackered as well. I'm not used to getting up at six.'

Maybe I should try and persuade him to leave his job once we find tenants. I realise I'd be asking a lot of him – giving up his career to project manage the house restoration with no guarantee he would be entitled to anything until we marry – but then he wouldn't have to make that journey. Generating an income from the house could take a while to establish but I'm optimistic and we wouldn't need a lot to live on. Besides, I'll still be earning a bit. If necessary we could rent out the coach house once we finish a couple of rooms and move into the Hall. At least we'd have a close neighbour then.

'How was your day otherwise?' I ask, hoping he'll say he didn't enjoy it too much.

'Work's good but it's going to be better. You know I've been more involved with the marketing of products at the festivals lately? Well, they've just called me and offered me a new job. It's a great opportunity.'

My heart plummets. I hear the excitement in his voice but I can't find the words to congratulate him. He definitely won't want to leave work now.

'Doing what?' I ask, knowing I have to show an interest.

'Managing the negotiation and delivery of sponsorship deals. Up to two million quid per festival!'

'What sort of sponsorship deals?'

'Beer, cars, fashion, food. It means I'll have to work away from home sometimes but I'm doing that now anyway.'

'How often will you be away? For how long?' I feel a stab of apprehension.

'I'll be going to Germany and Norway mainly, for about a week at a time but mostly in the summer. You don't mind, do you? Not now you're away from Luton?'

I want to tell him that of course I'll be fine. Haven't I been saying for weeks that I don't mind the isolation here? But the thought of being alone for a whole week at a time makes me feel… hollow. Unnerved.

I'm being pathetic, though, and unfair to Reuben as he proves a moment later when he asks, 'Aren't you pleased for me, Tash?'

'Of course I'm pleased.' I've got the Hall. It's only right that Reuben should have what he wants too. 'I'm just surprised. Did the offer come out of the blue?'

'Er, no…' Reuben pauses. 'I had an interview this morning.'

'You didn't tell me you'd applied for a new job!'

'I wanted to surprise you.'

He's done that all right. Hell, why am I feeling so shaken?

'I'll be earning a lot more than I do now,' he says, 'and I'll get a company car. You can have the Focus and we can resell that old crock we just bought for £500.'

I feel a sting of indignation. 'I love my little Renault!'

'You need something more reliable seeing as I'll be away a lot. You don't want to break down in the middle of nowhere when you're all alone.'

True, but I'm not keen on the Ford Focus. We haven't repaired the scratch yet so every time I look at it I'm reminded of Dean Rigby.

'You *are* okay about this job, Tash?' He sounds disappointed in me and with justification. It's hypocritical of me to want my dream and resent him wanting his. It's only that I'd hoped my dream would become his dream too.

'It's just the surprise,' I repeat.

'If you're worried about the Hall, we could look into getting a project manager,' he says.

'Good idea.' I force some enthusiasm into my voice but the fact is I don't like this new direction at all. 'Congratulations, by the way. We should celebrate.'

'We should.'

'I can organise the builders while you're away and it won't be all the time, will it?'

'Course not. Have you called any builders yet?' he asks.

I tell him about William's visit and the progress I've made researching companies.

'The two William recommended both sound good. I've arranged for them to come tomorrow morning and Thursday. I'll make notes for you in case I forget the details.'

'I've had to swap my days around because of the time I took off to attend the interview. I won't be home until Friday evening but I'm not back in work until Wednesday so we'll still have four days together.'

I try not to let the disappointment colour my voice. Friday evening is ages away. How will I feel when he goes for a whole week?

After we've wished each other good night I stare at the television for a while, not really taking it in. I *can* cope on my own. I *will* cope on my own.

I'm in the kitchen boiling the kettle when I'm suddenly plunged into absolute darkness. The power has gone off again.

Chapter 21

I grope around the kitchen for the torch but can't find it. Why didn't I think to keep it handy? I stand still for a moment, trying to decide whether to go straight to bed and tackle the problem in the morning or go over to the main house to throw the switch again. Will it matter if there's no electricity for a while? What about the food in the freezer? The weather's warm and it might defrost overnight and be ruined. I'll have to go to the house. I'm tempted to find the phone and call Kirsty and tell her I've got to brave the dark Hall, but it's late. She won't thank me for waking her up when she has to be in work early.

I stumble my way into the living room and feel along the sideboard. The torch isn't there so I pull open the drawer. There it is. I switch it on and locate the bunch of old keys. Trying to ignore the fluttering in my chest I slip out of the coach house and follow the torchlight across the yard. *Be brave*, I tell myself, *there's nothing to be afraid of.* This place is a lot safer than Luton. There the threat was real. Human and red-haired. Here the only threat is in my imagination.

Thick clouds cover the moon and the yard is so dark my weak torchlight doesn't reach to the other side. Which key is it again? I try two before I find the right one. The door opens with a creak that sounds loud in the still night. The darkness is so dense behind me I can almost feel it pressing against my back. I turn around, wildly flashing the torch about the yard to reassure myself that I'm alone. There's nothing to see but shadows looming in doorways as the light moves. A square black mouth yawns above the half-stable door. Something flies towards me through the torchlight and I duck. It must be a bat. Aargh! *Don't be silly*, I tell myself. *It's just a flying mouse.*

Stepping over the threshold into the scullery, I sense a movement of air against my bare arms and goosebumps rise up on my skin. Is there a window open somewhere? I try the light switch but no light comes on. I inch forward, my senses on high alert. God, this place is creepy at night but then so would any big old houses be with their histories and sinister dramas. *Stop it,* I tell myself. I need to think positive thoughts or I'll spook myself. I wonder if the house will be different when it's brightened up. But of course it will be. There'll be lights and warmth and sounds of television, music or radio. Now there's nothing but silence and darkness.

The kitchen seems endless as I walk through with just the torchlight. Shadows swell and shrink like demons from Hell as I shine the torch around the corridor and doorways and my heart beats faster. The smell of dust and damp fills my nose. When Reuben comes back I'll insist the electricity supply to the coach house is checked. This is ridiculous. The isolator switch must be dodgy. My irritation spurs me on but as I reach the old office doorway I stop. Did I hear something? I listen intently but there's no sound. Even so my disquiet is growing. Panic is building in my chest and my breaths are getting shorter. I need to throw the switch and get out again – back to the sanctuary of the coach house.

Wait. I definitely heard a scuffling sound coming from the dining room. Are there mice, or even worse, rats?

Footsteps?

I'm sure I heard footsteps. Oh Jesus, is there someone in the house? I run into the office and shine the torch at the meter cupboard. The isolator switch is off again. I reach for it but a sudden loud cry makes me leap in the air with shock. I flick the switch and whirl around. The lights in the main house remain off but my torchlight picks out the reflection of glassy eyes.

A cat! My heart hammers in my chest but I laugh softly. Nothing but a cat. How the hell did it get in? Is there a window open somewhere? The cat yowls again. It's an unusual woman-like cry but this is no ordinary cat. It has the pretty, striped face of a tabby but the rest of its fur is spotty. It must be a Bengal. I've heard a woman at work say how vocal they are. Expensive too. I can't imagine it being a stray, but where has it come from?

The cat shoots past my ankles and slips through the gap in the doorway to the dining room. Oh no. I don't want to go through there. Not with just a torch. Should I leave the cat in here? It can't come to any harm and it might eat the mice, if there are any.

'Here, puss,' I call softly. It doesn't appear so I head back along the corridor to the scullery and out into the yard. I'm about to close the door when the cat darts through, its tail the size of a toilet brush, as though it had feared being shut inside. I lock the door quickly and breathe a sigh of relief. The cat follows me across the yard and into the coach house and I'm thankful when the light comes on. I open the fridge and get out some ham.

'Here, puss,' I say again, flapping a slice of meat towards the cat. This time it runs to me, its tail reverting to its usual size, and delicately takes pieces of food from my fingers. It's well-mannered and friendly and doesn't seem starved. Maybe it's only recently wandered from its home. I put a bowl of water down and the cat drinks thirstily. I don't know what to do with it now. Should I let it stay in the coach house? It might soil somewhere or tear at the furniture and carpet if it can't get out. I can't leave it outside because what if someone has lost it and it wanders away? These are valuable cats.

I tip half a tin of tuna into a bowl and show it to the cat. It sniffs the fish and yowls once then eats it with enthusiasm. I look out of the kitchen window at the dark courtyard. I don't want to go out there again. Perhaps I'll keep the cat in here tonight and look for its owner tomorrow. It'll keep me company.

Chapter 22

The cat curls up at the end of the bed and sleeps there all night. I can't stretch out but I don't mind. The next morning it follows me downstairs and rubs itself against my legs to leave its scent. I look out of the window at the sunshine and I'm pleased I didn't call Kirsty. I'm quite proud of myself now it's daylight and the fear has gone. I faced my demons and survived and didn't pull any hair out. I'm getting stronger.

I fuss the cat then put some ham and cubes of cheese in a bowl and tempt it across the yard before shutting it in the old dairy with its breakfast. I don't want it to make a mess in the coach house. I'll let it out once I've discovered who it belongs to and I know just the woman to ask. I look at my watch. I have an hour and a half before the first builder shows up to price the renovation project.

* * *

The bell tinkles gaily as I enter the shop and Muriel looks up from her *Hello!* magazine. She hastily thrusts it under the counter and beams.

'Tasha! How lovely to see you. Have you got time for that cup of tea now?'

I almost hesitate in the doorway. I'm relieved my comment to Helen can't have got back to her but I feel exposed under Muriel's direct gaze, as though I'm the prey and Muriel the predator. I shake myself. How silly to feel uneasy with a woman who's nothing more than an old gossip. She is Julian's mum though and might want to glean information about me for Julian's benefit.

'Come in, come in. I won't bite. How's life at Black Hollow Hall?'

'I don't have time for tea today, sorry. I only came to ask if you know anyone who's missing a Bengal cat.'

'Oh.' Muriel's smile slides off her face. 'Have you found a cat then?' She frowns. 'The Newlands in Tanners Lane have a Bengal – they're the spotty ones, aren't they? I've seen it sitting in their gateway.'

'Where's their house? Can I walk there?'

'Easily, so you can spare a minute and I can tell you some history about the Hall.'

'It's okay. Old Bob is coming for tea today. He's going to enlighten me.'

Muriel's face is a picture. She looks like a fisherman whose ten-pound carp has just slipped the hook. I listen to her directions and leave with the promise to return for tea another day.

The directions take me to a pretty Georgian house behind tall, ornate black gates. I look about for an entry phone or doorbell but can't see anything apart from a 'Beware of the Dog' sign. I unfasten a gate, slip through and walk down the short, curved driveway, looking around to make sure there's no guard dog lurking to leap out at me with its hackles up and teeth bared. Maybe the dog and cat don't get on so the cat ran off. A smart blue BMW convertible is parked in the driveway and I wonder what the owner is like.

The doorbell clangs in a distant room and a minute passes with no reply. I'm about to give up and leave when I hear someone approaching. The door's opened by a woman with sleek blonde hair. She's wearing a white silk blouse and loose tan-coloured trousers. She must have been applying her make-up because one eye is emphasised with thick mascara while the other looks strangely naked.

'Yes?' Her tone is sharp.

'I was told you own a Bengal. I wonder if it's missing.'

'Have you found Morse?' The woman's tone completely changes. She grabs at my arm and pulls me into the house. 'Come in. We've been looking everywhere for him. My husband's out searching. I was about to go to the shop to see if that woman has heard anything. She seems to know everything that's going on hereabouts.'

'She's the one who told me to come here. I found a Bengal in my house last night. I've shut him in the dairy to keep him safe.. Great name by the way – I assume it's for Morse code rather than Inspector Morse?'

'Yes, dots and dashes. Dairy? Where do you live?' The woman's eyebrows rise as I tell her.

'But that's at least a fifteen-minute walk from here. He'd never stray that far. Sometimes he sits at the end of the drive but he doesn't leave our garden. Give me a minute. I'm Sandy, by the way,' she calls as she runs up the stairs.

Sandy reappears with full make-up on. Why bother when we live in the middle of nowhere? Clearly appearances are important to her. Sandy scribbles a note for her husband explaining to me that it isn't worth texting as the signal is useless, then takes me outside to her BMW clutching a cat basket.

'Do you have a dog as well?'

'God no. A cat's enough.' She notices the sign on the gate as we drive through. 'Oh that. We put it there to deter burglars and people selling rubbish at the door.'

'Are there many of those around here?'

'Actually no. We moved from Swindon so we weren't used to village life.'

Maybe that explains the need to keep up her appearance. She must think it very quiet around here with few people to admire her good looks. As we approach Black Hollow Hall Sandy's eyes widen and she sighs with pleasure.

'What a stunning house! I'd heard it was lovely but I've never seen it before. You must be so proud of it.'

'It needs a lot of work,' I say, but I can't deny the small rush of pride I feel at her gushing compliments.

'No wonder Julian is so desperate to buy it. He has a group of investors waiting to buy in to a house-to-flats scheme. This is the second one that's fallen through.'

I look at Sandy. 'Well, he won't get his hands on my place, I'm keeping it.'

'I'm sure something else will turn up for him, although I should imagine he's under pressure to find something soon. The investors won't wait around forever and he lost a lot of money on a piece of land recently in Cirencester.'

'How can you lose money on land?' I ask her. *How does she know all this?*

'He bought it expecting to get planning consent to build new houses but the palm he greased at the council had heart trouble and took early retirement. Julian was fuming.' Sandy gives a little laugh.

As we climb out of the car I marvel at the uncaring nature of Julian, and Sandy for that matter. 'How do you know all this?' I ask. Julian sounds dishonest and dodgy to me and I'm glad I have no business dealings with him.

'It's a small village.' Sandy shrugs and looks up at the old house with admiration.

I feel a shiver across my skin. How many other people want to turn Black Hollow into flats and build houses in the grounds? Who are these investors? I bet they weren't happy when I turned up. I lead Sandy across the yard to the dairy. Her face lights up when she sees the cat. She picks him up and he snuggles into her neck. I fear for the silk blouse.

'Thank you so much. I still can't understand how he got here though. I was beginning to think he'd been cat-napped.'

Cat-napped? And left in my house on purpose? A house in which the lights went out? No, I'm not even going to entertain the idea. The Rigbys made my life a misery in Luton. I'm not going to let lingering terror create fear out of nothing here. It must have wandered from home and got in a window. After all, I'd felt a draught, hadn't I? I'll check the Hall to see if any windows are open.

Sandy drops me back at my car in the village and suggests we meet up some time with our husbands for a thank-you drink. I don't try to explain Reuben and I are only engaged. I say a hurried goodbye and rush home, arriving as a large white van trundles down the drive behind me.

The builder, Michael Chambers, impresses me with his knowledge as we walk around the house and assures me the Hall would be his only commitment for the duration of the project. He studies the plans, surveys and engineer's reports thoroughly and looks at the quotes my father had received previously. He then asks several questions while he takes pictures of the documents with his phone.

I answer as best I can, wishing Reuben was here to assist, then I ask Michael questions.

He says he has a gang of skilled tradesmen working for him and as he's been given so much information he'll be able to email me a quote the following Monday. He's polite, efficient and not too pushy. He's also helpful when I ask for validation of his work from previous customers and says he'll request their permission to share their contact details.

'I have other builders to interview but I'll let you know my decision as soon as possible,' I promise.

After he's gone, I prepare a sandwich and look at my watch. I'll just have time to check the Hall more thoroughly for open windows before I fetch old Bob for tea. I'd glanced about as I'd shown the builder around but I needed to give him my full attention. I enter the back door and pause, waiting to see if a draught lifts my hair or brushes my skin. Nothing. Had I imagined it last night?

I look around the kitchen and test the windows are fastened securely. I don't want the cat to get back in – or anything else for that matter. I once heard a story about squirrels getting into someone's house through a window and causing all sorts of damage.

I check the boot room and office then walk through to the dining room. Heavy drapes are held by gold rope tie-backs, their huge tassels hanging low over the velvet. I move them aside to check the French doors and admire the view, sneezing as a cloud of dust tickles my nose. I look down, trying to get a tissue from my pocket when my breath catches in my throat.

There are footprints in the dust behind the curtain.

Chapter 23

I close my eyes to calm my racing heart then peer closer at the footprints. There's a thin layer of dust over them and surely it hasn't all come from the curtains? No, they were probably made months ago when my father was here. I'm not going to let them spook me. I'm here to stay.

Bob's waiting in the bar when I arrive to collect him and he gives me a wide smile. He chatters non-stop on the way to the Hall. It's as if he's been storing up conversations for months and now he can let them all out. He tells me about his knee and how much he misses his dearly departed wife. I park my little car as close to the coach house as possible but Bob wants to stand and admire the Hall before we move, much like Sandy did. I stare at it too and quash a small shiver of unease. *Don't be ridiculous. There's nothing to fear here,* I tell myself. Old Bob takes ages to hobble to the door. He must leave home early in the morning to get to The Dog House for his lunchtime pint. He pauses several times to rub his knee before sighing and setting off again.

'It's such a shame,' he says, 'I was keen to look around the old gardens to see how they've changed.'

I secretly think he might be disappointed if he did. William does a great job of mowing the acres of grassland and pruning trees with his extendable cutters but tending flower beds is a little trickier. He manages to hoe the weeds from his chair but getting amongst the plants to prune, support and deadhead them is too tricky. Bob's rose garden is overgrown – the plants leggy with no promise of the exquisite blooms he'd described on the short journey to the Hall.

Bob takes a large bite of Battenberg cake, washes it down with a mouthful of tea, and leans back in his chair. His eyes crinkle as he smiles at me. 'Forty years I worked here, and I loved every minute of it. It's so good to see the place again.'

'You must have known my family well.'

'I certainly did. Your father was a little scoundrel, always up to tricks with that friend of his, William. Only in fun though. Not like his brother. He always did have a mean streak.'

'Brother?' This is news to me. 'I didn't realise I had an uncle. Is he still around?'

'He's been gone for a very long time.'

I open my mouth to ask what he means – has he gone away or has he died? – when there's a knock at the door. I excuse myself and go to answer it. William sits waiting in his wheelchair; his arm outstretched and holding a catalogue.

'I thought we might plant some flowering shrubs around the grounds to add a bit of colour as I can't manage the flower beds. There are some lovely rhododendrons and hydrangeas in that brochure if you'd like to take a look.'

'What a wonderful idea. I've got Bob in here. Let's ask him for his opinion.'

'Bob?' William frowns.

'The old gardener. He remembers you.' I go back to the lounge to fetch him.

'Come and say hello to William, Bob. He can't come in, so could you come outside?'

'I'd love to.' Bob gets unsteadily to his feet then hobbles to the front door. *Why doesn't he use a walking stick?*

William has turned his chair and is trundling away.

'William, my dear boy,' Bob calls.

William pauses then swings his chair to face us.

'I haven't seen you for what... thirty years? I heard you were back.' Old Bob walks over to William and pats him awkwardly on the shoulder.

More pity. More remembering the man William used to be. William's mouth is pinched and he stares at his feet resting on the metal footplates. He glances up briefly and nods then looks away again. I've been insensitive and I feel awful.

'Remember when you and Andrew swapped my sugar for salt in the potting shed? I nearly threw my tea up.' Bob chuckles.

William makes an effort to respond, smiling grimly. 'I certainly do… you soaked us with the hosepipe as a punishment.'

Bob tips his head back, showing gaps between his teeth, and laughs like a barking seal. 'Little buggers, you boys were. Oops, pardon my French, Miss Tasha. One time they dug up all my neatly arranged bedding plants and mixed them all up. I'd spent ages setting them in groups of colour.'

William nods at the brochure. 'I'll leave it with you, Tasha. Well, must get on. Nice seeing you again, Bob.' He turned his chair and moved away.

I must remember not to impose any other visitors on him. Bob goes back inside to finish his cake. I sit opposite him and give in to my desire to bombard him with questions.

'Did you see much of my mother when you worked here? Sally, wasn't it?'

'Yes. Pretty slip of a girl, clouds of dark hair and big grey eyes, just like yours. She used to live in the village and visit with her sister, Lynn. Sally was sweet on your father and Lynn took a shine to William.'

'What about my uncle?'

'Simon? The girls didn't take to him. He was a surly, broody type. He was always jealous of your dad. Simon thought because he was the oldest he should be the apple of his mum's eye but she favoured Andrew. Sunnier nature, you see.'

'Is my uncle still alive?' I wonder why he hasn't inherited Black Hollow Hall.

'Far as I know, he is. Sorry to be rude but do you think you could run me home now? My knee's giving me gip and I need my tablets.'

I jump up. 'Of course! Perhaps you can come back another day when you're feeling better.'

'I'd like that.' He pats my hand and gets slowly to his feet.

I help him towards the car and as we leave he stares up at the attic window swallowing and blinking hard.

'Are you all right, Bob?' I ask, putting my hand gently on his arm.

He looks at me with watery eyes. 'Your grandmother jumped to her death from that window,' he says shaking his head. 'A very sad day, that was.'

I go cold all over and the backs of my hands tingle. Jumped to her death? 'What made her do that?' I ask, my voice betraying the shock I feel.

'She couldn't carry on once your grandfather died. Did you know he was murdered?'

Chapter 24

Bob peers at my face as I stare out of the windscreen. 'I'm sorry, I've said too much. You shouldn't listen to my ramblings. It was all a long time ago. Over twenty years in fact. Can you drop me at the third cottage on the left?'

'Murdered? In the Hall?' I'm stunned.

He pats my hand. 'I'll visit again soon.' Bob opens his door and tries to clamber out. I run around the car to help him and see him to his front door. He turns the handle and walks in, saying thanks for the tea, but I can't stop myself from reaching for his arm to detain him.

'Did they catch the person who did it?' I can't bear to think the murderer might have got away with it.

'Oh yes. He was put away for a very long time and as far as I know he's still there. Sorry, I've got to go. Goodbye miss.' He closes the door with a soft click and I'm left staring at the blue-painted wood.

Who killed my grandfather? I'll have to go home and look it up on online.

* * *

I search for hours but can't find anything. I also search for Simon Harrington but there are so many people of that name I don't know where to start. It's so frustrating. Bob knows a lot more but he's clearly reluctant to tell me. He could see he'd alarmed me and must have felt bad about it. But I need to know.

Luckily the power doesn't fail again because there's no way I'd go in the Hall tonight. I go to bed but sleep badly, my dreams taking on the surreal horror of the kind I'd had in Luton where

I was being chased by a man with a knife and my legs wouldn't carry me forward.

Relieved to see daylight creeping through a gap in the curtains, I think about asking Muriel for information. No. I won't do that. Muriel is bound to embellish the story and unsettle me even more. She's got a vested interest in scaring me away. I think she'd do anything to help her precious son to get his hands on the Hall. I'll ask William instead. I dress quickly and run up the drive to his cottage. When he answers the door my lungs are on fire and I can barely speak.

'Do you know who killed my grandfather?' I pant. 'Do you know how he died?'

William looks intently at me and is silent for a moment. 'I think you should come in for a minute. I'll make you a coffee.'

I perch on the edge of the sofa.

'Who's been telling you stories?' he asks. 'No, don't tell me. It'll be Bob.'

I nod miserably. I'm so disappointed Black Hollow has a sinister past. But hang on, did William say stories? 'Is it true?' I ask.

'It's natural to want to know what happened but really… name one good thing that'll come from knowing.'

'I'm not sure… but it would give me answers.'

'Feed your imagination, more likely. The past doesn't matter and we can't change it anyway. It's making the most of the future that's important.' William presses his hands to the sides of his chair and tenses his arm muscles to shift his bodyweight.

Is he referring to his own situation or mine? Perhaps I shouldn't keep badgering him.

'It was all so long ago, Tasha. Don't worry yourself with it. I was afraid Bob might start on those old stories. Just move on and enjoy the house for what it is. Don't let this spoil it for you. Did you look at those brochures?'

William's clearly not going to disclose more. I don't want to sour the easy friendship that's growing between us so I tell him which shrubs I'd like then return to the coach house to eat a quiet breakfast.

I don't want the radio or television on. I need time and space to think. There's so much I want to know. Where's my mother? How did my grandfather die? Who killed him? Is the murderer still in prison?

A loud knock at the door startles me. When I open it my heart gives a jolt and I step back, almost closing the door again at the sight of ginger hair. But it isn't a Rigby. Of course it isn't…

'Mrs Hargreaves? I'm Scott Dawson,' the visitor explains. 'The builder.'

I open the door properly, feeling foolish and not bothering to correct him about my title. Scott Dawson is young; a blue-eyed ginger nut. He holds out his hand and I take it, trying to force down my revulsion for a hair colour I'd rather liked before the Rigbys came into my life.

'I didn't realise the time,' I say, because I'm sure he must think me rude or a bit odd.

I close the door behind me and lead him to the Hall. He's as thorough and knowledgeable as the builder who'd called yesterday but as the minutes pass I realise it doesn't matter. I'm embarrassed and ashamed but I'm not going to give him the contract because every time I saw that red hair I'd panic that the Rigbys had found me. I know I've got to get over this ridiculous aversion but at the moment I need to focus on healing myself and strengthening my relationship with Reuben.

Scott promises to send me his quote but I'm too cowardly to tell him I've decided against him. I'll tell Reuben the first builder is the better option, though perhaps I'll be able to make things up to Scott by telling people it was a close-run thing.

I work at my computer for the rest of the day and find it calms me. When Reuben calls in the evening I assure him all is well. I can't tell him about last night after insisting I'd be fine here. I go to bed early and choose a family saga to read. The last thing I need is a scary psychological thriller. I try to lose myself in the Victorian setting but can't relax. I'm too tense listening out for strange noises. I really miss Reuben and can't wait to see him tomorrow. When he returns everything will be put back into perspective. We'll get the building project underway and start planning the wedding. I'm finally drifting off to sleep when my heart freezes and I can't breathe. Someone is in the woods. Screaming.

Chapter 25

I rear up in bed, the cool air prickling on my overheated skin. Had I really heard a scream or had I dreamt it? I hold my breath and wait. Oh, God. There it is again. A female in distress. Terrified, in fact. I want to hide under the covers but the woman needs help. I should call the police.

I turn on the bedside lamp, slide out of bed and creep downstairs, flicking light switches as I go. I reach the phone and pick up the receiver. But maybe I should call William first. He might know what's going on.

'Hello?' His voice is gravelly with sleep.

'William! Did you hear a woman screaming?'

'What?' He's silent for a moment as he takes in what I'm saying. 'Go back to sleep, Tasha.'

'We can't just leave the poor woman to—'

'It isn't a woman. It's a fox.'

'What?' I'm stunned.

'Haven't you heard a fox scream before? It's probably defending its territory. Wait until mid-winter. They make a terrible noise when they're mating.'

'I can't believe an animal would make a horrendous sound like that.'

'Have a listen on YouTube.' William yawns. 'You'll get used to all these weird noises eventually. You haven't heard the owls screeching yet.' He laughs softly.

I thank him and hang up, feeling foolish. Okay, this country living is going to take a bit of getting used to but I'll soon adjust to it. I wonder how many calls the police get from people mistaking foxes for women in distress. Loads, probably. Glad I'm not making one of them, I go back upstairs, turning lights off along the way but I leave a small nightlight on when I climb back into bed. I decide I won't tell Reuben about this embarrassing episode.

The rest of the night is peaceful and I wake to the sound of birdsong. I shower and switch the kettle on. Just a slice of toast and honey for breakfast, I think, because I want to take a proper look at the furniture in the house. I've lifted corners of dustsheets before but this time I'll remove them completely and take photos of everything. I'm going to compile 'before and after' photo albums.

I open the fridge and sigh with dismay. I forgot to get milk yesterday. I'll have to nip to the village shop. I pull on a pink cardigan and I'm suddenly reminded of the cashmere one I'd received for my birthday and used on Dean Rigby's victim. I shudder and try to push away the image of him holding the knife. I hope he's suffering in prison.

The thought of prison reminds me again of my grandfather. Was it a gruesome murder? I try not to think about the violence of it but can't stop wondering who did it. Perhaps I'll find a pretext to visit old Bob and ask him more questions. Perhaps I should make some cakes and take them round to him.

* * *

I enter the shop and go straight to the back where the fridges store the milk. Muriel must be in the stockroom because there's no one behind the till. I'm lingering by the chocolate trifle and lemon cheesecake when the bell rings to herald a new customer. I hear a familiar voice saying hello and Muriel apologising for being in the cloakroom.

'Has Julian got any further with his negotiations?' the woman asks Muriel. I was about to make my way to the till with a chocolate mousse but now I can't resist holding back to listen to the reply.

'He tells me it will all be sorted soon. You know as well as I do how persuasive he can be.'

They both laugh and I wonder what deal Julian is trying to pull off now. The situation here could become very awkward if

I stay hidden so I walk around the shelf unit and make myself visible. It's Sandy, looking elegant in a trouser suit – her sunglasses perched on top of her head. I contain a wry smile. It isn't even sunny this morning.

'Hi, Tasha! Lovely to see you.' She rushes over to me and lightly holds my shoulders then kisses the air near my cheeks, first left then right.

I feel a little foolish but step back and smile. 'How's Morse? Not wandered off again, I hope.'

'I've hardly dared let him out.'

'Wasn't it kind of Tasha to find your cat?' Muriel looks from me to Sandy, not wanting to be excluded from the conversation.

'Absolutely.' Sandy moves past me and jiggles her eyebrows up and down when her back's to Muriel.

I almost burst out laughing and have to disguise my spluttering as a cough. I didn't expect Sandy to have a wicked sense of humour. Maybe she'll be fun to know after all. I pay for the goods and wait for my change. Muriel pauses with her hand in the till, not ready to let me escape yet.

'Did you have Bob round for tea?'

'Yes, we had a lovely old chat. He's good company.'

'Well,' sniffs Muriel. 'It's a good job you saw him when you did. You won't be hearing any more stories from him.'

'What do you mean?'

'Didn't you know?' Muriel looks like her number has just been called at bingo on jackpot night. 'He's had a fall. He's in hospital with a broken leg and concussion. I doubt you'll be seeing him for a while.'

Chapter 26

How stupid am I? I knew Bob needed a stick so why didn't I say anything? I'd watched him struggle to walk, to gain his balance, even to get up and down off a chair. I'll go and see him in hospital – take him some grapes and a newspaper or something. I wish now I'd asked Muriel which hospital he was in instead of rushing out of the shop, but I couldn't tolerate that woman's look of glee. Muriel has clearly missed her vocation in life. She'd have made a great gossip columnist.

I search for NHS hospitals online as I'm pretty certain Bob won't have private medical insurance. He could be at the Cheltenham General or the one in Swindon. It's no good. I'll have to ask someone. Rather than go out again I ring The Dog House and ask the woman who answers the phone. She doesn't sound surprised at the question.

'He's in Cheltenham,' she says. 'If you visit him, send our love.'

I ring the hospital and I'm put through to the geriatric ward. I'm assured Bob is all right but needs to rest so it would better for me to visit after 4pm. It's only 10am so I decide to spend the next few hours checking the equipment in the kitchen and the furniture in the main reception rooms of the Hall. Before I start I go to the dining room. I scan the floor for new footprints and am relieved when I find none. *See!* I tell myself, *definitely old footprints.*

I go back to the kitchen, put a tatty cushion under my knees and open the heavy metal doors of the old cooker. I find grimy shelves and rusty baking tins. The door on the left reveals where the solid fuel is burned. A pile of ashes lies in the bottom. I wonder if the stove is still functional. I suppose if the flue's cleaned and serviced it might be. It would take some getting used to though.

Imagine trying to cook a quick meal only to find the fire has gone out? Perhaps I can keep it but have a small electric cooker as well. It's a shame there's no gas supply to the house. It means we need to plan for central heating too. The old electric storage heaters must be totally inefficient. Reuben has been looking into alternative energy sources and is very interested in ground-source heat pumps.

'It's costly to install but cheap to run and environmentally friendly. It would add value to the property,' he'd said but I hadn't commented. I don't want to talk about selling Black Hollow. I need him to fall in love with the place before it's finished and I wonder how long I've got to persuade him. The builders think about six months to have it habitable but it might take longer for the finishing touches. I just hope we have enough money. I remove the rusty baking tins from the oven and stack them near the wall then move on to the cupboards.

When Mr Jarvis had told us there was £400,000 to do up the house it had sounded a lot of money but looking into the costs of everything it will probably be eaten up very quickly. We need to be careful if we want to bring in craftsmen towards the end of the project to match and replace some of the ornate plasterwork and carved wood, and sorting the rutted driveway out will be costly. The quotes for the general building works will be back on Monday and I'm looking forward to sitting down with Reuben to devise a detailed budget plan and timetable. At least I'll know what I'm up against then.

Cursory glances into the kitchen cupboards reveal piles of plates, dishes and cookware. I look at the chipped edges, old-fashioned gadgets and rusty knives, deciding most of them need to be binned. I open a double length cupboard and am surprised to discover items of food that look more recent – packets of pasta, jars of sauce, peanut butter – and I wonder if they were my father's supplies. They certainly haven't been here for twenty years. I wonder why he didn't keep them in the coach house kitchen, but perhaps they belonged to the workmen who repaired the chimney.

Back in the dining room I tie a scarf over my nose and mouth and pull at the grey-coated sheets, trying to catch the dust in folds as best I can. It still billows up in clouds and I wonder where it all comes from. When I was little my friend told me it came from the moon, which was just a giant ball of dust. I'd believed her for a while, but then I've always been gullible.

The dining table and chairs are the first items uncovered. I use the sheet to wipe a layer of dust off the table revealing a deep caramel-coloured mahogany. It's curved at both ends with an extension piece in the middle. What a simple design yet so elegant. The twelve chairs in a matching wood have crest-shaped backs with a delicate fretwork design and striped fabric seats. It's all a far cry from the little pine table and two chairs we have in Luton. I sit down and immediately jump up as a sharp spring stabs my bottom. I'll have to get the chairs reupholstered.

Next I uncover a huge sideboard with multiple drawers and cupboards. Inside I find silver cutlery, napkin rings and place name holders, all in need of a clean but in good condition. It speaks of a long-lost way of life and I wonder what conversations have gone around the table, what dresses the women have worn and what hidden dramas their lives might have held. Like murder. I stop pulling items out of the cupboard and sit back on my heels. I look over my shoulder and shiver. What happened here? Which room was my grandfather murdered in? I wonder if his spirit is still here then push the thought away. I don't believe in ghosts and the afterlife. It's enough coping with this life. I refocus on the task in hand and pull open another cupboard. There are matching candelabras and boxes of tall white candles too. Wow. I can't wait to hold a fancy dinner party. I carry the silverware to the kitchen ready to be cleaned.

My mum and dad would love all this. Another six weeks and they'll be home. I can't wait to see them. Communication has been quite sporadic from the cruise ship as the internet doesn't always work. I miss my long chats with Mum and sage advice from Dad. I wish the Hall was habitable so they could stay but maybe I can find them a nice hotel nearby.

I move on into the large drawing room. Light streams through the massive window and illuminates the dust motes like a laser beam stage show. I adjust the scarf around my mouth and nose and pull off more dust sheets. Underneath is a plush dark green sofa with an ornately carved wooden frame. The fabric is worn in patches and it looks as though a family of mice has taken up residence there. I poke tentatively at the stuffing spilling out near the back of the cushion, wondering if the sofa can be recovered. Maybe it isn't stuffing. It appears to be shredded paper. How odd. I go into the kitchen then come back with a silver fork. I don't fancy putting my hand in there. I'm not afraid of mice but I don't want to be bitten.

Hooking out a pile of nibbled paper I suddenly realise what it is. Old £50 bank notes. Lots of them. They're no longer legal tender but it wouldn't have made a difference if they were. The mice have made a cosy nest by shredding them up and none of them are in one piece. I hold a handful of paper in my palm and stare. Why would anyone hide so much money in the sofa?

Chapter 27

The nurse points to a bed at the far end of the ward and continues on her way. I thank her and smile at the tiny, frail people in the beds on either side of her. Some smile back as though hopeful I might pause and spend a precious few minutes with them, others lie with their eyes shut, either asleep or having given up on the world.

Bob's face is pale and his eyes are closed as I sit on the plastic chair next to his bed but they fly open as soon as he hears the chair legs scrape on the floor. He sees me and his whole face pleats into one big smile.

'Hello, miss.' He tries to turn towards me and winces. 'It's so kind of you to visit me.'

'Please. Call me Tasha,' I say again. I suppose old habits are hard to break and I am the lady of the house in his eyes. Oh well, it's better than ma'am. I move my position slightly to stop him twisting around. 'How are you feeling?'

'I've been better but I've been told I'll live.' He touches his head. 'I've still got a corker of a headache and my leg's giving me gip, but I'm fine in myself. I mustn't grumble. They're looking after me really well.'

'I've brought you a few things to make your stay more comfortable,' I tell him as I pull items out of a carrier bag. I put a punnet of grapes alongside a chopped fresh fruit salad, a bottle of cordial and a selection of savoury and chocolate biscuits.

Bob's eyes shine with gratitude and appreciation. I imagine he isn't used to many treats on his small pension and what money he does have over each week he probably spends on his daily pint of beer to buy himself some company. He reaches a hand towards me and I take it.

'Thank you, Miss Tasha, you're very kind to me.' He squeezes my hand and I'm dismayed to see tears pooling in his eyes. 'Sorry, I'm a foolish old man. It's just that most of my friends and family have passed away. It gets very lonely when you're eighty-five and the last one to go.'

'It's never too late to make new friends. When you're better you'll have to come for tea again. I enjoyed your visit. Oh, I nearly forgot. The lady at The Dog House said they all send their love.'

'Really? Well it's nice to be remembered.' He sinks back into his pillows with a smile.

'I brought you these as well.' I hand him a newspaper and a crossword book. 'I don't know if you like crosswords.' My dad does but it may not be old Bob's idea of fun. He looks at them then puts them on the table and pats them.

'I do like them but I haven't got my glasses. I think they got broken when I fell.'

'What happened, Bob?'

'I don't rightly know. I was making a bite of supper when the power suddenly went out. I got a bit wobbly in the dark – couldn't work out where I was. Then next I knew I was lying on the floor. My head was pounding and my leg was agony. I must have bumped into the table or hit a chair on my way down. I had to drag myself to the phone in the hallway.'

'Has your power gone off before?' Maybe the supply to the village is unreliable.

'It's not the first time. I think my toaster's a bit dodgy and it tripped the fuse. I need to buy a new one.'

I make a mental note to check his toaster. 'Has anyone else been to see you, Bob?'

'No. Sadly, Jim, the man I play dominoes with, is staying with his daughter for a while. He's getting forgetful and she's worried about him. He leaves his stove on and forgets to take his medication. The other day he forgot where he lived.'

I dread getting old and possibly losing my memory. I try to think of something more cheerful to talk about.

'We've ordered some pink rhododendrons and blue hydrangeas for the gardens to give them some colour.'

'Aah. Now there's a thing...' Bob tilts his head and looks at me. 'Do you drink that real coffee stuff? You know, where you get the leftovers; grounds, I think they call it. If you want a blue hydrangea you need to throw the grounds on the soil otherwise the flowers will turn pink.'

Bob's soon in full flow, plying me with gardening tips. Maybe I should take more interest in the garden. I could restore the flower beds under Bob's guidance. I want to spend more time with him and hear his stories about Black Hollow. He spent a lot of his own childhood there when his dad was the chauffeur and he knows so much about my family. Before I go I want to find out more about my grandfather's murder, but I don't want to upset Bob when he's clearly so vulnerable. Despite William saying there's nothing to be gained from knowing more, I'm creating all sorts of scenarios in my head which are probably far worse than the reality. And what about the money I found stuffed in the sofa? Is there a link between that and the murder? Perhaps I should skirt around the subject to see if Bob will divulge information without being pressured.

'What was it like for my father growing up at the Hall? Was it a happy place?'

'He had a wonderful childhood. His parents doted on him and he and his friends ran almost wild in the woods and grounds. They even had a boat for the lake. It was picture postcard perfect. The only problem he had was trying to avoid his brother. Simon wasn't able to make friends easily so he often tormented Andrew and his chums. He used to hide the cricket bat so they couldn't play or make up stories saying someone had rung and the friend was needed at home.'

'Where's Simon now? Was he around when my grandfather was killed or had he already left the area?'

'He was around all right. After Andrew left for college and then university Simon had his parents to himself. He took every penny of theirs he could lay his hands on. He got in with a group of serious gamblers over in Cirencester and built up massive debts. His father refused to pay them off. I heard them arguing about it once and my Nancy, who was the cook and housekeeper, said they were always at each other's throats.'

Maybe that explains the money in the sofa. Perhaps Simon's parents were hiding it from him. What an awful way to live.

'I wasn't going to tell you this but I suppose you have a right to know.' Bob frowns as he thinks what to say. 'It was your uncle Simon who killed your grandfather in a terrible rage one night. He'd got a gun from somewhere. Said he only intended to frighten his father with it and it went off by accident. He was found guilty of murder though. Simon's in prison serving a life sentence. He got twenty years.'

Chapter 28

I can't stop thinking about my uncle killing my grandad. Was it really an accident like Simon had said? But the courts found him guilty so it can't have been. Reuben and I have talked about it but I still feel the need to pick over the information again in my head. There might be a morsel I've missed or failed to analyse.

'Tash!'

I shift in my chair and realise I've been lost in thought and not paying attention to Reuben.

'You're not bloody listening. I said Scott Dawson's quote is much better value. Look.' Reuben plucks the sheet of paper off the dining table and points at the figures on it. 'He even itemises everything so you know what you're paying for. Tell me again why you prefer the other one.'

I bite my lip, my mind racing to think up a plausible reason. 'Michael Chambers was the more knowledgeable about old buildings. He had a real feel for the place. And I think I could work well with him. Which is important seeing as you'll be away for—'

'Come on, Tash. What's the real reason? I know you judge people sometimes without giving them a chance to prove themselves.'

'No I don't! I'm open-minded. Who have I judged?'

'That woman in the shop for a start.'

Damn. He's got me there. 'She's an old busybody.'

'Or just chatty and friendly.' Reuben takes my hand in his and gives it a little shake. 'Tell me what the real problem with Dawson is.'

'I just… I didn't feel comfortable around him.'

Reuben stiffens. 'Why? What did he do?'

'Nothing.'

'He must have done something. Did he touch you? Make suggestive comments? I'll kill the little shit if he–'

'No, Reuben! It was nothing like that.' Hell. I can't let poor, innocent Scott Dawson get a reputation as a pervert. But I'm out of other ideas. Which leaves the truth. I breathe out slowly. 'He has red hair.'

'Come again?'

'He has red hair. Ginger hair. Which–'

'Reminded you of Dean Rigby. Christ, Tash, you can't go through life avoiding people with ginger hair.'

'I know that.'

'And I thought we were here so you could get over the Rigbys? If you're not getting over them, there's no point in staying here. We might as well sell up quickly – that Julian bloke might still be interested – and buy the house we always wanted. The house I still want if I'm being honest. Not in Luton itself but not far from it. Best of both worlds, I say.'

'Reuben, I am getting over the Rigbys! I've made heaps of progress since we came here. But you can't expect me to get over what happened in an instant. I need a little more time.' I've stopped plucking hairs out for a start. Surely that's a good sign?

'Maybe you're coming at this the wrong way. Instead of avoiding people with red hair, maybe you need to confront it head on and get the problem with it over and done with all the sooner.'

I suppress a shudder. 'I still think Michael Chambers is the better man for the job. You could talk to him. Let him show you how–'

'What's the point?' Reuben tosses the quote aside. 'It's your house and your money, and you've clearly made your mind up.' He stands and goes to the kitchen, where he fills the kettle.

'It's home for both of us,' I call after him. I don't want tension to build between us before Reuben leaves for work again. We've had a good weekend but today it's as if there's an undercurrent to all our interactions with each other. I can sense Reuben's restless. He keeps looking at his mobile phone and complaining at the lack of signal then getting up halfway through television programmes to check his emails. I suppose he's feeling isolated and homesick.

'What will you do if one of the workmen has ginger hair?' Reuben's voice carries from the kitchen. 'Kick him off the premises? You say you're making progress but frankly, Tash, I'm not seeing it.'

'I'm a lot happier,' I insist. 'I've been staying here alone, haven't I?' Even as I say the words I'm struck by an echo of the terror I've felt at times. When I had to creep into the Hall in the dark when the lights failed… When I saw those footprints in the dining room… When the fox screamed in the woods…

I've told Reuben nothing of those incidents and thank God for that. He'd have us back in Luton in a heartbeat. It hadn't crossed my mind that Michael Chambers might have workmen with ginger hair. I'll just have to hope he hasn't. I follow Reuben into the kitchen, anxious to put things right between us. I snake my arms around his waist. 'Let's not bother with coffee. Let's go to The Dog House for an early lunch.' We can look at the finances for the project later.

'I've made the coffee now.'

'Throw it away. Let's go out for a while. Meet some more people.'

He sighs as though he's not in the mood for socialising but then he tips the coffee into the sink and I take it for acceptance. Reluctant acceptance, though. It worries me and the smile I fix on my face is more than a little desperate. 'It'll be fun.'

* * *

Someone calls my name as we walk into the pub. I turn and see Sandy, half out of her chair, waving at me. Next to her is a tall, thin man with a mop of dark hair and glasses. He sends me a tentative smile.

'Come and join us!' Sandy calls. 'This is my husband, Timothy.'

Timothy stands with rounded shoulders, his head nearly scraping the ceiling. He puts out a hand and Reuben takes it.

'I'm Reuben.' He gave a cursory nod to Timothy. 'Nice to meet you.'

Reuben offers his hand to Sandy who ignores it and leans in to grasp his shoulders and kiss him on both cheeks. Reuben takes a step back, looking startled. She kisses me too but all I get is an air kiss. She looks at Reuben again for too long. She fancies him.

'Sit here, Tasha, next to Timothy.' Sandy directs Reuben to the seat next to her.

I do as I'm told but would prefer to sit next to Reuben. Still, I think this is the correct form for table etiquette. I suppose I'll need to learn more if I want to host elaborate dinner parties.

'How are you both settling in?' Timothy asks. 'It's a beautiful house with so much potential.'

I cringe inwardly. I hope he's not going to talk about bloody flats as well.

'It's wonderful. So peaceful,' I say, wanting to add that I feel safe.

'Very quiet,' Reuben says at the same time. 'And remote,' he adds. 'What do you do for entertainment around here?'

'Oh, we make our own entertainment, don't we, Timothy.' Sandy giggles suggestively and somehow her hand lands on Reuben's thigh.

The kiss had surprised him earlier but to my dismay I see Reuben is warming to Sandy. In fact, his gaze drops momentarily to her cleavage, which her low-cut blouse is doing little to hide. Timothy is watching them too; his shoulders slumped and his mouth set in a straight line.

Oh, God. Is Sandy the sort of woman who has affairs? Reuben has never been the sort of man to look at other women but that was when we were happier.

'So,' I say brightly, 'do you have any children?' I know this isn't a polite question to ask but I can't think what else to say and I want to take her attention away from Reuben.

Sandy and Timothy exchange a glance then Timothy says, 'We decided against children. We chose to focus on our careers instead.'

'Oh!' I say in surprise. I'd somehow assumed Sandy was a housewife and I'm ashamed I've stereotyped her. 'What do you do?' I ask her.

'I dabble in stocks and shares, business start-ups and investments. You know the sort of thing. I'm a venture capitalist.'

I'm not sure I do fully understand but my antennae have gone up. Investments? Is she one of the private investors funding Julian's projects?

'Sandy had a generous inheritance so used her funds to make more money,' Timothy explains.

'You've got to speculate to accumulate, I always say,' Sandy laughs.

Reuben looks at her with open admiration.

'Do you have children?' Timothy directs his question at Reuben.

'Not yet, but we will. Once Tasha agrees to marry me.'

'I have agreed. I just want to wait until we've finished Black Hollow.' I don't want to have this conversation in front of almost strangers. Reuben is trying to put me at a disadvantage and I'm irritated.

I make a huge effort to be bright and bubbly over lunch but as soon as we've eaten I pick up my handbag. 'It's been lovely but we need to be heading back, Reuben. We've got to sort those figures out before you go tomorrow.'

'Figures? If you need any help, Timothy's an accountant.' Sandy nods in her husband's direction, eliciting a weak smile from him.

'I don't think corporate auditing is quite what they're looking for,' he says.

We pay for our food at the bar and wave goodbye then get in the car.

'You were flirting with her.' I fold my arms and look out of the side window.

'Hardly. I was only being sociable. You want us to make new friends in the area, don't you?'

'Not ones with a double D frontage on display. You couldn't lift your eyes higher than her collarbone.'

'Don't be daft.'

'Okay. What colour eyes did she have?'

'A lovely shade of blue.'

'Huh, lovely were they?' I know I'm being childish but I can't stop myself.

'I'm teasing, Tash. Why would I look at another woman when I've got you?'

I try to smile but I feel rattled. Reuben enjoyed the attention from Sandy and that bloody woman had been like a wasp around a jam jar. I'll have to keep an eye on them from now on and not give him any reason to feel aggrieved by anything. Things are quite strained between us; he even told me he was too tired to make love the other night. I don't want to push him further away. Who knows where he might end up?

Chapter 29

'We need to hire a skip,' I say, sitting next to Reuben at our small dining table and writing *skip* into my notebook. 'There's a ton of stuff in the Hall to get rid of. In fact, we'd probably be better off hiring a van and taking it all to the local dump. I'm writing a to-do list for us.'

Reuben rolls his eyes. I know he hates my lists but there's so much to do that we have to prioritise tasks to fit in with the building works. I also want him to feel more involved.

'Is there anything you want to add to it?' I ask.

'Wouldn't it be best to go through the whole house first?' he asks. 'See how much there is to dispose of?'

'That's what I'm doing. I've done the kitchen, pantry and dining room and started on the drawing room.'

'Ooh, get you! Drawing room.' Reuben tuts. 'It's a lounge to us mere peasants.'

My cheeks grow warm. 'That's what they were called years ago. "Living room" or "lounge" doesn't sound right for that fantastic room.'

'It would have been fantastic if we'd got to these banknotes before the mice did.' Reuben has pulled all the remnants of the £50 notes out of the sofa and currently has them spread across the table, trying to piece them together.

'I don't know why you're bothering with that. They're no longer legal tender.'

'The Bank of England will take them. I just have to find at least half a bank note with the number on it to get an exchange.' He smooths a fragment of paper and scrutinises it then places it next to another piece.

'You've been doing that for ages and still haven't got even a quarter of a note. You're wasting your time.'

'I've been trying to estimate how much money there was but it's so difficult to tell. There must have been thousands of pounds worth stuffed in there. And I still can't get my head around your uncle shooting your grandad. It's shocking, isn't it?'

'Yes, but like William said, it isn't good to fixate on the past.' I don't tell Reuben that the horrific event keeps invading my thoughts. 'Nothing positive can come of it.'

'Wise words indeed. Isn't this exactly what I've been trying to say to you about the Rigbys these past months?'

'That's different. I still worry about the Rigbys finding me.'

'Even here?' he asks.

'Not as much as in Luton, but yes, sometimes,' I confess.

'You'll be suggesting we move to Scotland next.'

A wave of tiredness hits me. 'No, I won't, but I would appreciate a bit more understanding.'

Reuben sighs. 'I'm sorry. I'm trying Tash, but it's not easy. You keep seeing things that aren't there. You interpret daily occurrences as personal threats to your safety.'

'What do you mean? Give me an example.' Has William told him about my panic over the screaming fox?

'The knife in the newspaper, the eggs thrown at the front door, the scratch on the car.' Reuben stops fiddling with the bits of paper.

'Okay, maybe, but what about the knife attack and the Rigbys threatening me. What about my phone being snatched out of my hand?' Weren't they real threats?

Reuben looks me straight in the eye. 'Yes, they were, but they weren't necessarily all connected,' he says, his voice flat. 'But I'm still concerned about the way you overreact at times.'

'Such as?'

'Thinking I fancy Sandy for a start. I think you're becoming paranoid, Tash.' Reuben looks away and rubs his chin. 'I worry about you being here on your own. I can't see the benefit of living here for either of us. You need to be nearer to our families so they can support you.'

I'm so glad I haven't told him of my fears since we arrived and I certainly won't tell him if anything else frightens me. I need to be strong and rational and I have to make sure I don't pull any hair out in his presence because he knows I do that when I'm anxious. 'I'm fine, Reuben. I don't think the Rigbys can find me here. Like you say, they're small time crooks. They're hardly likely to trek right over here and comb the countryside for me. I'm sure they've got far more important things to do.'

Reuben picks up a chewed piece of fifty-pound note and puts it next to another piece then tosses it aside.

'William told me you called him the other night in a panic but it was just a wild animal making a noise.' He looks at me with his eyebrows lifted.

Damn. Why did William have to tell him? I feel betrayed somehow. 'You didn't hear it, Reuben. It sounded like someone being murdered. Was William cross I'd woken him up?'

'No, he thought it was funny, but even so…'

'Can you move some boxes in the attic for me before you go?' I say, wanting to get off the subject of my supposed paranoia. 'I'll start on the bedrooms this week and if they don't take long I'll sort through the attics.' I just hope there aren't too many spiders.

Reuben stands and stretches his arms to the ceiling then rubs the back of his neck. 'We'll do it now, before I seize up completely sitting here.'

'You sound like an old man.' I laugh, trying to lift the tension between us. I'm reminded of Bob and wonder how he's doing. I haven't visited him again with Reuben at home but I plan to go tomorrow. Reuben made sympathetic noises when I told him about Bob but he didn't fancy giving up part of his weekend to visit someone he's never met. I'll try to help Bob settle once he's discharged home.

* * *

The sun's low in the sky as we cross the yard to the house. I pause by the stove as Reuben walks through the kitchen heading for the attics.

'Do you think we'll be able to get this working again?' I ask. 'We could gather firewood from the estate and it would warm this room and possibly the adjoining ones.' Surely the thought of saving on the heating bill will elicit some enthusiasm from Reuben.

'Possibly.' He shrugs. 'You'll need to research it and call someone out.'

It seems as if I'll be organising most of the restoration. Oh well. I'm capable, but wouldn't it be wonderful if Reuben was as excited by the Hall as I am? I'm at a loss as to how to change his view of the place from seeing it as a short-term project to make extra money to the Hall being our forever home. We could have such fun choosing fittings, enthusing over the old features and craftsmanship, planning exciting projects, setting up a business. The only time he became animated was when I showed him the sofa stuffed with money and told him about the murder that had taken place. Still, at least he'd offered sympathy when I told him of my grandmother's suicide.

We pass the office. 'Wait, can you check the isolator switch?'

'Why?'

'I… er,' I haven't told Reuben about the power cut the other night and after our earlier conversation I'm not going to. 'Just to make sure it won't turn itself off again.'

We stand in front of the grey plastic box with the large red handle.

'Look Tasha. This is down and in the 'on' position.' He talks slowly as though I find it difficult to understand. 'These switches don't flick off by themselves. It takes some force to move them.'

Is that true? Reuben must be wrong because if he's right it would mean someone deliberately moved the switch that night the power failed for a second time. Dread rises up my spine with icy licks and I separate a hair from the lock on my shoulder before winding it around my finger. Who would cut off my power? The answers rush in on me though I try to push them away. A man whose business is failing might do such a thing to force me out. Or a family whose son was locked up because I gave evidence in court might do such a thing to mess with my head. Had Lewis Rigby followed Reuben here or pretended to be a prospective tenant to find out where we are?

No! I'm not even going to entertain ideas as crazy as those. Reuben's no expert. He must be wrong about the switch. He must.

Chapter 30

The dust is everywhere but this isn't the sort of dust I was dealing with when I uncovered the old furniture in the Hall two weeks ago. This dust has left a sticky, gritty layer over everything and clings to my clothes and hair. It hangs in the air and I can feel it crunching in my teeth. It's even worse when the builders are knocking through the walls to create new doorways. I walk along the corridors, saying hello to workmen as I go and stepping over holes in the floors where new pipes and cables are being laid. Thank God none of them have red hair.

I can't wait to get in the shower to rinse it all off but first I need to clear out belongings in the bedrooms. All my good intentions to tackle this task a couple of weeks ago had to be set aside for more pressing matters. The builders had pushed for an early start as they'd just finished a big project and they needed me to make decisions before they got on with the work. I've had to visit showrooms to find suitable bathroom fittings then drag Reuben around with me to make the final decisions. I've created design boards for each room with colour schemes and samples of fabrics and paints.

As well as choosing tiles and flooring Michael has involved me in the positioning of the bathroom equipment, the timetable of the project and managing the budget and finances with him.

On top of all this my boss wants me to produce a new theme for greetings cards targeting the older buying market. I've started designing a new set of cards which, for the time being, I've called 'The Turning Worm.' They depict a late middle-aged couple performing mundane tasks around the home but with the husband taking revenge on his wife for nagging him. They're a tad sexist but might appeal to that demographic. I was inspired by Bob's tales and had the husband putting salt in his wife's tea or aiming the hosepipe over the hedge at her as she berates him for not doing his chores. I've finished eight pictures in total and will leave Laura to write the greetings. I was delighted when my boss praised my designs and he said he's more than happy for me to continue working two days a week from home so thankfully I'm only in Luton one day a week.

The first bedroom I enter contains a four-poster bed with richly woven hangings sadly damaged by mould. They'll need to be removed and new drapes made. The mattresses will have to be thrown away as will the rugs which are threadbare in patches. Carpet beetle, maybe. My parents' wool rug was eaten by those a few years ago. I'll need to get the whole place fumigated as soon as the floorboards are back down. I sigh heavily. Sometimes I feel overwhelmed by how much there is to do. I stand on the bed trying to unhook the drapes but can't manage it. Reuben will need to help me when he's back.

The smell of mildew is very strong. The house seems damper up here but this room is under the spot where the chimney had damaged the roof and it's evident rainwater has been dripping through the ceiling. There are lumps of plaster on the bed and floor. Furniture has been moved aside in places to expose the floorboards ready for pipes to be laid, adding to the mess. I open a huge old wardrobe and peer inside. A waft of mothballs hits my nose and I screw my face up. *Yuk.* I'd forgotten how much this stank the first time I took a quick look round all the cupboards. The rail is full of old clothing. It's hard to believe no one has ever sorted through all this stuff. It's as if the front door had been locked following my grandparents' deaths and not opened again for twenty years. I wonder if my father even went to his parents' funerals.

'Tasha,' a male voice calls up the stairs. 'There's someone here to see you.'

I close the wardrobe door and go to the top of the stairs. Adrian, the plumber, is at the bottom looking up at me. He has an open, smiling face and lovely blond hair.

'He says he's here about the stove.'

'Brilliant!' I run lightly down the stairs, jumping over a pile of floorboards at the bottom.

'Careful! That board's loose. We don't want you getting injured.' Adrian wags a finger at me and I laugh. 'You should be wearing a hard hat too. These ceilings could come down at any minute. I'll find you one.'

I like having builders around the place. It helps to ease my solitude when Reuben's away for his three-night stints in Luton. He has his first festival in two weeks' time and I'm not looking forward to being on my own all week. Daytimes are fine as there are plenty of people around and I regularly visit Bob now he's back home but the nights are long and, on occasions, a little creepy. Sometimes I hear strange sounds downstairs but assure myself it's just the old building creaking as it settles for the night and the knocking sounds are just the pipes expanding and shrinking with the changes in temperature. *Aren't they?*

The main house is quite sinister in the dark so I avoid it. Thankfully, the electricity supply hasn't been switched off again so there's no need to go in there. I've bought candles and matches just in case. I can't wait for the wiring to be finished and the electricity supply to the house to be connected.

A man with an old navy corduroy cap and bushy eyebrows stands on the doorstep. He touches the peak of his cap. 'Hello. Miss Hargreaves? I'm Derek. Shall I take this round the back?' He points at his pushbike leaning against the wall outside the front door. It has a selection of poles with round brushes on the ends tied along its length.

'Oh!' I'd expected a shiny van for some reason. I give the chimney sweep directions then meet him in the kitchen. He spreads his sheets around the bottom of the stove although I'm tempted to tell him not to bother as the floor's filthy anyway. He gets brushes ready then unscrews the front plate of the flue.

'Oh dear.' He takes his cap off and scratches the back of his head.

'What?' I peer over his shoulder.

The flue is full of twigs. Derek pulls a handful out, bringing more down, and puts them on the sheet.

'I'll leave you to it,' I say. 'Call up the stairs when you've finished but be careful of the holes in the floors.' I'm a little disappointed as I'd had the childish urge to run outside and watch the brush pop out of the chimney. I can hardly wait outdoors for ages without making it obvious what I'm doing. An hour later Derek calls me back and takes me into the yard to show me the huge mound of sticks he's pulled from the flue.

'There must have been crows nesting up on the chimney for years. Taken me ages, that has. I suggest you get bird guards on the pots.' He wipes his brow. 'The chimney's swept now. You just need to clean the range then it should be in working order. It's a basic piece of equipment. Light the fire, turn the dial to let more air in if you want it hotter and move this lever to dislodge the ashes.'

I'll call someone in to clean the ovens. At least we now have some form of heating for the kitchen and adjoining rooms and a cooker of sorts. As well as a huge pile of sticks for kindling.

'While I'm here I might as well do the other fireplaces,' Derek says, gathering up his tools. 'Save me cycling all this way again.'

I agree and show him into the drawing room then watch as he screws the poles together and pushes the brush up the chimney. He hasn't got very far when his brush snags on something. He jiggles it and a loose brick falls into the fireplace followed by a flurry of old mortar and soot. Derek picks up a small brush and sweeps it to one side then stops and leans forward to pluck something out of the rubble. It looks like a thin piece of string. He rubs it on his jacket and I realise what it is – a broken gold chain with a large oval gold locket hanging from one end where the clasp is. He swings it towards me and lets it trickle into the palm of my hand.

'Someone's hidden that in there,' Derek says. 'Probably been there decades.'

I pick up the locket and try to open it but the clasp is jammed. I don't want to force it so I take it into the kitchen and lever it open gently with a knife. Inside is a tiny photograph of a dark-haired girl. I'm about to close it again when I realise there is another layer. I pull it open and see two more portraits. A headshot of a young man with dark hair and a new-born baby wearing hand-knitted clothing and bonnet. Who were they? I'll have to see if the young lad resembles any of the portraits hanging up. Is this my father? Is this me?

I slip the necklace into my pocket and I'm heading back upstairs when Adrian stops me.

'I don't suppose you've seen my crowbar have you?' He scratches the side of his head. 'I left it with my tools in here before I went home yesterday. Morris can't find his drill either. We thought the tools would be safe here at night. Have you seen anyone hanging around lately?'

'No.' I frown, hating the sense of unease that creeps over me. 'It's a big house. Maybe you left them somewhere else or someone moved them?'

'Maybe.' Adrian shrugs then turns and walks away.

'You're right!' Morris calls from the study then appears again, holding the drill triumphantly. 'God knows how this got to be three rooms away and I still can't find the crowbar.' A thought strikes him and he grins. 'Maybe you've got a poltergeist,' he jokes, 'because I definitely didn't leave my drill in there.'

Ghoulish humour is the last thing I need but I manage a faint smile and leave Adrian searching for the crowbar.

Get a grip, Tasha, I urge myself as my imagination begins to take hold. I resume my task of clearing out the rooms upstairs, puzzling over the builders' tools. Is someone moving them? I throw the mouldy old clothes from the wardrobe straight out of the window onto the driveway ready to go into the skip. Progressing on to the next bedroom I'm surprised but relieved to find the bed linen isn't damp as it's further away from the water damage. Pulling the counterpane off, it strikes me that the bed looks as though it could have been slept in only recently as the bottom sheet is creased and there's the indentation of a head in the pillow. The thought takes hold and I wonder if I'm looking at the indentation of my father's head. I stare down at it and swallow. But I realise it's unlikely my father slept here when he had the creature comforts of the coach house available. Maybe it was one of the builders who repaired the chimney.

I pull open a deep mahogany drawer to find piles of T-shirts inside. These don't look as old as the stuff in the previous room. I lift one out and unfold it to examine the label. ASOS? My skin tingles. ASOS is relatively new, isn't it? Surely ASOS T-shirts weren't around twenty years ago. I hold up another T-shirt and almost let go again. On the front is a gruesome looking skull with '*I love the dead*' written underneath. I turn it over and feel a stab of alarm. In the shape of a coffin is a list of dates for the '*Alice Cooper – Spend the Night Tour.*' The first date for the UK tour was last November. The building works were done before that. Maybe I really have heard footsteps. But who do they belong to? Is someone squatting here? Are they moving the tools?

Chapter 31

I close the front door of our Luton house and look up at the 'To Let' board as I walk down the path. It's odd we haven't found a tenant yet. I thought there was a shortage of rental properties in the area. I look up and down the street for any sign of red hair then make my way to the train station. My heart rate increases as it does every time I see the bridge and I take deep breaths to calm myself. There are loads of people around. No one is going to attack and rob someone in broad daylight, are they?

I sit on a bench on the platform so that no one can creep up behind me, then wind a hair around my finger and tug. Every sense is on high alert and my palms are sweating. The train arrives on time and I brush the loose hairs from my jacket then scurry on, relieved when I find an empty seat. I hate this journey. I study the people around me. They look harmless enough but who knows what lies beneath their bland expressions and ordinary appearance. I watched a scary TV programme the other night that said possibly one in four people are psychopaths which means at least four of the people are in this carriage. Are they harbouring evil thoughts right now? I shrink into my seat and wait for my stop, remembering the old man who had frightened me that fateful night. He was harmless after all. Just an old drunk looking for someone to have a drink and a dance with. Probably.

I arrive at the office early and make myself a coffee before I switch on my computer. Amanda stops at my desk on her way in.

'How's the building work coming along?'

'Messy,' I say, 'but I think they're making progress.'

'Has Reuben warmed to the place yet?' she asks.

I let out a deep sigh. 'Sadly not. I'm trying to think of ways to change his mind but he hates being so isolated and he finds all the toing and froing exhausting. The last thing he needs after a busy week is an almost three-hour drive to get home. I wish he'd reduce his working week but he's taken a promotion so is working even more hours.'

'Oh well, at least you've cut your hours.' Amanda looks around the empty office but still lowers her voice. 'Between you and me you're better off out of here at the moment.'

I look at Amanda in surprise. 'Why?'

'That bloody Laura is getting right on my tits.'

A smile tugs at the corner of my mouth. I sensed last time I was here that there was tension between them.

'She's got Ian wrapped around her little finger. Laura this and Laura that,' she quotes. And a word of warning – she took the credit for the new range of cards you've just designed.'

My smile disappears. 'Bloody cheek!' Maybe I should come in more often if she's playing that game. I think of the journey on the train. No, once a week is enough.

'Don't worry. I've got your back. If she does it again I'll tell Ian they were your idea.'

I thank her and she goes to the kitchen to make herself her usual two cups of coffee. I settle down to work wondering how I can get the better of Laura. My phone pings and I see a text from Kirsty asking if we can meet up for a drink before I head back to the Cotswolds.

* * *

'What a cow!' Kirsty says, as we sip cocktails.

I'm unable to drive now so I suggested to Reuben that we stay in Luton tonight. He was delighted and has gone to his local to see his mates.

'I need to find a way to stop her claiming the ideas are hers,' I say.

'Why not find a range in the shops and copy it then send it to her. When she tells Ian they're her idea you can tell her she's copied it from the Clintons display.'

'Brilliant. I'll do that. You can be quite wicked, Kirsty.' We laugh and Kirsty calls the barman over.

'This is my last one,' I say. 'I want a clear head tomorrow.'

'How's life in the Cotswolds? Are you happy there? Doesn't it get a bit creepy at times?'

I want to paint a rosy picture of my idyllic life so I don't tell her about my scary moments and my worries that there may have been a squatter, in case word gets back to Reuben again. I also don't want to put her off visiting sometime. Somehow though, I find myself telling her about my grandparents.

'That's awful,' she says, her eyes round and her mouth agape. 'Thank God he's locked up now.'

* * *

Kirsty comes back to the house with me and waits for Reuben to come home before she calls a taxi to take her to the station. I've offered the spare room for the night but she says she'll be fine on the train back to London. I envy her ability to take life in her stride.

Reuben collapses into bed as soon as he gets in and I'm disappointed that the only intimacy between us is listening to him fart and snore. I get up at 9am and take him a coffee but he lets it grow cold and sleeps on. I'm itching to get back to Black Hollow. The street outside is noisy and I haven't slept well. I can't relax here. An hour later I throw his coffee away and make a fresh one.

'Come on, Reuben. Don't waste this coffee as well.'

He groans and drags himself to a sitting position. 'Haven't I told you how exhausted I feel?' He rubs his eyes and leans back against the headboard. 'Do we have to go back to the Cotswolds? We could stay here for the weekend. Rob's having a bit of a bash around his place tonight and I quite fancy it.'

'I'm not staying here on my own all evening,' I say. 'We've already stayed an extra night and Mum and Dad said they'll take a detour and call in to Black Hollow tomorrow afternoon on their way home from Portsmouth. I'm looking forward to showing them the Hall. If you're so exhausted maybe you should drop a day a week. Take a bit of time off.'

'Don't be ridiculous. My new boss is a complete moron. I need to be around otherwise we'll lose people on the team.'

'Do you like your new job?' I ask tentatively.

'Of course I do, but managing others is more complicated than I realised. Sometimes it would be easier and more enjoyable to organise stuff myself. Anyway, the extra money is good.'

'But we don't need the extra money. It isn't worth being in a job you don't like just for the money.'

'I didn't say I don't like it. I'm just having a few problems with my new manager, that's all – but nothing I can't handle. I need to earn more to feel good about myself, okay? It's all right for you, everything landing in your lap. Some of us have to work hard to get it.'

'But what's mine is yours, Reuben.'

'Is it? I feel I'm making all the sacrifices and putting more into this relationship than you are. I don't feel you're committed to us as a couple at all.'

'Would it help if I wrote a will leaving everything to you?'

'It's not about the money. I feel I can't mention our future together in case you think I'm just after your inheritance.'

'I don't think that at all,' I say, and I vow to myself that I'll arrange to see the solicitor and sort out my will.

Chapter 32

I stand at my bedroom window marvelling at the glorious grounds bathed in sunshine. Now I'm back in the Cotswolds my mood has lightened considerably. As much as I love Reuben I'm finding his company quite oppressive lately and I wasn't as sorry to wave him off to work this time. Seeing Mum and Dad was wonderful though. They were so excited to view the place. They'd hired a car from Portsmouth where their ship docked so they could take a detour to visit me.

I showed them around the whole property and grounds then they stood chatting in the drawing room. They loved the setting, although they, too, are worried about my isolation with Reuben away so much.

'It's a stunning house but won't you get lonely, love?' Mum had asked. 'You're a long way from your friends and family.'

'I'm making new friends locally,' I told them. I don't add the two women I've met aren't to be trusted. One's after information for her husband and the other is after Reuben. Maybe I should invite Kirsty to stay as soon as the house is habitable.

'Do you think Reuben will settle here?' Dad had asked, looking up with admiration at the tall mullioned windows.

'I hope so. It would be a wonderful setting for our wedding and a fantastic place to raise a family.' I didn't tell them about his lack of enthusiasm for the place and his reluctance to live here long-term.

'I can see how much you love the old building already.' Dad had patted my shoulder then walked through to the kitchen. 'Have you got the range working yet?' he asked, as Mum and I followed.

'We lit it one evening and it seemed to work well. The weather's been too hot to light it since then but at least we know we've got heating and cooking facilities in here.'

I'd introduced Mum and Dad to William and he'd charmed them with his positive outlook and protective attitude towards me.

'Don't worry, I'll always look out for her,' he'd assured them, and I'd felt a warm glow in my chest. It feels lovely having someone who wants to watch over me even though he's limited in what he's able to do. Still, he's always at the end of the phone and he's a great listener.

It had been a wrench saying goodbye to Mum and Dad but we'd all agreed they'd come for an extended stay when some rooms were habitable in the main house. In the meantime they're making the most of a rare English summer and staying in Devon for a few weeks with friends. They lead a wonderful life now they've retired.

It hasn't rained since the end of May – almost a month ago now – and the stunted grass is showing patches of yellow. In contrast, the sunlight dapples through the trees, casting cool blue shadows and dancing lights across the grounds like a nightclub glitter ball. William has admitted to me that he misses mowing the lawns but says he'll turn his attention instead to clearing undergrowth and pruning back the tall shrubs.

I watch him now across the gardens as he lifts the long pruning pole, fits the shears around a bough and pulls at the rope to close the blades. The branch falls and William dodges to one side. I wince. Did that just catch his head? Maybe I should go and see if he's all right. I want to ask him if he knows anything about the clothing I found the other day. Maybe the T-shirts were my father's. I won't come straight out with my concerns though. I'll tell him about the building work first.

Reuben had set his heart on the ground-source heat pump which means the garden to the side of the house leading down to the lake would be dug up and pipework laid to absorb the warmth from the earth. William was against the idea, saying it would be difficult for him to restore the lawns to their current condition. He suggested Calor gas instead but I felt the need to stand by Reuben's decision because it was the first time he'd shown any real interest in the project.

Unfortunately, the plumber told Reuben the ground wouldn't provide enough heat for a huge, draughty old house like Black Hollow. The radiators would be lukewarm and the pump would struggle to provide water hot enough for showers and baths. Reuben had shrugged but I could tell he was disappointed.

'Are you all right?' I ask as I reach William.

'Never better.'

He seems to be okay, I think with relief. I smile at him in anticipation. He'll be delighted with my news. 'I've come to tell you we can't go ahead with the underground heat source.'

William beams, his teeth glowing whitely in his dark beard. 'What will you do instead?' he asks, lowering his cutters and fixing them into hooks on the side of his tank chair. He rubs the side of his head.

'Did the branch hit you?'

'It's only a scratch.' He looks at me expectantly. 'Well?'

'We're going to opt for a variety of things but still aim to be self-sufficient. We'll put wood burning stoves in the main rooms; we'll have the AGA in the kitchen and solar panels on the outhouse roofs to provide hot water and heat to the radiators.'

'Good idea. There's plenty of firewood in the grounds. I'll have to see if I can manage a chainsaw.' William mimes waving a chainsaw around.

Crikey! I don't think that would be a good idea. I can envisage all sorts of horrific accidents.

'Is something wrong?' William is watching me closely.

'No. I just found some stuff in the house which puzzled me. I think I'm letting my imagination run away with me.' My laugh sounds forced but I don't want William telling Reuben I'm getting paranoid again.

'Tell me what's bothering you, Tash.'

It feels strange hearing William use my shortened name. It's usually only Reuben who does that. I find it familiar and reassuring.

'Will you promise not to tell Reuben? He thinks I'm over-reacting about everything.'

'Did I put my foot in it telling him about the fox?' He presses his lips together and raises his eyebrows.

'A little maybe.' I tell him about the food in the cupboard and the clothing in the bedroom and how it unnerved me.

He looks at me, his head tilted to one side. 'So you haven't spoken to Reuben about it?'

'No. I don't want him to think he can't leave me alone here.' I can't admit to William I daren't in case Reuben insists we move back to Bedfordshire. Yes, there's a lot of money to be made but money isn't a big motivator for Reuben. Friends and family are more important to him.

'Is that all that's bothering you?'

I take a deep breath and find myself describing the stabbing in Luton and how I needed to get away from the threat of the Rigbys then I tell him about some of the strange happenings at the Hall with the power going off, the footsteps in the dust and Morse. It's a relief to unburden myself.

William does his best to reassure me that Black Hollow is safe but the clothes in the bedroom are a puzzle to him. He says they certainly didn't belong to my father as he preferred pop and hated rock and he hasn't seen anyone about the premises. I think this would be unlikely anyway as he's a five-minute walk away along the drive.

'Maybe they stayed a few nights at the beginning of last year. Got in a window or something. I didn't move here from Tetbury until April last year so it could have been before that. They're probably long gone.'

I'm not convinced. The T-shirt tour dates were more recent than that. There are also the packets and tins of food in the kitchen that don't look very old. I'd just accepted they must have been bought by my father as no more have been eaten and no new food has appeared but now I'm not so sure.

'Either that or one of the builders stayed over. Or maybe a squatter took advantage of the property being empty,' he suggests helpfully.

I don't think so. Why would a local builder want to stay here and it feels too far off the beaten track for a squatter? But hey, perhaps William's right and the 'visitor' has gone. I hope so.

I leave William to his pruning and turn towards the Hall. One end is currently covered in scaffolding as the rest of the chimneys need to be repointed and rebuilt in places. It still looks beautiful though. Waterfalls of blue wisteria blooms tumble over the yellow Cotswold stone and honeysuckle tangles its way through a trellis by the front door. Sunlight sparkles off the many paned windows and the air is full of birdsong. Everything is so beautiful on the surface but now there seems to be darkness underneath. *Stop it!* I tell myself. *Stop being fanciful.* This place is my dream home and I won't let it slip through my fingers.

William has swivelled his tank chair around and he pulls up alongside me. We watch with interest as a man climbs a ladder towards the roof where the scaffolding extends to surround the chimney. He reaches the top then walks across the planks to the platform, holding on to the handrail as he approaches the brick stack. Initially I think my eyes are deceiving me. For a second it looks as if the platform shifts. I blink and stare. It's like watching a slow-moving film as the poles and planks come apart and begin to fall from the roof with a crash and clatter. I hear the man shout then he's falling, down over the edge of the roof to the platform on the scaffold tower below.

'Jesus!' William exclaims.

I gasp and put my hand over my mouth then I run towards the house with William zipping along behind me. More workmen have gathered outside and one is climbing the ladder to reach his mate. The man on the platform doesn't move.

'Has anyone called an ambulance?' I shout as I get nearer.

'No signal. Have you got a landline?' The plumber, Adrian, turns to me, his face ashen.

'I'll call from the coach house. Who's fallen?' I call over my shoulder as I run.

'It's Michael.'

* * *

The paramedics reassure me Michael's injuries don't appear to be life threatening, which is a huge relief. I watch the ambulance team drive off, taking the rutted driveway slowly to avoid jarring their patient. The gang of workmen stand beside me until it's out of sight then glance at each other. They look completely lost and I remember that Michael is the project manager. How is the work going to move forward now?

Chapter 33

'I'm afraid all building work will need to be suspended pending a full investigation.' The Health and Safety Executive officer smooths greasy wisps of hair across his balding head and looks from the scaffolding to his clipboard. 'We'll need copies of all the risk assessments, plans and method statements.'

My heart sinks. I'll ask the workmen but it's unlikely they'll have the information as Michael has organised all that. He hasn't given me copies of anything and for a fleeting moment I wonder if Scott would have been a better option after all. His paperwork was far superior to Michael's. Thankfully, Michael has only sustained concussion and a broken arm. The hospital is keeping him in for observations but they'd insisted I report the incident to the health and safety people as I have a duty of care as the owner of the premises.

I wish Reuben were here. He'd handle this much better than I can but he's halfway through a week-long project, organising food stands for a rock concert. He'd been shocked when I'd told him about the accident over the phone but blamed whoever constructed the scaffolding. That person was Curly, a funny nickname given that he's completely bald.

'I've been doing this job for thirty-two-and-a-half years and there's never been a fault with my work,' Curly had told me as we stood looking up at the scaffolding. 'You ask the others. I built that tower with utmost care.'

But of course he'd say that.

He'd leaned closer to me even though we were standing on the lawn alone. 'Personally, I think someone might have tampered with it.'

'Surely not!' I'd stepped back and stared at him.

'And did you cancel the order for the plasterboard and the sand?'

'No, of course not. Why would I do that?'

'Someone did,' he'd muttered, turning away.

I'd felt goosebumps on my skin as Curly's words brought all my worries into the light of day and had to fight the urge to pull my hair to calm myself. The missing tools, the cancelled order, the scaffolding. Was someone trying to disrupt the building project? Has Lewis Rigby found me? Or is it Julian, perhaps, so he could step in with another offer to buy the Hall? Would he risk another man's life for the sake of his business, though? Julian couldn't have known Michael would only fall as far as the first platform.

'How long will the investigation take?' I ask the officer. I need to know the cause for my own peace of mind. I haven't warmed to this officious little jobsworth standing in front of me and I have a feeling he'll drag the process out. *No. I'm being unfair. He's only doing what he needs to do to keep everyone safe.*

'If people fit in with the timetable for interviews and you allow us easy access to the premises I'd say two weeks for the enquiries then another week for the report. That's if we don't get a fatality to investigate in the meantime.'

'Three weeks?' By then the workmen will all be tied up on other building projects. This is a nightmare.

'We need to investigate what caused the accident, stop it happening again and, if necessary, bring a prosecution.'

'What!' I press my hands to my cheeks. Prosecution? Would I be liable? A prosecution would certainly put me off continuing the project. I dread telling Reuben about this. He'll definitely want to call it a day.

Another thought strikes me. Ugly, mean and outrageously disloyal. Isn't this accident playing right into Reuben's hands? He could have– *Christ, what am I thinking? Reuben wouldn't arrange an accident. He's a good man. My future husband, for God's sake.* The Rigbys then. They wouldn't think twice about injuring someone.

Are they tormenting me? *No. No. It must have been an accident. I have to stop thinking people are out to persecute me.*

'We need to find out if there's been negligence or tampering,' the health and safety man continues. 'The police might need to be involved but we'll decide that later.'

I feel numb as I say goodbye and watch the little man drive away. The place is eerily quiet after all the noise and bustle of previous weeks and I have a sudden urge to get away too. I fetch my keys and purse and head to The Dog House.

* * *

'Did you get the result you were hoping for?' Roger leans in towards Julian but his voice still carries to me as I cross the lounge bar. His black Labrador looks up momentarily then puts its head between its paws again. It must be missing Jim's poodle.

'Yes, but we won't talk about it now.' Julian frowns at Roger and turns to see who's within earshot. 'Tasha. Good to see you. How's the building work going?' He smiles warmly at me.

'Okay thanks,' I mutter. I certainly don't want to get into a conversation with him. With the way the jungle drums work in this village he probably already knows about the accident. In fact, from what I've just overheard he might have first-hand knowledge.

I order a soft drink and a sandwich then look around the room for someone to talk to. To my relief Bob's sitting by the empty fireplace staring at me hopefully.

'Bob! I didn't expect to see you here. How are you?' I've visited Bob a lot since he left hospital. I've run a few errands for him and spoken to his carers to check all is well and have been surprised at how cheerful he's been. He doesn't look happy now though. His leg is stretched out in front of him and he winces as he tries to shift his weight.

'How did you get here?' Surely he hasn't hobbled here on crutches. I look around but can't see any.

'Julian fetched me in a wheelchair. He's put it outside out of the way. He's a good lad.'

I raise my eyebrows. 'Really?' I glance across the room at him and he lifts his glass an inch and nods at me. Is he mocking me? I nod back and look at Bob again.

'I've got a big favour to ask you, Miss Tasha.' Bob leans forward and grasps my hand.

'Of course. You know I'll do anything I can to help you.'

'It's about Jim. He phoned me to say he's staying at his sister's permanently but he was almost in tears.' Bob's eyes glisten as he speaks. 'She's got two cats, see, and said she couldn't keep Bonnie. She's put her in the local rescue centre.'

'Bonnie? Is that the red poodle I saw in here?'

'Beautiful dog she is, and so intelligent. She'll be pining for him. He wants me to have her and I need to fetch her quick before someone else snaps her up or they have to put her down.'

'Are you sure you can manage a dog?'

'Please, Miss Tasha. The carers would feed her and maybe you could take her for a walk every day. She can sleep on my bed and we'll be company for each other. She knows me.' A tear pools in his eye and rolls down his left cheek. A puddle in the other eye threatens to overflow.

'Where is this rescue centre?'

'It's in Aspley Guise, Bedfordshire. A Home for Unwanted and Lost Animals – they call it HULA.'

'But how would you get there? You can't get in my car with a broken leg. They might not let you have her anyway in your condition.'

'They'd let you have her, though, and we could put the seat right back to get my leg in. Now you've got your boyfriend's car there's more space. I'd like to try.'

My mind's racing. This is a crazy idea but if I can make two old men and a dog happy I'll give it a go. I need some happiness at the moment. Besides, I quite fancy the idea of walking a dog every day. It'll give me a sense of purpose and some exercise. It might de-stress me with everything else that's going on.

'Okay. When would you like to go? I could probably spare the time tomorrow.'

'We need to go today. Something else might happen to her otherwise.'

'What?' Crikey. Today hasn't turned out as I expected. 'We need to phone them first. We can't just bowl up and hope they'll see us.' *And we need to check the dog's still there.*

'Rachel behind the bar will let you use the phone. She's a kind girl.'

Rachel is pushing fifty but I don't correct him. She calls HULA and tells us we can visit so I look around for Julian for help with getting Bob in the car. I'm sure he was standing nearby a minute ago. I can't see him so I look outside to see if he's in the car park. He's at the far end of the building talking to someone. Wait, isn't that one of my builders? He certainly looks familiar. I step back, my head buzzing. What's Julian doing talking to one of my builders? *He's planning further sabotage*, a voice whispers in my ear. *He's trying to get information out of him.* I don't trust the pair of them. I'm going to keep a close watch on that builder from now on. I go back inside. Bob is sitting on the edge of his seat watching me so I approach Roger.

'I don't suppose you could get Bob in my car, could you? He wants me to take him somewhere.'

* * *

Bob stares out of the car window then looks at me. 'How about some music?' he says, his eyes twinkling. 'We might as well enjoy ourselves. It's not often I go on a trip out.'

I'm glad to see Bob's cheerful nature returning. It'd been a shock seeing him so upset. I reach for the dial and turn the radio on. A heavy metal song blasts through the speakers and we both jump. I'd forgotten I'd had my music so loud last time. I quickly turn the volume down and switch to another radio station.

'Bloomin' racket.' Bob shakes his head. 'I prefer a bit of Perry Como myself.'

'I don't think I've ever listened to Perry Como. I'm more of a Muse fan.'

'Never heard of them. Your father used to listen to Perry with me when it came on the radio. Such a sweet lad he was. Not like Simon. He used to constantly play an awful song about not going to school.'

I think of the Alice Cooper T-shirt and my imagination runs ahead with possibilities.

'Ooh, Abba. I like this one.' Bob wriggles happily in his seat. 'Can you turn it up a bit?'

Chapter 34

I'm quiet for the rest of the journey. I need to digest the information about Simon. Did he like Alice Cooper? Thank God he's locked away in prison. The T-shirt can't possibly be his. I'd be unable to cope being alone at Black Hollow Hall otherwise, especially now the scaffolding accident has taken the threat to another level. I think all the strange happenings must be linked and now people are getting hurt. I take one hand off the steering wheel to wrap a hair around my finger. Will I be next? Or is Reuben right and I'm being paranoid? It's funny how we use that term in such a blasé manner. Now it's beginning to take on a much more ominous meaning.

The car bounces up and down as it tackles the long, rutted drive to the rescue centre. Bob clutches the door handle and puts his other hand to the side of his leg but he doesn't complain. He leans forward, peering out of the windscreen at the approaching house and outbuildings.

'I'm not sure if we'll manage to get you out of the car and into the wheelchair, Bob.'

His smile fades.

Oh, heck. 'I'll ask them if I can bring the dog out to you,' I add, and his smile brightens again.

I go to the office and introduce myself. I explain about Bob already knowing the dog and how I would be looking after it with him. There's no one strong enough to lift Bob from the car and I don't want to risk anyone getting injured so I ask if we can take Bonnie to him. I leave Bob waiting and follow the girl, who introduces herself as Sarah, to the sheds where the kennels are.

The smell of urine is strong when the doors are opened and I can imagine how difficult it must be to keep the place fresh, especially in this heat. We pass a cage containing a husky type of dog who immediately starts barking at us.

'It's okay, Daisy, we're only passing by. She's a little nervous of strangers,' Sarah explains.

The next cage holds a Staffordshire bull terrier who jumps up at the bars and sniffs at us. The third cage appears empty, then I see the red poodle curled up in a basket at the back. She lifts her eyes to look at us but her chin stays on the edge of her bed.

'She's not been very happy since she moved here yesterday. I think she's missing her owner. She hasn't eaten a thing yet.'

I feel a lump in my throat. The poor dog – wrenched from her owner like that. How could Jim's sister be so heartless? Sarah opens the cage and clips a lead to the collar.

'Come on, Bonnie. We've got some people who want to see you.'

Bonnie climbs out of her bed and walks slowly to the door, her head hanging low. She sniffs my hand and half-heartedly wags her tail then we all file out of the building. I'm glad to get back into the fresh air and Bonnie lifts her head to sniff the breeze. We walk her over to the car where Bob sits with his door open. Bonnie sniffs again then suddenly becomes animated. She pulls on the lead, straining to get to Bob.

'Bonnie!' he cries. 'My lovely girl.'

Bonnie dances around in circles and gets tangled in her lead. The girl lets go and Bonnie launches herself into the car, climbing up onto Bob's chest to lick his face.

'Oh my word! What a difference in her,' Sarah says. 'I'm not sure where we go from here. We usually like to do checks and phased introductions.' She attempts to take the lead and bring Bonnie out of the car but the dog buries her head under Bob's arm and burrows her curly-haired body into his. He puts his arms around her.

'Please don't take her. Please.' His eyes are moist and pleading. Sarah looks at me.

'What if you called Jim and asked him?'

'I'm not sure. I suppose we could as she only came in yesterday.'
She disappears and is back within minutes.

'I've spoken to my supervisor and Jim has already called to say he wants Bob to take her. Everything's fine. I'll fetch the paperwork and we can do it out here,' she says. 'Have you got all the equipment for a dog?'

'She's going to sleep on my bed and I've got bowls. What else could she possibly need?' Bob looks perplexed.

'She should have a harness for the car and she'll need a collar and lead. I'll check if she came in with any. I think the bed in the kennel is hers.'

Sarah returns with forms to complete and a car harness. 'I've made an exception in this situation and we're going to loan you the harness. We'll need a deposit but we'll refund you when you return it.'

Bonnie sits behind me on the journey home, clipped into her safety harness, her pink tongue hanging out of her smiling mouth. Bob had wanted to cuddle her all the way back but I'd been insistent. I don't want any more accidents on my conscience. Sarah has written a list of requirements for the dog, including grooming brushes and treats for good behaviour. She also said we'd have to find a grooming parlour as Bonnie is in dire need of a trim to keep her paws and ears healthy. I'll have to sort all this out and I'm beginning to wonder what I've taken on. I'd been tempted to ask about the big husky that barked. Maybe I need a guard dog at the Hall. My mind has been temporarily distracted but now I'm deeply worried again.

'You did say Simon was in prison, didn't you?' I ask Bob.

'Yes. He was sentenced to life with a minimum of twenty years but that was nineteen or so years ago…' Bob's voice tails off and he looks at me.

'What?' I say, with a jolt of alarm.

'…So I suppose he could have been released earlier for good behaviour. It does happen sometimes.'

Chapter 35

'You didn't answer my call last night. Where were you?' Reuben asks. 'I rang a couple of times this morning too.'

'I'm sorry. I went upstairs for a nap and fell into a heavy sleep then I got up early and went out.' I bite my lip, hoping he'll believe me. After asking the landlord for assistance and dropping Bob and an excited Bonnie home, I'd gone straight back to the coach house and packed an overnight bag. I needed time and space to think through everything and I didn't feel safe at Black Hollow.

I'd booked bed and breakfast at the Kings Arms in Didmarton and stayed in a gorgeous little apartment in one of their converted outhouses. I'd been made to feel really welcome and had been fussed over with a huge and delicious cooked breakfast. The change of scene had done me good and I was then able to think more rationally.

On my way back I'd gone to a hardware store and bought window locks and a huge bolt for the front door. I'd rung Adrian who'd called round after he'd finished work and fitted them for me. I'd like to have attempted the task myself but didn't have any tools. I'd asked Adrian what all the workmen were doing and he'd said they were mostly taking on small jobs until they could return to Black Hollow Hall. I was touched by their commitment and loyalty, and was pleased to hear Michael was home again and recovering well, but I was annoyed with myself for not remembering the name of the builder I'd seen with Julian at the pub. I could hardly describe him and ask what he was up to without it seeming suspicious.

No doubt Reuben will ask why I need extra security and I'll have to be honest with him this time. Or maybe I could say there are occasional dog walkers about and I need to keep my work laptop secure. Yes, that's believable. He'll be back tomorrow and I can't wait to see him. I look at my watch. It's 7pm. Reuben has called two hours earlier than usual. He must be worried about me.

'Are you okay, cherub?' he asks. 'You don't sound quite yourself. Is something worrying you?'

'I'm fine. I've been helping Bob.' I launch into the story of the dog rescue to assure Reuben that I'm all right.

'Who'll look after the dog if anything happens to old Bob?'

'I thought perhaps we could. She's a gorgeous dog.'

'Hmm. I'm not really into little poodles.'

'She's medium-sized and she's shaggier than the typical clipped poodle. We can take her for walks together. Don't worry; she won't ruin your street cred.' I laugh.

'What street cred? There's no one to impress around there, unless you count Sandy and Timothy and we both know we won't be spending much time with them. We hardly know anyone else.'

'It's early days yet. When the house is finished we can invite people around to celebrate.'

There's a long pause. 'We'll see,' he says. 'I need to go. I'm meeting someone for dinner.'

'Someone? Male or female?' Are they staying in the same hotel?

'Female. No one you know but don't worry. She's definitely not my type.'

'Not a double D chest, you mean.' I could bite my tongue as soon as the words are out.

I hear Reuben sigh. 'I have no interest in big chests, Tash. I'm a 34B man and always will be.'

I apologise and we say goodbye. I'm annoyed with myself for being so petty but I can't help feeling jealous of Sandy and the way Reuben looked at her.

I pace restlessly around the small living room then decide to go for a walk around the grounds. Perhaps if I get some fresh air and exercise I'll sleep better. It's still bright sunshine and very warm outside. I'll go and fetch Bonnie and take her out. She'll be good company.

Bonnie's pleased to see me and runs in circles when I show her the lead. I strap her into the car and drive back to Black Hollow. I'll have to buy another harness so I can return this one or I'll need to find some walks local to Bob's cottage.

We skirt the edge of the lawns with Bonnie stopping to sniff at rabbit holes, fallen branches and clumps of fern. I wait for her and look into the woods. It's quite shaded beneath the trees and I peer into the gloom for any movement. I realise I don't actually feel comfortable standing here. I try to pull Bonnie away but the dog suddenly goes rigid and stares into the trees. A low growl emits from her throat and my knees weaken. Oh, Jesus. Is Simon Harrington in there or Lewis Rigby? It would be easy for someone to hide in there. Someone who wants to watch me. I know I'm being ridiculous but the hairs on my arms lift and I get a strong urge to run. I tug harder at the dog's lead and set off at a jog across the lawn towards the house. I'll take Bonnie home then lock myself into the coach house.

'Was she well behaved?' Bob asks when we get back. 'She's usually very good but she does have a habit of growling at the birds.' He chuckles. 'It used to tickle Jim. He phoned a little while ago. He asked me to thank you for all you've done. You've made him a happy man.'

I can barely get a word in but my thoughts are whirling. Perhaps Bonnie had been growling at a bird. I must stop worrying so much.

'Would you like to stay for a cup of tea, Tasha?'

'Sorry Bob, can I come for one tomorrow instead?' I want to get home before the light fades.

'You're welcome any day and every day.' Bob gives me a wide smile.

I pat Bonnie on the head and leave. I park in my usual spot and walk briskly around the side of the Hall to the coach house, then stop in horror. My hand flies to my mouth and my legs buckle.

Lying on the doormat is a large headless rat.

Chapter 36

'We didn't expect to see you back so soon.' The landlady at the Kings Arms is all smiles as she hands me a key. 'Change of plan,' I say without elaborating. I can't think of a believable story so I don't bother to offer one. The woman will think I'm crazy if I say I'm there because I found a headless rat on my doorstep. I eat a quiet supper then go straight to bed. At least Reuben has phoned early this evening so won't wonder where I am again. I lie rigid, staring at the ceiling and trying to put my thoughts into a coherent order. Everything that's happened to me could have a plausible explanation which Reuben would doubtless use to dismiss my fears but I can't shake off the feeling that someone is out to frighten me and possibly even cause me harm. There's been too much going on for it all to be a coincidence or easily explained away. Surely one person couldn't attract this much bad luck?

And now another headless rodent.

Is it a message? It has to be the Rigbys making good on their threats. But how have they found me? I take a deep breath and point out to myself that I've no evidence at all to indicate that the Rigbys are responsible for what's happened. Morse might simply have come back and left me a thank-you gift for feeding him. Yes, it's Morse. It has to be.

I breathe in and out slowly and try to relax; ignoring the doubts that crowd in on me because the way I feel isn't just about a rodent. It's about an accumulation of happenings that put together...

Think of something else, Tasha! I think of Reuben but find no comfort because my mind hones in on what he'd said about dinner with another woman. Who? I pick over our conversation. No one I knew, he'd said. Was it a work colleague? Were they staying in rooms near each other? I've never had cause to be concerned about Reuben's faithfulness since I've been with him and I trust him. I definitely trust him. It must be to do with work. He'd hardly tell me he was going for dinner if he was having an affair. I'll ask him about the meal tomorrow by dropping it casually into a conversation. I have to stop thinking the worst. I'm worried I'm driving Reuben away with my neuroses and insistence on staying at Black Hollow – but how can I return to living in Luton when the place terrifies me? I'm between a rock and a hard place.

* * *

I wake early, after a fitful night's sleep, with the covers tangled around my legs. I get unsteadily out of bed and stumble to the bathroom to splash cold water on my face. I rub my temples where the skin is sore from pulling out my hair. My head feels muzzy and I haven't even drunk any alcohol. Perhaps I'd have slept better if I had.

I eat breakfast, avoiding more than a superficial conversation with the landlady, and go out to my car. It smells of warm plastic from the sun shining through the windscreen. The weather is already hot and I soon feel clammy and grubby. I had a quick shower in the room but hadn't got clean clothing to change into. The novelty of this relentless heat is wearing thin and now I long for a cool breeze and gentle rain. I sit in the driver's seat, the car fabric hot through the thin cotton of my top, not quite sure what to do or where to go next. I ought to return to the coach house and do some work but I feel nauseous after the cooked breakfast and can't face the dead rat yet.

I start the engine and pull out of the car park. At least this car has air conditioning. I set it on full blast then begin the drive back to Black Hollow but as I reach Tetbury I see the sign for the M4 and on impulse I follow it. I'm fed up with my limited summer wardrobe. I hadn't planned for a heatwave when I'd packed up belongings to take to the coach house. I'll drive back to Luton and fetch some of my old summer clothes. The house still hasn't been rented out and I'm getting sceptical about Reuben's assurances that 'there's nothing wrong with the property, it's just that the market is dead at the moment'. Are the agents doing enough?

'Everyone's staying at home to enjoy the sunshine,' he said. 'People aren't thinking about moving house in this heat.'

He's probably right and at least we haven't had to sort out the rest of our belongings. The Hall isn't in a fit state to store our old house contents yet.

As I drive, I can't help but admire the display of trees and fields passing by my window. Everywhere still looks lush and green despite the lack of rain, until I pass through villages and see scorched lawns and plants frazzled in the heat. I look about with interest. It's good to get out into the big, wide world and I promise myself I won't become too reclusive at Black Hollow. A weekly trip to the office is not enough.

As I approach the outskirts of Luton I instinctively find myself scanning the streets for people with ginger hair. I see no one to cause me alarm and my mind wanders back to the estate agents. I'll check the number on the 'To Let' board when I reach the house and give them a call.

I turn into our road and before I've even reached the house I can see there's something missing.

There is no 'To Let' board.

Chapter 37

'I was wondering if you have any properties for rent in the Marsh Farm area,' I ask the receptionist. I had to call Mum to look up the number for me. Thankfully I was able to remember the names of the estate agents. I miss my decent phone with the internet connection and curse the motorcyclist again for stealing it.

'We have a one-bed flat and a two-bed maisonette,' the girl says.

'No three-bed houses?'

'Not at present. We have in other areas though. Would you like me to take your details?'

'Not at the moment, thanks.' Maybe the house has been recently rented and Reuben's forgotten to tell me. 'Have you rented any others in that area recently? I just wondered what sort of price they go for.'

'We had one on the market for just over a thousand a month in that area but the owners withdrew it a few weeks ago.'

Reuben and I had been asking £1,050. This is too big a coincidence. I thank the girl and hang up then look around the house. There are signs of Reuben's occupancy everywhere. He isn't the tidiest of people. The bed is hastily made, there are clothes on the floor and a towel slung over the banisters. In the kitchen there are plates and mugs in the sink and a loaf of mouldy bread in the bread bin. The house is clearly not being presented to prospective tenants.

Why hasn't he told me he's taken it off the market? What's he planning to do – stay here? I've never questioned Reuben's honesty before but only last week I'd asked if there was any news from the estate agents. He could have told me then. And if he's deceiving me over this, what else might he be doing behind my back? I'm in no position to judge him though. I haven't been totally honest myself. I feel a wave of sadness. When exactly did the foundation of trust in our relationship start to crumble? Is Black Hollow Hall driving a wedge between us or is he growing tired of me? Can we get back to where we were? If only Reuben would agree to stay at Black Hollow I'd be able to tell him honestly if I felt scared and he'd be able to make me feel safe.

While I'm here I make a quick call to the solicitor to enquire about writing a will. He's in Thailand for two weeks so I make an appointment for when he's back. I collect a few summer outfits from my drawers and wardrobe and pack them hurriedly into a holdall. The little house suddenly feels claustrophobic and I need to get out. I glance around the living room and kitchen before I leave. The place seems tiny, cheap and basic and I can't help but compare it to the lofty-ceilinged opulence and craftsmanship of the Hall. I'd been so happy and contented when we'd bought this place but now I never want to live here again. I close the door with a firm click and walk down the path without looking back.

As I near Black Hollow I decide to ask William to move the rat for me. He doesn't answer the door but his car's there so I presume he's working in the grounds. I progress slowly along the pot-holed driveway scanning the woods and meadows to left and right. There's no sign of him by the house, so I park the car and walk with trepidation to my front door.

The rat isn't there. Instead, lying on the coir matting is a piece of grey tree bark that looks like it has fallen off a log from the nearby log pile. Is this what I'd seen yesterday? I screw my eyes up in concentration, trying to recall the memory. Is my mind playing tricks on me?

No. I definitely saw a headless rat. I remember the blood and gristle. What's going on? William must have seen it and cleared it up for me. I kick the piece of bark away and peer at the doormat for traces of blood. Nothing. Where's William? I walk to the front of the Hall and around the other side towards the lake. There, in the distance is William in his tank chair holding an extra-long handled rake extended over the water. I watch him pull it towards him, dragging weeds with it.

'You're fighting a losing battle there,' I say as I approach. The lake has become choked with algae and blanket weed recently with all the sunshine. 'I think we'll need to hire someone to sort this out.'

His mouth sets into a firm line and he flings the rake into the water again – his muscles rippling through his shirt. I know William hates the idea of bringing in outsiders for tasks he wants to do but is incapable of.

'The lawns don't need cutting and I need something to occupy me,' he mutters.

'I've come to say thank you,' I say.

'What for?'

'For moving the dead rat.'

'Rat?' William shakes his head. 'Sorry, I don't know what you're talking about.'

Chapter 38

'It's so good to be with you, Tash.' Reuben's fingers gently stroke my hair as I lie on his chest. His heart is a steady, reassuring rhythm and I feel safe for the first time in ages. I've decided I shouldn't get too hung-up about the house not being on the market. I'll give him a chance to explain tomorrow and I'll be calm and rational. I'm sure Reuben must be finding it hard dealing with my neuroses and I don't want to push him away further. I need to show him the old me again so he knows what he'd be missing if he left me.

A gentle breeze drifts through the open window and cools our skin. It's been a lovely evening. We took Bonnie for a long walk and Reuben enjoyed throwing a ball for her to fetch. She had a ten-minute mad spell where she tore around the lawns, zig-zagging left and right to avoid Reuben plucking the ball from her mouth.

'Bob calls it the zoomies when she does this,' I'd laughed.

'She's probably glad to get out of his cottage and into the fresh air.'

'It's been too hot to take her out during the day and I'm not great at early mornings.' Besides, I haven't been here the last couple of mornings but I'm not going to tell Reuben that. After our walk Reuben had pushed Bob in his wheelchair to the pub where we treated him to dinner. Bob kept patting my hand and telling Reuben what a wonderful girl I am and how I've made him a happy man. He's such an old charmer.

'I think you've got a new admirer,' Reuben had teased as we'd driven back to the coach house. 'I'm jealous he gets to spend so much time with you.'

I'd been tempted to say that if he rented out the house and gave up his job to help with the building work he'd see a lot more of me, but I swallowed the retort. It could wait until the weekend. I haven't seen him all week and don't want to spoil the evening by picking a fight.

'Do you still like it here?' Reuben's voice sounds a long way off as I begin to drift off to sleep.

I sit up and wipe my face. Oh no. He isn't going to suggest we leave again, is he? 'Of course I do.' The truth of it is I'm scared and I'm not sure if being here is good for me either. After the incident with the rat I'm seriously beginning to doubt myself. Am I seeing and hearing things that aren't there? 'Why do you ask?'

'You've got that edginess back. Like you had in Luton. Do you really feel safe here?'

'Of course I do,' I lie. Thank God I paid cash for the two nights' bed and breakfast. I couldn't risk him seeing that on my bank statement. How would I explain it? 'I went to Luton this morning to fetch some more summer clothes,' I say. 'I definitely couldn't live there again.'

'Did you?' He sounds surprised. 'Like I've said before, there are plenty of other places where we could live once you sell the Hall.'

'I noticed there wasn't a 'To Let' sign anymore.' I can't wait until tomorrow to discuss this after all. I need to get it off my chest now and I refuse to talk about selling up.

Reuben hesitates and I hold my breath. Is he going to lie to me?

'There were a few problems with the agent so I withdrew it from them. I haven't got around to sorting out another one yet.'

'Problems?'

'Viewings booked and no one turning up after I'd spent ages cleaning. Then people turning up on a different day when the house was a mess.'

Having seen how untidy the house was earlier I could understand why he'd be annoyed.

'You haven't mentioned this before.'

'Yes I did. On the phone the other night.'

I don't remember that conversation but then I have been distracted recently. I feel guilty now for mistrusting him. I have to be mindful of the pressure that's building up inside me. It's sapping my self-confidence and I'm not thinking straight.

'Besides, I want to be sure you definitely want to stay here before I contact another agent. I get the niggling feeling you're not telling me stuff. Has something happened?'

'Of course not,' I lie again, 'and I definitely want to stay here. The house has so much potential and I love the grounds.' I want to raise a family here and for us to run the house as a business together but I don't tell him that. He hasn't fallen in love with the place like I have. Yet.

'How was your meal last night?' I hadn't intended bringing this up either but I want to distract him from my anxieties about Black Hollow and I'm desperate to know who this woman is.

'Okay. Gina's steak was a bit tough but it was hardly a five-star hotel.'

'Gina?'

'She's over from America. She's one of the directors and she wanted to meet me and hear how the week had gone. Don't worry. She's almost old enough to be my mum.'

Almost. I chide myself for being so suspicious.

'I think she fancied me though,' Reuben laughs.

I punch his arm and he tickles me until I beg for mercy but it's far too hot for play fighting. Eventually we sprawl across the bed, our limbs barely touching under the thin cotton sheet. I find myself drifting off to sleep again when I suddenly hear a loud voice.

'Tasha!'

I jump and sit up. Reuben continues to snore softly beside me. I gently shake his shoulder. 'Did you hear that?'

He groans. 'What?'

'Someone called my name.' It had sounded like a command. The sort of tone Mum would have used when it was time to get up for school. But this was a man's voice.

'You were probably dreaming. Go back to sleep.'

I lie awake for a long time worrying about the voice I'd heard and wondering if I should go and look downstairs. It had seemed so real but if it was why hadn't Reuben heard it? My skin shrivels as though a cold wind has entered the room. I pull the sheet tighter around me. I'd been dismissive when Reuben had suggested I should see a doctor or counsellor all those months ago. I'd thought all I'd needed to get back on an even keel was to get away from Luton and the Rigbys.

I still love this house and think I could be happy here. I think Reuben could be happy here too if only he'd open his mind to the advantages. But the fact is I'm not back on an even keel. Far from it. I'm seeing things and hearing things, imagining perils, threats and betrayals. There's only one word to describe what I feel and I don't like the sound of it at all. Paranoia. Perhaps the time has come to get some help otherwise I risk losing Reuben, the Hall, my sanity and everything else.

Perhaps I should see the doctor.

Chapter 39

'It's quite common for people to hear voices as they move from consciousness to sleep and back again.' The face on the screen is expressionless, the voice flat.

I wonder if this online doctor is qualified but it doesn't matter. I feel a massive weight lifting from my chest. His words are comforting. Reassuring. According to the internet almost a third of the population hear voices at some time or another and this doctor on YouTube says it doesn't mean they have a mental health problem. I think I was overreacting last night. Everything always seems worse in the middle of the night. Maybe I'm just stressed. I haven't quite managed to find plausible explanations for all the other incidents where I've seen or heard things that might or might not exist but it's probably just a matter of spending a few more hours researching the internet.

A key sounds in the lock and I quickly shut the lid of my laptop before standing up.

'I can't smell bacon cooking,' Reuben calls from the kitchen. He enters the lounge and looks at me. 'What have you been doing?'

'Checking emails. Did you get a fresh loaf?'

'Yes. It was the last one. You should have seen Sandy's face when she saw me at the till. She'd walked there just for bread.' Reuben laughs. 'I offered to share it with her but she declined.'

I can't help feeling a twinge of annoyance at the mention of that woman's name. When we went to the pub for a drink last night she'd fawned all over Reuben again – like a teenage fan with a rock star. It was pathetic. Yes, Reuben's wide-mouthed, easy smile, dancing blue eyes and blond cherubic curls are lovely, but he's mine.

'I don't know why Muriel doesn't order more in. She always sells out,' I say.

'Doesn't want to be left with some that haven't sold, I suppose, and it keeps the customers competing to get there first. Come on. Get a shift on. Mum and Dad will be here soon.'

I jump up from the table. I'm really looking forward to their visit. I pull the bacon out of the fridge and lay slices under the grill. It's a shame there is still so much rubbish around but Reuben has ordered another skip for the smaller items and it's filling up quickly. We've already taken a van full of rotten furnishings and mattresses to the dump.

The house is looking and smelling better without so much mildewed old clutter and it makes it easier for the workmen to move around. Not that there is much damp at the moment. The dry spell has continued and we're still in the grip of a heatwave with temperatures reaching thirty degrees. Thankfully, the thick walls and high ceilings of the Hall make it a comfortable working environment and I often take my laptop over there to work in more tolerable conditions.

It's lovely having the workmen back too. The health and safety officer hadn't been able to find any evidence of poor workmanship or tampering but had insisted Curly attend a day's training on scaffold building at the local college. Curly had bristled at the suggestion but accepted it as a necessity if he wanted to continue working. He still insists the tower had been tampered with and I feel a dart of unease each time he says it. He attended the course, though, and returned with a swagger.

'I knew more than the bloody trainer!' he'd exclaimed with his chest puffed up. The other students had respected his knowledge and experience, he'd said, and asked him numerous questions. He'd even signed one up as an apprentice labourer.

'Are you ready yet?' Reuben calls up the stairs after washing the breakfast dishes. 'Mum said they'd be here at ten and I want to wait at the end of the lane for them in case they have difficulty finding the place.'

'I'm just sorting out a load of washing. I'll be two minutes.'

I come downstairs with my arms full of dirty clothes and damp towels and take them into the kitchen. I thrust them into the washing machine then notice a thick line of dust on top of the machine where it must have shuddered from under the countertop the last time I used it. I grab a cloth and wipe it, hoping the movement doesn't mean a problem is developing. I've got enough to think about already. I add powder to the drawer then switch it on, relieved when it gurgles into life. Reuben stands watching me from the doorway.

'Ready now,' I say.

* * *

I pinch the front of my blouse, wafting it in and out to cool my skin, and brush damp hair from my forehead. I wish I had a sunhat. 'I'm going to wait under the trees. It's too hot on the road,' I say. I look at my watch. They're twenty minutes late.

'They're here,' Reuben says excitedly and I feel a pang of guilt that I've isolated him from his family.

They turn into the driveway and stop. We climb in the back of the car and Reuben leans forward to kiss his mum's cheek.

'What fantastic gates!' exclaims Margaret. 'Is the house as grand as the entrance?'

I follow Reuben's gaze to the lopsided gates tangled with weeds and catch an expression of surprise on his face. My heart lifts. Margaret can see beyond the damage and neglect to the beauty underneath.

I watch Margaret's face from the back seat as we approach the house and I'm delighted when her eyes widen and she takes in a breath. This is what I'd hoped for when Reuben first saw it.

'Oh my word,' she says as Graham stops the car. 'What a beautiful house.' She swivels towards me. 'Tasha, you must be thrilled. I'd love to live somewhere like this.'

Before I can reply she's out of the car and gazing up at the tall drawing room window.

Reuben and I exchange a glance then get out to stand next to her. Graham joins us and pats Reuben on the back then gives me a hug.

'Stunning,' he says, nodding his approval. 'Sorry we were late. We couldn't find the place.'

Showing Reuben's parents around the property is everything I'd dreamed of. They ooh and aah like children at a firework display and gush over every little detail and piece of craftsmanship. At first Reuben looks bemused but it's as if their enthusiasm is contagious and before long he's pointing out features, talking about the plans and smiling. It's as if he's seeing the place through different eyes. I so wish his mum and dad had visited sooner.

'Jessica will adore this, and little Alfie... well, he'll be in seventh heaven. All this space to charge about in. It's a wonderful place for children.' Margaret looks from Reuben to me then her eyes stray to my stomach.

'One day,' I laugh. 'We're not quite ready yet.'

'Do you want a cuppa?' Reuben asks. 'Or shall I show you the lake? I thought we'd go for lunch at The Dog House.'

'We've had soft drinks in the car. A walk would be lovely, do you agree, dear?' Graham looks at Margaret.

'Absolutely. A lake. How romantic.' Margaret's eyes are shining. 'This would be a fabulous venue for weddings. Will you have yours here when the place is finished?'

I look at Reuben. It's almost as if I've written Margaret a script. She's saying everything I want and need her to say.

'I suppose we could,' he says thoughtfully. 'It would save the expense and worry of hiring somewhere.' He glances at me and I grab and squeeze his arm. I feel so happy I could run and click my heels together in mid-air.

'Let's talk about it over lunch,' I say.

* * *

I'm sorry to see Graham and Margaret leave but they're visiting a friend in Cheltenham this afternoon. I think Reuben is coming round to liking the place. I might be able to persuade him to stay.

We walk arm in arm around the side of the Hall towards the coach house, then stop abruptly. A large pool of water is shimmering on the flagstones, ripples moving across the surface as more water joins it from the threshold of our front door. Reuben swears, then splashes through the water and unlocks the front door. The ground floor of the coach house is under two inches of water.

'Where's the stop cock?' he shouts, even though I'm only a few metres away.

'I… I don't know.' Oh God, this is terrible. 'Shall I phone William and ask him?'

'How would he know? He can't get through the doorway.' Reuben sloshes into the kitchen, the water soaking into his trainers, and opens a cupboard. He pulls items out and dumps them roughly on the worktop where they leak water – the box of washing powder creating a white puddle that grows then trickles over the side to join the water on the floor.

'Here it is.' Reuben sounds relieved. He fiddles about then pulls his head out of the cupboard and surveys the scene around him. 'We will never, ever, put the washing machine on again if we're not in the house.'

I kick off my flip-flops then step into the kitchen, gasping as the cold water covers my bare feet, and look around in dismay. I walk through to the lounge and see a tide mark of moisture as it seeps upwards into the sofas and curtains.

'Why would it leak like that?'

'The waste pipe has probably got dislodged at the back. It must have been pumping water out for ages though, so perhaps the machine's valve is faulty. Whatever caused it, we can't stay here now, Tash.'

Chapter 40

'**I**'m not moving back to Luton.' I jump to my feet and glare at Reuben. I'm determined about this.

'We can't stay at this B&B indefinitely.' Reuben sinks down onto the end of the bed and runs his hands through his hair. 'We've already been here a week and it's costing us a fortune.'

'If you'd made more effort with the house we could have rented it by now and we wouldn't be so skint.'

Reuben looks at the floor and doesn't respond. The bed and breakfast we're staying at in the village next to Lower Bramcote is pricier than the King's Arms at Didmarton but I can't risk taking Reuben there. He'll find out I've stayed before. I sigh and sit back down on the end of the bed next to him.

'I'll speak to the solicitor to see if he'll release some more funds for living expenses, after all, it's not our fault the coach house has flooded.' I could kick myself for not telling Reuben the machine had bounced forward. But then I wouldn't have expected him to know so much about washing machines. His knowledge of plumbing is usually quite limited.

It's going to be at least six weeks before we can move back in. Large dehumidifiers have been installed to soak up the moisture but it will take time for it all to dry out and then the place will need redecorating and possibly new flooring laid. The B&B had been a novelty initially but now, a week in, it's becoming tiresome. We're constantly driving back and forth to the Hall to supervise the project and collect essentials and we're continually snapping at each other. We've also exhausted the menu at the local pub and long for the convenience of our own kitchen.

'We could go back to Luton for six weeks then return when the coach house is habitable again. We could keep the house on the market and if we find a tenant we can stay at my parents' place,' Reuben says.

'But I need to be here to make daily decisions about the building work and I have a responsibility for Bonnie.'

'Sandy could walk her.'

'No.' Definitely not. I know I'm being unreasonable because Reuben didn't have any say about Bonnie but I'm not giving Sandy the chance to win my dog's affections. It's bad enough that she's pursuing Reuben. 'I've been thinking… we could move into the Hall.'

'What? It's little more than a building site. It's not safe.'

'Yes it is. The loose ceilings have been removed along with the damp plaster on the walls, the floors have been relaid and the place has electricity now. We could live mostly in the kitchen and dining room.'

Reuben stares at me. 'God, you're serious.'

'We can buy an electric cooker for the kitchen and take utensils from the coach house. We can move our bedroom furniture into the dining room and buy a second-hand sofa to tide us over. In fact, the insurance is paying for new furniture so we could buy a new one.' I pause to let the idea sink in.

Reuben opens his mouth to object but then closes it again. 'What about a bathroom?' he says after a long pause.

'We've got the downstairs cloakroom in the Hall and we can still use the bathroom in the coach house for baths or showers when the workmen have left for the day.'

'You've really thought this through, haven't you?' Reuben looks at me with a mixture of grudging admiration and resentment.

'Yes, the large dining table can go in the drawing room for now to create space and we can eat at the kitchen table.' I sit back in the small armchair and can't resist a smug grin. 'You must be fed up with being confined here by now.' I wave my arm at the small room.

* * *

It doesn't take long to move the furniture in and buy a second-hand cooker. The weather is far too hot to contemplate lighting the AGA. I ask Reuben to climb a ladder and take the heavy dining room drapes down then I carry them outside and beat the dust off them. They're threadbare in patches but thankfully most of the damp is at the other end of the house so they're relatively intact, as are the floors and ceiling joists. The side window has no curtains. I'll need to find something to cover it. I sweep and clean and tell the plasterer he'll have to replaster the dining room and kitchen last. The rooms looked a mess with no skirting boards and bare walls to waist height but it's still better than Luton.

'We should have bought some more table lamps,' Reuben grumbles. 'It's too dark in here.'

He's right. The ones from the coach house are inadequate in such a large room and the overhead lighting is a long way from being installed. I snuggle up to Reuben on the cheap IKEA sofa and kiss his cheek.

'I'll go to Cirencester and buy some tomorrow,' I say.

The first night spent in Black Hollow Hall is a strange experience and neither of us sleep well. The house creaks and cracks around us as it settles for the night and I find it hard to relax. I need to get used to it though as I'll be on my own when Reuben goes back to work in two days' time.

'Can't you book another day's leave?' I ask as Reuben drifts off to sleep.

'I've already put myself behind by taking tomorrow off,' he mumbles groggily. 'I've got another big festival coming up in two weeks' time.'

My heart sinks. That means I'll have another whole week on my own soon. Maybe I can invite Kirsty to stay if she doesn't mind sharing my bed.

I lie still, listening to the strange sounds. What's that? My heart jumps against my ribcage. Can I hear footfalls on the other side of the house? Surely not. It must be the new pipes shrinking as the night cools. I focus all my concentration on the sound but can't hear it anymore. I must be imagining things again. Now all I can hear is Reuben's breathing. He sounds snuffly, as though he's getting a cold. Within ten minutes his snoring rasps and saws through the silence, leaving my nerve endings frayed and tattered. I watch him in the moonlight that shines through the side window. He's sleeping as soundly as a teenager, I think with resentment, while I'm being kept wide awake. I fidget and tug sharply at the cover. Reuben stops snoring then lies sighing for a long time. In the morning we're both heavy-eyed and lethargic.

'If I don't sleep well tonight, I'm staying in Luton tomorrow night, otherwise I'll be fit for nothing when I go to Germany on Wednesday.'

Reuben's tired and grumpy for the rest of the day and we constantly bicker and snap at each other. We don't sleep much better the next night but who does when the weather is so hot? Reuben complains about the new living conditions at every opportunity – the water's cold, the milk's off as there's no fridge, it's such a pain trekking to the coach house for the shower – that I'm almost relieved when he announces he's returning to Luton after an early dinner.

'If I stay here I'll have to get up at five to catch my flight and I'm already totally knackered. I don't feel that great either. I'm sorry, Tash. I'm going home for an early night. I'll be back late Friday evening.'

I say nothing. Home. He'd called Luton 'home'.

Chapter 41

I need to keep myself busy after Reuben has gone so I go to the attic to fetch a box of old photos I stumbled across this morning and haven't had a chance to look through. I put them next to the sofa in the old dining room, ready for when I return from taking Bonnie for a walk. They'll take my mind off being alone.

Bonnie twirls and jumps up when she sees me and tries to wriggle into my lap as I squat down to ruffle her ears. Bob stands in the doorway, leaning on a stick and chuckling at us. He's recovering quickly from his fall and claims it's because he has someone to get up for in the mornings.

'Bonnie has given me a whole new lease of life,' he tells me. 'I phone Jim every day to tell him what she's been doing and he talks down the phone to her. She cocks her head on one side then barks at the phone like she's having a conversation with him.' Bob's eyes crinkle with merriment.

'We'll have to take Bonnie to see him one day when you're fully recovered,' I promise. I wait until Bonnie stops spinning then clip the lead onto her collar.

'I'm going to walk about the village tonight,' I tell Bob. I need to be around civilisation and hope there'll be someone to say hello to.

'We've got storms coming,' Bob warns me. 'See how the wind has picked up and the sky has gone a funny shade of yellow? You'd better not be too long. I think this heatwave is about to break.'

I walk around the village green that should really be called the village yellow as the heat and drought have scorched it to a straw-like colour and texture. Even the nettles and bindweed in the hedgerows have shrivelled and the pond has a thick frame of dried and cracked earth around it. It reminds me of the stream at Black Hollow which has shrunk to the smallest vein of mud and, according to William, the lake is the lowest he's ever seen it. I flap the front of my dress to cool my damp skin.

Bonnie tugs and pulls me to the waste bin and lamp post to inspect other dogs' calling cards. She sniffs appreciatively then moves on to the next vertical object. I'm getting bored with this. I look about for a diversion and see Roger getting out of his 4x4 with his black Labrador in The Dog House car park. Bonnie must have seen her doggie friend because she strains at the lead and pulls me towards the pub.

'Okay, I'll just have a quick drink and you can see your friend,' I tell her. I'm really hot and the thought of a chilled glass of cider is tempting. As we enter the bar the black lab rushes over and stands nose to nose with Bonnie. Roger looks across and nods politely then resumes his conversation with a man I haven't seen before. The man turns to look at me then realises I've spotted him and looks away. They're talking about me. I collect my drink then sit down nearby. Roger has lowered his voice but I don't think he realises how loud he is and I can hear every word.

'They've given him a week to find something or they're all pulling out of the deal. Between you and me if he doesn't get this place he'll be finished. The land he purchased in Cirencester was refused planning and he's lost a fortune.'

They're talking about Julian. They look as surprised as I am when the door opens and he walks in. He scans the room and lifts a hand to Roger and the other man then his eyes linger on me longer than is comfortable. I take a gulp of my cider and pull Bonnie closer then take my cheap mobile phone out of my pocket to see if there is a signal. It's only got one bar but I pretend to be looking at stuff. I must look in desperate need of company and the last thing I want is Julian's.

'Hi, Tasha.' He's standing in front of me, blocking the light from the window and casting a shadow. 'Can I have a quick word?'

'I'm about to leave,' I say.

He glances at my almost full glass of cider. 'It won't take a minute.' He pulls a chair over and sits down.

'I'd like to revise my offer…' he says.

'It's not for sale.'

'…to 2 million.'

Crikey. That's £400,000 over the value. Mind you, quite a bit has been spent on it already. It's a good thing Reuben isn't here. He'd want me to accept.

'I'm sorry. It's still not for sale.'

'You're making a big mistake, Tasha. You might regret refusing this generous offer.' He pinches his lips together and the edges whiten.

'Excuse me, I need to go.' I stand and catch my leg on the table causing it to wobble and cider to slop over the top of the glass. I stride away with Bonnie without a backward glance. Julian is beginning to unnerve me. Have I swapped the Rigbys for him?

The sky's turning everything a strange yellowy colour, as though I'm looking at it through a Quality Street sweet wrapper. I need to get back and settled for the night. It won't be dark until ten and will be light again at five. That's only seven hours of darkness to contend with. I take Bonnie back and let myself into the Hall. The silence wraps around me like a tomb and I give an involuntary shiver.

I want to be prepared for my first night alone in the house. I go over the whole property ensuring the windows are shut and the doors locked. The French doors in the study facing the lake have no key and there isn't one on the bunch to fit the lock. I try the handle but it won't open. I'll need to get a locksmith in as it would be a shame if we can't ever use this door. I continue around the house. The front door and scullery have huge bolts so I slide them across.

I've bought more table lamps and soon the dining room is lit up like a Las Vegas hotel. I've also got a supply of candles and a couple of hurricane lamps to hold the candles safely in case the power goes off again. Lastly, I have a supply of drinks and snacks so I won't need to leave the dining room after my last visit to the cloakroom just before dark. I'll get over this hurdle of my first night alone in the big house then I'll be okay. Black Hollow is my dream home and I'm determined not to be driven out by fanciful thoughts and worries.

Sitting with my feet curled under me on the sofa, I pull the box of photos towards me and start to lift them out one at a time. The photos are difficult to decipher as I have no idea who anyone is. There are sepia ones with family groups staring solemnly at the camera – the father standing upright with his hand resting on his seated wife's shoulder. Their clothes are tightly buttoned from the neck to the waist and the children are wearing knickerbockers and white lace. Are these my ancestors? Maybe I should trace my family history.

I feel a deep longing to know more about my real mother. Do I look like her? Is she in any of these photos? Maybe if I track her down she'll meet up with me and we can build a relationship. I skim past pictures of gun dogs, the gardens as they used to be – Bob would like to see those – and babies with chubby thighs then stop and catch my breath as I see a photo of three teenage boys, all tall and dark-haired, and a girl. They're standing in front of the lake, holding fishing nets on sticks. A golden retriever lies at their feet. They're all smiling except the boy on the left who's standing a little apart from the group as though he doesn't want to be there. Are these people Simon, William, Andrew and Sally? Was Lynn, Sally's older sister, holding the camera? My heart beats faster. Is this my mother? I stare at the heart-shaped face, the cloud of dark hair and the huge grey eyes – just as Bob described her. It's difficult to comprehend that this girl could have given me life. She looks so young but he's right. I do look like her.

I stroke her face with my fingertip then put the picture carefully to one side. I rummage through the rest of the pictures but, disappointingly, I can't find any more of the young girl. I pick up the group photo again then get the locket out of my purse and flip it open. I stare at the picture of the young man, or rather boy, then study the photo again. I'm sure that's the same one. Is that my father? I'll ask William tomorrow or maybe Bob. He'll know if it's them. I peer again at the young girl and can just make out a flash of light at her throat. Is it this locket?

My eyes feel sore so I put the photos back in the box and set it on the floor. I'm beginning to feel tired. I'll watch some television then turn in for the night. I switch the channel from a crime drama to a light-hearted quiz show where comedians go head-to-head to create the longest word out of a jumble of letters. The quiz is inane and the comedians' exploits ridiculous but it makes me laugh and forget my fears of being in the old house alone. When my eyes grow heavy I wrap myself up in my thin summer duvet and fall into a deep sleep.

* * *

A sudden loud noise jars me awake but I'm not sure what I've heard. I try to replay the sound in my mind but it slithers away outside the grasp of my consciousness. A second later a flash of lightning illuminates the room, followed by a loud clap of thunder. That must be what had woken me. Bob was right about the storm. I slip out of bed and go to the side window. There's still no curtain and I suddenly feel exposed even though there's no one out there. I'll nail a sheet over it tomorrow. The lightning flashes again and I can see across the empty lawns and flower beds to the dark woods beyond. It's quite eerie in monochrome. The thunderclap comes almost immediately, making me jump. The storm must be right overhead.

Within seconds the sky tears apart to release a torrent of water. It falls in heavy, straight lines and obliterates my view. I turn away from the window and crawl back into bed. William will be pleased. His lawns are desperate for rain. I feel quite cosy in the warm and dry, listening to the rain outside. I'm just sinking into unconsciousness when there is a loud bang somewhere in the house. My heart pounds and I curl into a ball. What the hell was that? I pull the cover over my ears but the sound comes again, echoing through the downstairs rooms.

There must be a door or window open, slamming in the strong winds. I don't want the old door or window to break or the rain to get in and ruin the wooden flooring. It's no good. I'm a brave thirty-two-year-old woman, not a little kid, and I need to look after the house. I'll have to go and investigate.

Chapter 42

I unfurl my legs and lower my feet over the side of the bed to push them into my slippers, then pull on my dressing gown, more for the illusion of cosiness it brings than for the warmth.

I cross to the sideboard to get the torch but when I pull open the drawer it isn't there. Reuben must have moved it. Oh Jesus. Why didn't I check the torch was there? I'll have to take one of the hurricane lamps. I light two tea lights and put them inside then lift it by the handle and move to the door.

I hesitate. I know the crashing sound is just a door or window banging in the wind. No intruder would make a racket like that. Even so I feel vulnerable. I look around the room, my gaze falling on the poker in the fireplace. It feels surprisingly light when I pick it up. The heaviest part is the handle so I hold it upside down and, feeling braver, I open the door. Shadows dance and leap around me but I ignore the shrinking sensation that comes over me and listen for the banging to come again so I can get an idea of direction. The bang, when it comes, echoes around the great hall and almost has me spinning on my heel and running for my bedroom. Then a lesser thud. The door must have swung against the frame again and at any moment the wind will snatch it once more and fling it against the outer wall.

I pick up speed. The sooner I get the door or window fastened the sooner I can get back into the safety of my bed. Huh. Who am I kidding? Only children believe blankets offer security. I cross the hall and enter the small sitting room then through to the library. Nearly there. A draught of cold air wraps itself around my feet and I shiver, goosebumps rising on my arms and legs. It's so dark, as though all the colours of the daytime have been layered one over the other like printing ink until the only colour left is black. The lantern barely lights a foot in front of me. Maybe Reuben was right. I should have gone back to Luton, at least until the overhead lighting is sorted.

The tall French window smashes into the wall again and this time glass shatters. *Damn.* I hasten across the room to secure the door to prevent any more panes breaking but before I get there I spring away to my right as something moves to the left of me. Still backing away, I bring the lantern round to see what it was. Or who…

The light from two tiny candles is pitiful. It barely penetrates the darkness but I'm too afraid to step forward again.

'Who's there?' I can't help asking.

No one answers. Of course they don't. The storm continues to rage outside and gusts of air surge through the open door to make the candles flicker. To make the shadows flicker too. Was that what I'd seen? Am I literally afraid of my own shadow now? I step to the door and with glass crunching underfoot I reach for the handle. It's cold and wet in my sweaty palm. I'm exposed here and the rain soaks into my wrap while the strong wind flaps it around my legs. I scrape the soles of my slippers on the door sill to dislodge any fragments of glass then drag the door shut. I click the latch then test it to see if it holds. It seems fine but I puzzle over why I couldn't open it earlier. The wind continues to throw rain through the broken pane but I'll have to sort it out in the morning.

As I turn back to face the room a sudden flash lights up the wall of the library and I see a man-shaped shadow. My shock turns into a scream then I run, the poker bashing painfully on my shin and my wet slippers skidding on the wooden flooring as I bolt through the sitting room doorway. I catch my shoulder on the frame and pain erupts down my arm. A door creaks behind me but I don't stop. I weave in and out of the furniture in the drawing room and rush into the dining room. The candle flames gutter and die as they drown in liquid wax. I slam the door behind me and throw the poker and lamp on the floor then grab a dining chair and tilt it, ramming it under the door handle.

It isn't enough. One push from the other side of the door would send it flying across the room. The chest of drawers. They'll be better. My breath's coming in short gasps now and sweat trickles down my sides. My left arm feels numb. I run to the chest of drawers and lean all my weight into it, pushing it across the floor. The feet scratch the polished wood but I don't care. It crashes into the dining chair sending it skittering away. With the furniture positioned across the doorway I turn and look wildly around. I need something else to go across the other doorway that leads to the kitchen but no. It won't work. This one opens outwards.

Under the bed.

No. Too obvious.

The cupboard.

I grab my thin duvet and rush to the huge sideboard. I open one of the doors and crawl inside, grateful I've emptied it of old rubbish, and tuck the cover under and around my sodden robe. I find a screw head on the inside of the cupboard door and use it to pull the door shut. I wrap my arms around my knees and hunch into as tiny a ball as possible. I rock slowly back and forth, blood pounding through my veins. I'm trembling all over.

I listen.

Nothing.

I put my head on my knees, silent tears soaking into the thin duvet and then lift my head in horror.

I can hear the unmistakable sound of laughter. Deep and male. There's no doubt about it now. I'm not going crazy or suffering from paranoia. There's someone in the house.

Chapter 43

A layer of sweat coats my skin but I'm too afraid to move, to push the cover off my damp body. Instead, I sit perfectly still and focus on the trails of moisture tickling my skin as they run down my sides and back. I try to breathe slowly, to calm my pounding heart. Will he go around the house and through the kitchen to get to me? Does he know the layout of the building? Can he get in? No, I don't think so. The doors are all bolted. I wait, tugging hairs out one at a time, concentrating. Listening for footsteps or the sounds of a search.

Who is it? A Rigby, Julian, newly-released Simon or a stranger…?

The house gives nothing away. Time has no relevance. My whole world has shrunk to the inside of this musty cupboard and I'm either safe or I'm not. Cramp sinks its teeth into the back of my calf and I bite the cover to stifle my moan of pain. I knead my fingertips into the muscle, trying to break the spasm. I have to stretch out. I can't stay here all night. I'll count to 1,000 then I'll come out.

That's not long enough. Perhaps I'll count to 2,000 or even 3,000… Four thousand beats later I push the door open an inch and listen.

Silence.

No laughter, no footsteps. I ease myself out of the cupboard, my legs too stiff to straighten, and roll quietly onto the floor wrapped in the duvet. The poker is a short distance away so I roll towards it and snatch hold of the handle.

How long have I hidden in there for? It's difficult to tell. An hour? Two? My feet and buttocks begin to prickle as the blood flows more freely. Surely he would have got me by now if he was coming for me? Or did I imagine it after all? The room is so bright it hurts my eyes. I blink and rub them then look at the doorway to the kitchen. The door's still firmly shut. I peer under the bed. I'm alone in the room. I'd have heard if anyone came through the kitchen door. I let out a long breath then sit up and look at the window above me. The sky is dark and full of heavy clouds. No stars, no moon. Rain bounces on the flagstones outside and water spews from a blocked gutter above, splattering on the window in huge drops. If the rain carries on like this there'll be flooding as the ground's too hard and dry to absorb the deluge.

I crawl towards the bed, dragging my duvet after me. I climb onto the mattress and curl up like a baby, hugging a pillow to my chest. I'll face the door and stay awake. *But wait*. I didn't check behind the curtains. I clutch the poker tightly and climb out of bed again. My legs feel weak and I have to steady myself before I step forward. I creep towards the curtains then, lifting the poker aloft, fling the left one aside.

Nothing.

I do the same on the other side then breathe heavily with relief. I close the curtains again then fall back into bed, still clasping the poker.

* * *

A blade of sunlight cuts through the window, turning my eyelids red. I cover my face with the duvet and roll away from the light, then sit up abruptly as I feel something hard digging into my ribcage. The events of the night before rush into my head and I see the chest of drawers in front of the door. The physical reminders tell me I haven't imagined it all – the lamp on its side on the floor, the poker in the bed and the sideboard cupboard yawning wide open, littered with loose hairs. I have survived the night. I get unsteadily to my feet and pull the belt of my wrap tighter around my waist. It's six in the morning – too early for workmen to be on the premises. I look all around the room and listen. A wood pigeon coos outside the window and I'm struck by a strange smell. It's almost like that of a wet dog. I go to the French doors and move the curtain aside, peering from left to right for any sign of another human being. The place is deserted. The smell's stronger now and seems to be seeping through the ill-fitting door frame. Wet earth after heavy rain.

I think I'll feel safer outside. I open the door and step onto the terrace, lifting my face to the sun. What a relief to be in daylight. It has stopped raining but there are massive puddles everywhere. Sunlight sparkles on the surfaces and lights up beads of water on the leaves of the wisteria. The grounds are dark and sodden. The fresh summer air is like balm and the horrors of last night begin to recede in my memory.

I go back inside and shut the doors, feeling stronger and more in control of my fears. I need to check the house to make sure there's no one else in here and inspect the damage to the study door. I'll ask the workmen to fix the lock and replace the glass. I shove the chest of drawers back then walk silently through the house. Sunlight pools on the floors, warming the still air and bringing a sense of normality and tranquillity. I look around the room. The French door in the study is still closed but the pane of glass is missing, apart from two jagged shards attached to the frame. A warm summer breeze drifts through, smelling of the honeysuckle that grows around the doorway.

The room is empty. Empty of threat and menace. I look behind the armchair for traces of an intruder but there are so many footprints in the dust that I can't tell. I stand by the French doors and study the room. Could I have been wrong? Could I have mistaken the tall standard lamp with the drape of dust sheet for a man? Not really, although in my heightened level of fear last night anything is possible. And what about the laughter? That had sounded real. I consider calling the police to say I had an intruder but apart from the broken glass there really isn't any evidence, and it smashed because the wind caught it. Nothing is missing and there is nothing worth stealing. I don't want to waste their time.

I open the door and step outside, careful to avoid treading on the glass, then look beyond the terrace along the banks of grassland that lead down to the lake. Wait. Was that Morse I just saw down by the water? Maybe he's a regular visitor after all and he might have left the rat. If it is him, I'll bring him back to the house and call Sandy. I hurry to the kitchen and tip some tuna in a bowl then rush to my makeshift bedroom to pull on shorts and a T-shirt and a pair of trainers.

The lake seems higher and I'm surprised so much rain has fallen in so short a space of time. The ground is still hard underfoot, the water unable to soak into the compacted earth. I'm beginning to feel better now – the terror of last night diminishing in the beauty of the surroundings. Up above me an aeroplane draws a graffiti line across the clear blue sky. It looks like we're in for another hot day. I walk around the edge of the lake, calling Morse.

There's no sign of him and I begin to wonder if I saw a fox and not a cat. I tilt my head to one side and listen carefully for the angry squawking of a territorial blackbird, a sure giveaway of the presence of a cat, and I'm surprised to see a constant circle of ripples moving steadily across the surface of the lake. The stream must be full. I approach with caution. The ground seems to have shifted and earth and stones are washing down to the lake. The stream looks more like a river now. Water tumbles and gushes over rocks; swirling leaves and twigs getting caught in broken branches only to be released again to continue their journey.

I wander upstream at a safe distance then come to an abrupt halt. Up ahead, a tree has toppled, exposing a tangle of roots. The soil holding it steady must have shifted because of the prolonged drought, leaving it vulnerable to the furious gales of last night. I study the roots and the shapes they form. How strange. That small bleached branch of twigs poking out from the newly-exposed bank looks exactly like a skeleton's hand. I might take it home and draw it. I move closer, carefully negotiating my way through the snaking roots, and bend down to peer at the detail of the structure. My heart stops beating. A scream echoes inside my head like a fire alarm and my stomach turns inside out. I back away, tripping over in my haste and nearly falling.

It is a human hand.

Chapter 44

'Here, drink this.' PC Mills hands me a mug of sweet tea then sits next to me at the kitchen table. 'It must have been a terrible shock for you,' she says. Her green eyes are warm and full of genuine sympathy.

I nod and sip my tea. 'How long do you think it's been there?'

'It's difficult to tell. The pathologists will need to examine the bones and run some tests but from what I saw it looks as though the skeleton is intact and has been there some time.'

'Oh?'

'The tree must have grown around it after it was buried. It wouldn't have been possible to dig a big enough grave through all the roots.'

Dig a grave? My skin contracts as though I've got into an ice bath. 'Will they be able to find out who it is?'

'Sometimes we can track people through old dental records. Sometimes they might be wearing a distinctive piece of jewellery or belt buckle that links them to a missing person record on police files.'

'What about DNA?'

'Highly unlikely. It was only in 2013 that a separate database was set up to record the DNA of missing persons and I think the body has been there much longer than that.'

I sit in silence for a few minutes trying to take it all in. Someone else had been murdered at Black Hollow Hall. 'How long will it be before we know?'

'It's likely to be at least a week or two for all the tests to be run and analysed. Do you have anyone to stay here with you? I'm sure it must all be very unsettling.'

I need to phone Reuben. 'I'm not sure. Can I make a phone call?'

'Of course, go ahead.'

'I'll have to go to the coach house. There's no phone here and my mobile doesn't work.'

'No phone signal? Don't you feel cut off?' She looks around the vast kitchen and rubs the back of her arm.

'Do you think I'm in danger here?' I ask her.

PC Mills' eyes widen in surprise. 'From whoever buried those old bones out there? I doubt it.' Her eyes narrow now as she looks at me, then she asks, 'Why? Has something else happened?'

Lots of things. But I'm not sure where reality begins and imagination ends. 'How can I find out if someone is still in prison or not?'

'There's a Prisoner Location Service but it doesn't give information out to the public without good reason. Who are you trying to locate?'

'My uncle. My dad's brother. He was put away for twenty years for murdering their father. Do you think he could have had anything to do with this... skeleton?'

'I'm sure we'll look into all the angles.' She puts a comforting hand on my forearm. 'This must all be very difficult for you.'

PC Mills' sympathy pulls a thread in the tight weave of denial I've built around myself. I need to tell someone the truth. 'I keep thinking there's someone in the house but I'm not sure if I'm imagining it. Last night I thought there was an intruder. The door to the library smashed in the storm.'

'Do you want to show me?'

I lead PC Mills through the house. Her neck cranes from left to right as she takes in the splendour of the old building, so I explain how I've come to own it and the conditions of the will.

'I can see why you don't want to give up on the place,' she says. 'It's absolutely beautiful.'

When we reach the study doorway she looks around, careful not to disturb the scene in case she destroys evidence.

'Did you say the door was swinging about before the glass broke?' she asks.

'Yes, it shattered while I was in here.'

'In that case I can't see any sign of a break-in, Tasha. There are no marks on the frame and there are so many footprints and scuff marks from your builders it would be difficult to work out if a stranger was in here.' She looks at the tall lampstand and squints. 'Might you have mistaken this for a person? In the dark, I mean. You said you only had a couple of tea lights.'

'I might have done,' I admit. *But what if someone had draped that sheet over it on purpose to make it look like an intruder?*

'What else has happened?'

I tell her about the power going off and the cat in the house but it sounds so weak I can't go on. Was the laugh real or had I imagined that as well? I need to seek help. I lead her back to the kitchen.

'I'll take a statement from you as soon as you've made your call,' PC Mills says as she sits back down at the kitchen table.

'I'll be as quick as I can.'

Reuben sounds stunned when I tell him I found a skeleton in the grounds. 'What? For real? You mean a human skeleton?'

'I found a hand sticking out after a tree got uprooted in the storm but apparently the rest of the skeleton is there too.'

'Jesus, Tash. Are you okay? Are the police with you?'

'They've got a team here.'

'Do they know who it is? The skeleton, I mean.'

'Not yet, but they think it's been there a long time.'

'You must feel terrible,' Reuben says. 'Why don't you go back to Luton and I'll ask my boss if I can come home too?'

I certainly don't want to stay here for another night on my own but neither do I want to go to Luton unless I'm sure Reuben will be able to get back. He's only just landed in Germany for a three-day stint. I suppose I could stay at Reuben's parents if he can't.

'Okay.' I let out a long breath. 'Let me know what your boss says and I'll pack a few things.'

'I'll call at noon. Make sure you're by the phone.'

I give my statement to PC Mills then wander down towards the lake. A tent has been erected over the skeleton and a wide area has been cordoned off with crime scene tape. Metal squares are laid on the ground like tiles to form a walkway. A large man dressed all in white with equipment slung over his shoulder is lifting the flap of the tent. Probably going in to take photographs. I shudder at the thought of a body being concealed in my own garden. As I turn to look back at the house my emotions are in turmoil. In the light of this real trauma, my terrors of last night seem pitifully unreal. I'm going to do what I should have done months ago – make an appointment to see my doctor. Anxiety is running away with me, threatening my well-being and my relationship too. I need to put a stop to it once and for all.

* * *

Back in the coach house the shrill of the phone startles me even though I'm expecting it. God, I'm a nervous wreck.

'Not great news,' Reuben says. 'My manager isn't happy with me leaving at what is a critical time in the project. Besides, there aren't any direct flights until tomorrow. Even if I got one with stop-overs I wouldn't be back in the UK before 2am.'

My mind's racing. I can't afford any more stays in a bed and breakfast so I can either stay on my own here or go back to Luton. What sort of choice is that?

Chapter 45

'Don't worry about it,' I've told Reuben. 'I'll sort something out.' But I'm not having much luck. I sigh then cough. I mustn't breathe too deeply because the smell of stale water is overpowering. Mum and Dad are still in Devon, and I don't fancy being on my own in their house so I ask Reuben's parents if I can stay overnight.

'I'm so sorry, Tasha,' Reuben's mum says when I call. 'We've already got people using the spare room tonight. Graham's brother and his wife are coming for our anniversary dinner. They're staying over and we're all spending the day at Woburn for the Homes and Gardens event.'

Damn! I've completely forgotten about their anniversary. We should have sent them a card. 'Not to worry! I'll be fine. I'll make other arrangements.' The brightness in my tone sounds unnatural and Margaret isn't fooled.

'I could always make you a bed up on the sofa, love.'

'No, don't be silly.' The last thing I want to do is to gatecrash their celebratory dinner. I decide not to tell her about the skeleton. I don't want to add to the pressure of her trying to sort out somewhere for me to stay.

'I know you get anxious on your own, love. It's been months since the court case now though, and the Rigbys have probably got new victims in their sights. They'll have likely forgotten all about you.'

I doubt it. 'Yes, you're probably right. I'm sure I'll be fine.' I thank her and hang up. I'll go back to Sandford Road for a few days. I'll manage for one night on my own and Reuben may be back tomorrow.

I walk through the house and tell the builders the police are there.

'Bloody hell. A dead body?' They stand with their mouths open and their hands redundant by their sides. I ask them not to talk to anyone about it in case the local press gets wind of it. The last thing we want is the place swarming with reporters.

'I'll be away for a few days but while I'm gone can you fix the glass in the study door and change the lock?' I ask Curly, who nods slowly. 'I don't have a key for that door and it was blowing about in the storm.' It's strange I couldn't open it, though. When I checked, the house was secure.

As I get in the car I look up at the window my grandmother jumped from. This house has seen so much tragedy and sadness that I long to transform it to a bright and happy home for Reuben and our future children. The beautiful building deserves better.

There's no sign of William so I post a note through his door telling him what has happened. I wonder where he's gone. Shopping probably. Before I set off for Luton I call in to see Bob. He's horrified when I tell him about the skeleton in the grounds.

'Who do you think it could be?' I ask him.

'I wouldn't like to guess,' he says, his gaze sliding away from mine.

Realisation and horror hit me with full force and I take a step backwards. 'Do you think...' My voice trails off but I blow out air, take another breath and try again. 'Do you think it could be my mother out there? The police said the body has been there a long time. What if she didn't run away? What if someone killed her and buried her in the grounds?'

'Don't let your imagination get the better of you,' he says. 'Your mother wrote a letter saying she was leaving. I heard she took clothes as well.'

'Did she? You've not told me this before.' I frown.

'Don't be cross with me, Miss Tasha. I was afraid of upsetting you, that's all.'

'I've brought a photograph to show you.' I pull the photo of the three boys and a girl from my bag.

He puts on his reading glasses and peers at it.

'That's William, Andrew and Simon,' he says, pointing at the boys. 'And that's Sally.'

It is my mother which means it's also her in the locket. I look at her delicate face and my stomach twists with a mixture of joy and sadness. Where is she? Hopefully not being dug up from under the tree.

I stand up. 'I need to head off now, Bob.' I have to get away from the worry that the skeleton is my mother, that she might have been murdered too. 'I've arranged for Roger to walk Bonnie with his black Labrador. She'll like that.'

Bob's happy with the arrangements but follows me to his front door.

'You will come back?'

'Of course. I just need a few days away to get over the shock of this morning.' *And last night*, I add in my head. I kiss his prickly cheek and he puts his fingers to the spot and smiles.

* * *

I take the scenic route to Luton to distract me from the gruesome memory of a hand poking out of the soil. I'm glad I've made the decision to see a doctor. Whether it's pills or counselling I need, I'm relieved to think I might soon be back to the old Tasha. The woman who enjoyed life and didn't see threats around every corner. The woman who Reuben fell in love with.

I unlock the front door, stepping over the mat even though the headless mice are no longer there. The house is cramped and stuffy and smells of unwashed socks and Indian takeaways. For a moment my heart slumps but I open all the windows and load the washing machine then put the rubbish out. The thin veneered doors, plastic framed windows and Formica worktops look cheap and tacky after Black Hollow Hall's quiet splendour but as I potter about the house it suddenly seems so familiar that the last few months feel surreal. Unreal, almost. But not quite. I might have let my imagination get the better of me in the Cotswolds but the stabbing was very real and so was the way the Rigby brothers threatened me. I switch the radio on and get the hoover out. I need to fill the house with sounds so it doesn't seem so empty.

Two hours later the house is presentable again but I still don't want to be here. I grab my keys and go to the car. I'll get an anniversary card and a bunch of roses, and call in to see Margaret to offer her some help preparing her meal.

* * *

Margaret has everything under control so I have a quick cup of tea with her and finally tell her about the skeleton.

'Oh my word! That's awful, Tasha. I feel terrible now. You must be so upset by it all. Go and fetch your stuff and I'll make you a bed up on the sofa.'

'No, really. I'll be fine at home. I'm going to have an early night as I didn't sleep very well last night. I had to get up because a door was banging in the storm.' I don't tell her everything. She'd be appalled if she knew I'd hidden in a cupboard for hours.

On the way home I call in to the doctors' surgery and ask for an appointment the following day. There are none available so I put my name on the list for a cancellation slot.

I check every window and door of the little house to ensure they're locked before darkness falls and can't help but compare this task to last night's one. It doesn't take long this time and I'm thankful we have high security here. Because of break-ins in the area all windows have locks and the doors have five-lever mortice locks. I go to bed early with my phone next to me. The room is stifling but I daren't leave the window open. I throw off the duvet and find a thin sheet instead. I read a few pages of a comedy romance novel before giving in to exhaustion.

It seems I've only been asleep for an hour when I hear voices outside. At first they sound jovial so I don't take much notice. It's bound to seem noisy here after the silence of Black Hollow but soon the pitch changes and they become heated and aggressive. I slide out of bed, my heart thumping, and scurry to the window, opening the curtains a mere fraction so that I can see into the street without being spotted. Two men are out there face to face circling each other. Strangers. Oh God. I hope they don't have weapons. My knees weaken. I can't face being a witness again. I'm tempted to close the curtains and crawl back into bed but I can't draw my eyes away from the drama unfolding before me. I'm like one of those drivers on the motorway who can't help but slow down to look at the accident on the other side.

One man steps forward and throws a punch but the other man ducks and steps sideways. The first man staggers, pulled forward by the momentum of his swinging arm, and almost trips over. The second man uses the opportunity to shove him hard in the back and he sprawls into the gutter. He's probably drunk. *Walk away, please,* I silently beg the second man. He hesitates then aims a kick at the man's rump and walks off. I let out a long breath as the first man stumbles to his feet and carries on along the road shouting obscenities. *Thank God, thank God.*

I'm as tense as when I'm in the dentist's chair – every muscle taut. It takes me ages to relax and when I do, I sleep fitfully and dream I'm back on the bridge watching the knife slide between the man's ribs. I run but my legs don't take me anywhere and I wake up panting with my hair plastered to my forehead. I stare at the light coming from the landing and realise where I am. I hate this place. I definitely don't want to be here. All I want is to feel safe and enjoy peace and quiet. The trouble is, when my mind sees nothing but danger, is anywhere safe?

Chapter 46

'I'd like you to keep a diary over the next few weeks,' the doctor says. 'It's what we call "Watchful Waiting" and it's all about helping us to understand your symptoms. Record any feelings of anxiety, what the triggers are and anything that happens to you, real or possibly imagined, such as voices, seeing things that frighten you, sensations of being watched and so forth. This is the first step of an assessment and will hopefully enable us to eliminate post-traumatic stress disorder and paranoia to perhaps look at a diagnosis of anxiety instead. We can then look at ways to reduce the cause.'

'Could I please have a piece of paper and a pen?' I ask the doctor. I need to write this down. He passes a pen and notepad over the desk.

'You've been through some very traumatic events, Miss Hargreaves, and sometimes the mind deals with them by replaying them to try and make sense of them – especially at night, hence the nightmares – or by increasing the chemicals in the brain that cause anxiety as a way of heightening the body's flight mechanism to avoid future danger.'

This sounds logical to me. I'm ready and willing to accept a diagnosis of anxiety. I feel that, with help and time, it's a diagnosis I can come back from in a return to normality. But paranoia? He doesn't mean it in the way most people talk about being 'a bit paranoid'. He means it as a serious mental health condition and I don't like the sound of that at all. It troubles me when I think back to the voice I heard – or thought I heard – and the figure in the library on the night of the storm. I wonder if they're actually symptoms of paranoia. Doctor Anderson says self-diagnosis from the internet is a dangerous thing but what if I am going crazy? I feel a rush of anger. It's all bloody Dean Rigby's fault. Before the stabbing I was a rational, sane human being.

'I've also noticed you pulling at your hair.' The doctor nods at my lap and I look down with dismay at the visible layer of hair draped across my legs. I touch the side of my head and rub my scalp with my fingertips.

'How long have you been doing that?' he asks gently.

I shrug. 'Since I was about four, I guess. I managed to stop for a long time but just lately…'

'It's a condition called trichotillomania. Have you heard of it?'

I shake my head, surprised there is a name for something I don't notice myself doing half the time.

'Some people pull out hair from their head, others their eyelashes or eyebrows. It can be a symptom of anxiety or a compulsion. It would be helpful if you write in your diary how often you do it and how much hair you pull out. I'd like you to come back in two weeks' time and bring your diary so we can look at the whole picture,' Doctor Anderson continues. 'At that stage I'll decide whether to refer you for a mental health assessment or not. In the meantime, I'll refer you to a well-being clinic locally or if you'd rather you can self-refer. They can offer talking therapies, cognitive behavioural therapies and various workshops. There's usually a six to ten week wait but feedback tells us that eighty per cent of attendees find the service helps to reduce their anxieties. This leaflet explains what they can offer.'

Six to ten weeks? That's ages. I don't know if I can wait that long. 'Apart from keeping a diary is there anything else I can do in the meantime?' I ask.

'Eat a healthy balanced diet, drink lots of water, have a good sleep routine and get plenty of fresh air and exercise.'

I immediately feel a pang of longing for the Cotswolds and Bonnie. I love walking her around the grounds and village, admiring all the natural beauty around me. What can I do for exercise in Luton? Run in the park I suppose, but I'd need to join a group. I wouldn't feel safe on my own. But would I be fit enough to keep up with a group? I feel completely knackered today. It took me ages to get back to sleep after the skirmish in the street last night and afterwards every little noise pulled me upright in bed, my blood pulsing in my veins and my mouth dry. I inspected the doors and windows twice in the night to check everywhere was secure. I've got dark circles under my eyes and I feel spaced out, as though I'm not quite in the room.

I'm clearly not because the doctor has been speaking and I've not heard him. 'Sorry,' I say. 'Can you repeat that?'

'I'd like you to read these self-help leaflets before your next appointment.' He holds out pamphlets with the headings *Making Sense of Mindfulness, Cognitive Behavioural Therapy* and *Taking Care of Yourself.*

I take them and stuff them into my handbag. He swivels his chair back to his computer and starts typing. 'Would you like me to refer you to the well-being clinic or would you rather do it?

'Can I think about it?' I need to decide if I'll be staying in Luton for a while or returning to the Cotswolds. Perhaps my diary will help me to analyse where I feel safest and happiest. Reuben is coming back tomorrow evening as the flights were too expensive today but I'm staying at his parents' house as usual tonight so at least I won't be alone. Reuben and I are going to spend the weekend here to sort out some belongings and catch up with friends and family.

Before I go home I visit the shops and treat myself to a flowery hard-backed notebook and a free-flowing pen. Maybe this diary exercise will be a form of therapy in itself. Maybe I'll get my head sorted out so that I can live at the Hall without fear.

Chapter 47

I watch Reuben moving quietly and efficiently around the kitchen. He looks different today and I can't decide what it is. He tips a heap of onions into hot butter and my mouth waters as the delicious smell fills the room. He then sets to work dissecting a large red chilli. He's a good cook when he puts his mind to it and it's nice to have a night off from preparing the meal. He lifts his hand to rub his eye then stops and grins at me.

'Woah! That was close,' he says.

I grin back. 'Make sure you wash your hands before you go to the toilet! That could be nasty.'

He laughs. I know what's different about him. He looks happy. Relaxed and happy and totally at home. Because this is home to Reuben in a way Black Hollow Hall has never been. I turn away and open the fridge. Guilt at dragging him away from his home, family and friends settles on me like a heavy duvet. I suddenly feel hot and can't breathe freely. 'Fancy a chilled glass of wine, chef?' I ask.

'Please! Shall we go to the pub later? A few of the lads will be there and I think Sue and Amy are going. It'll be a proper Saturday night.'

I always feel like a spare part with Sue and Amy as they work together and are best friends. I try to join in their conversations but it's often about their colleagues and people I don't know. Never mind. I'll just have to try and interest them in a different subject. 'That will be lovely,' I say. 'It'll be good to catch up with them.'

I'd prefer to spend the evening with Kirsty. I should call her and arrange to meet soon. I've neglected our friendship lately and don't want us to drift apart.

When we enter the pub I see Amy across the room. She notices me then leans over to Sue and says something. Sue laughs then looks up. I hope they're not laughing at me. I look down at my thin cotton dress. It's too hot for much else but I'm wearing similar clothes to a lot of other women so it can't be my appearance. Reuben heads to the bar. I approach their table and they give me bright smiles that fade quickly.

'Tasha! How lovely to see you,' Sue says.

I can't help thinking her greeting sounds too enthusiastic and fake. This is going to be a long night if they think I'm in the way. I ask politely what they've been doing since we last met, how are their jobs going and have they holidays planned? They answer but don't reciprocate with enquiries about my life. They know I've inherited a huge old house but I don't want to be the first to talk about it in case they think I'm boasting. A pause in the conversation becomes uncomfortable so I tell them the story about Bonnie and how Bob and I rescued her.

'Aw, bless. I'd like a dog,' Sue says. 'Have you got a picture?'

I borrow Reuben's phone briefly, explaining mine was stolen, to show her some images of Bonnie and I relax a little. Perhaps the evening will improve. My optimism is short-lived.

'Did you see Adam's face when Gary called him into his office?' Amy asks Sue and I'm excluded again.

It's like playing gooseberry to a married couple. I look across at Reuben. He's listening to his mate Steve, a full pint of beer in his hand, and throwing his head back in a roar of laughter as the punchline is delivered. As I watch him I realise this is more like the Reuben I used to know. I hadn't been aware that I was trying to change him as a person as well as change his residence. Have I changed too? Maybe it's an inevitable consequence of what happened to me and we need to find a way to move forward together. I don't think my anxiety has helped. If only the doctor can sort me out, I can find a way to make the Hall more attractive to Reuben. Perhaps we'll find a way to keep both houses and make some new friends in the Cotswolds that Reuben can relate to.

Amy is still going on about some poor team clerk who got a verbal warning for being late and I tune out. The lads all roar with laughter again. It looks much more fun over there. I make my excuses to Sue and Amy, who barely pause to acknowledge what I've said, and go over to Reuben. He looks at me with surprise.

'Everything all right?' he asks as he plucks a couple of loose hairs from my dress.

'I just thought I'd spend some time with you. I haven't seen you all week.'

He puts his arm around me and gives me a brief squeeze then carries on chatting to Steve about the latest Arsenal game. God, I feel as included over here as I did over there. I want to go home.

Another two hours of banter and nonsense pass before Reuben finally suggests it's time to leave. I've tried to drink more and join in but the prosecco has made me feel queasy. I'm such a bloody lightweight I'm annoyed with myself.

It's a treat to get out of the pub and into the fresh air. I link my arm through Reuben's and my mood lifts now that we're going home. The night is still warm and I marvel that I'm out this late in just a cotton sundress.

Reuben's next words puncture my mood like a tyre running over a nail. 'What was the matter with you? You had a face like a baby sucking a lemon all evening. Why can't you relax like me? I've had a great night.'

'Lucky you,' I say. 'I just don't enjoy listening to office gossip about people I've never met nor am likely to meet.'

'Better that than spend time with those stuck-up bloody Hooray Henrys in the Cotswolds. At least people around here know how to have a laugh. No wonder Amy says you think you're better than everyone else now you've got your big inheritance.'

'I do not! When did she say that?' I feel hurt. I've tried hard all evening to get on with everyone. Reuben shrugs and says he can't remember. His gait is unsteady and he leans heavily on my arm. He's drunk. It would be stupid to get into an argument with him now.

A group of teenagers are clustered on the corner ahead and I tense and grip his arm tighter.

'They're fine. They won't hurt us.' Reuben straightens and picks up speed as he approaches. My hand slips out of the crook of his elbow. 'All right, lads?' He nods at them and marches through. They part like the Red Sea and I scurry after him. 'You just need confidence,' he says, as a balled-up bag of McDonald's chips hits him on the back of the head. Remnants of food land on the pavement.

'Good shot!' he laughs.

The teenagers snigger then turn away, jostling each other as they walk off in the opposite direction.

'See!' He grins stupidly at me.

'You wouldn't be laughing if they'd thrown a bottle at you.' I rush past him, eager to get into the relative safety of our house. Once we're inside with the door bolted I face Reuben. I know it isn't sensible to talk when he's been drinking but that stupid, antisocial behaviour in the street has brought the Rigbys back into my head in full technicolour. 'I don't want to be here, Reuben. I know you like Luton and all your friends and family are here, but it's not for me anymore.'

'Well, I'm not living in the back of beyond. Not even while the house is being finished. I hate it there. Hate it! It's so bloody boring, our accommodation is shit and it's too far away from everything that's important to me.' He staggers into the lounge and flops down on the sofa.

I stare at him agape. I knew he wasn't keen on being at Black Hollow but I hadn't realised he felt this strongly about it. The alcohol must have loosened his tongue.

'Where do we go from here then?' I ask, feeling totally helpless and out of my depth.

'Sell the bloody place and we'll buy something else around here. It's either that or you'll have to live there on your own. You've made it clear you don't want to get married yet, if at all. Maybe you think more of your bloody mansion than you do me.' He tilts his head back and shuts his eyes.

I'm rooted to the spot and don't know what to say. I grapple for a reason to keep the house. 'But if we do it up then sell it we stand to make a load more money. You could give up full time work, we could travel and have fantastic holidays – have money to raise a family.'

He opens one eye and looks at me. 'You don't know me very well, do you Tasha. It may surprise you but I'm not interested in being rich or owning a bloody big house and I certainly don't want to give up work. I know it hasn't been easy with my new manager but I love my job.' His voice is slurred but his meaning is clear. 'And how much money do we really need to raise a family, eh? Other people manage on far less and I wouldn't want my kids to grow into spoilt brats. The choice is yours. You can live in or around here with me or you can live at Black Hollow on your own.'

Chapter 48

I lie on crumpled sheets watching the sun brighten the outline of the curtains, feeling as tired as when I went to bed. Reuben's decision not to live at Black Hollow, even for the duration of the renovations, has circled around and around my head for hours like washing stuck on a spin cycle. Reuben or Black Hollow. Reuben or Black Hollow. But even if I agree to sell, it could take ages which would mean living back in Luton with the fear of the Rigbys casting an oppressive shadow over my daily existence. I'd be watching out for danger whenever I walked down the street and be on edge in my own home. I can't live like that.

But do I feel safe at Black Hollow? I have to be honest with myself here. I feel safest when I'm with Reuben regardless of which house we're in and safety is what I crave the most. I also can't throw away all we've planned for the future for a mere house. But Black Hollow isn't a mere house. It's my family inheritance. My history. I've never had a history before. No. That's looking backwards. I need to look ahead.

My line of thought jumps back and forth then stutters and stalls. I sigh. I can't let go of my dreams this easily. A pony in the stable, our children making camps in the woods, family picnics by the lake, huge dinner parties. Building a business together – how amazing would that be? A whole wonderful, colourful, exciting life. Why can't we share the same desires in life? It would make the situation so much easier but he just wants a small house near his family and friends and for us both to work for other people. It used to be enough for me but not now I've experienced something better. I'd also like to run my own business from home when we eventually have kids. I can only hope he won't remember his ultimatum when he wakes up. It won't be the first time he's forgotten a conversation after a gutful of beer. I won't mention it and I'll avoid anything that might trigger his memory. I slip out of bed to put the kettle on then take him a drink.

'I've put a bit of sugar in yours,' I say, knowing he likes it sweeter when he's got a hangover.

He grunts and rolls away from me. That's not a good sign but I'll just carry on as normal. I'll cook us a full English breakfast then perhaps we can go out somewhere.

Reuben is quiet but he doesn't admit he's got a hangover until I catch him downing painkillers.

'Let's go for a walk,' I suggest. Maybe the fresh air will revive him.

'It's too bloody hot to go out walking,' he mutters.

'We can go to the park. It'll be cooler under the trees.' We need to be occupied so that last night's conversation doesn't break through the thin veneer of normality to reveal the messy conflict underneath.

He agrees reluctantly and I almost change my mind when we get into the hot, stuffy car, but the air conditioning soon cools us and Reuben begins to relax as his tablets take effect.

The park looks strange with its bleached white grass shimmering in the relentless sunshine. I take off my sandals but it's brittle and prickly underfoot so I put them on again. I've enjoyed the heatwave but I'm getting tired of it now and miss the soft, velvety lawns that usually caress my bare feet.

'The trees are stunning, aren't they?' I say. 'I'm amazed they look so healthy when it hasn't rained for nearly ten weeks here.' I could kick myself for this. Luton didn't get the storms like the Cotswolds did. I'm trying to think of a subject that won't lead the conversation back to the Hall but I've failed miserably.

'You must have had quite a storm in Lower Bramcote if it uprooted trees. It must have been a terrible shock for you, finding that skeleton, and sadly it might put buyers off.'

Put buyers off? Damn. He has remembered.

He stops walking and looks directly into my eyes. 'I'm sorry, Tash. I think I was a bit harsh and over the top with you last night. I apologise.'

My spirits lift. Perhaps he's prepared to stay in the Cotswolds after all.

'I'm not giving you an ultimatum but for the sake of our relationship and future together I'd like you to consider selling Black Hollow sooner rather than later. I don't like being so isolated and I don't have the same emotional attachment to it as you have.' Reuben takes hold of my hands. 'I know you don't want to be here but I don't want to be there. I miss calling in to Mum and Dad's, seeing Jessica and Alfie, nipping to the local for a pint with the lads. I miss going to the gym. We were happy here before. We could be again and we can live locally in a nicer area.'

It's no good. I'm going to have to resign myself to the fact that I can't keep the Hall if I want us both to be happy. I know in my heart I want to marry and have kids with Reuben and now I know my parents were so young when they had me, I no longer fear that I'll have inherited a gene that would make me a bad mother. I can't jeopardise everything we have together. If I insist on us living there, Reuben might be so miserable that he leaves. I may never meet or love anyone else and end up a lonely old spinster rattling around in a huge, ancient house. I carry on walking with heavy feet. I need to be positive. Six months ago I didn't even know Black Hollow existed. He's right. We were happy then. We can be happy again.

I wonder what tomorrow will bring. Will the police have any news about the body? I doubt it. PC Mills said it could take a couple of weeks. I don't suppose we can even begin to market the house until we know. I could talk to some agents though – get a valuation – ask for advice. As a last resort I could sell to Julian but I baulk at the thought of him turning the Hall into flats and even worse, building more houses in the grounds. I still can't be sure he hasn't been behind some of the unsettling incidents. If I'm not imagining stuff, then someone has been trying to scare me and drive me out.

'It's not all that great anyway. The place has a dodgy history,' Reuben continues. 'Not many people find skeletons in their garden.' He sounds almost pleased. This situation couldn't have suited him better if he'd planned it. I take a sharp inward breath as a terrible thought slithers into my mind. What if Reuben has been trying to frighten me to get me back here? It's a possibility. No, that's ridiculous. Reuben loves me. Yet he doesn't love me enough to move to the Hall with me, does he? All the sacrifices are mine.

Stop it! Don't think this way. This is Reuben, for pity's sake. But what if…?

I'm so confused by everything but the doctor encouraged me to write things down and maybe doing so will help me gain some perspective. As soon as we get home and Reuben is distracted by sport on the television I fetch a sheet of paper, write each incident into one column then write Reuben's whereabouts on each occasion into another column.

I lean back in my chair and close my eyes in relief. Reuben wasn't even in the country when some of the incidents occurred. Guilt strikes me anew. Why am I even considering Reuben as a suspect? He's the man I love. The sooner I get help from the doctor the better. Not that the doctor will be able to make me like Luton any more than he could make Reuben like Black Hollow. I tear the sheet of paper into tiny pieces and put it in the kitchen bin. Reuben would be mortified if he saw the list. This house is driving a wedge between us. Reuben's right – I do need to sell it.

What about the builders though? We'll have to stop the renovation project and they've been so hard-working and loyal. I'll feel terrible dismissing them and we've signed a contract. Maybe I'll have to let them finish it but visit once or twice a week. Bob will be disappointed. But it can't be helped. I have to focus on my fiancé and building a life with him.

* * *

Reuben takes a call late on Sunday evening. His boss wants him to go to Budapest tomorrow morning for ten days to prepare for a huge festival there. It wasn't on his original schedule but someone else has taken ill and they need cover.

'Surely you can say no if it wasn't on your schedule. I really don't want to stay here on my own,' I say. Ten days is such a long time.

Reuben sighs. 'I'm sorry, Tash, but this is important. If I provide cover, it shows I'm committed and reliable. I could go a long way in this job. Things are a bit tricky at work at present. My manager is a bit of an arse and people keep leaving or going off sick which creates more stress for me. He said if I cover this one he'll get someone else to cover the next trip so I won't be away any more than originally planned. It's just brought forward a bit. Besides, I've always fancied seeing Budapest.'

Huh! When I mentioned travelling before, he didn't show any interest. 'Maybe I could join you for a few days? I could do with a holiday.'

He pauses for a moment then says, 'That wouldn't work, I'm afraid. I barely get any free time so you'd be on your own in a strange country. We can't afford the airfare either.'

I know he's right, but I'm stung that he expects me to give up Black Hollow Hall, but he won't put me before his career.

'And you're worrying unnecessarily about being on your own. The Rigbys have already got one son in prison so they won't want to risk another one being sent down. I think it would be bad for their "business" if they lost Lewis.'

I'm going to have to find other ways to feel safe. I'll get myself an attack alarm for starters and maybe I'll join a self-defence class. I'll also call Kirsty to see if she fancies staying for a few days. We could go to Black Hollow while Reuben's away or we could stay here and visit local places. Not as exciting, I know, but it's worth asking her. Kirsty's down-to-earth good sense will stop my mind from going in wild and dangerous directions.

Chapter 49

We chat for ages on the phone. We've got so much to catch up on. Kirsty has some holiday due and says she can take a week off as August is always a quiet month in the fashion industry. She says she'd prefer to stay in Luton as there's more to do locally. Now I only have one night on my own. I survived last time so I can do it again.

I kiss Reuben goodbye with a lighter heart. He gives me a tight hug and kisses my forehead. 'We're all good, aren't we, cherub?'

'Of course,' I say.

Reuben runs his fingers through my hair and frowns. 'Your old habit is back and you're heading for a bald patch,' he says. 'I'm worried about your state of mind, Tash. Are you sure you'll be okay?'

It's difficult to hide things from Reuben as he knows me so well. He remembers how anxious I'd become on a school activity trip where we had to abseil, canoe and crawl into tunnels. I'd been convinced a terrible accident was going to befall me and I'd pulled my hair so much it showed. Reuben had been wonderful, though, and given me the courage to try new things. He'd pointed out that strict safety measures were in place, and that no one else was getting hurt.

'Do you really think your parents would have let you come here if they'd thought you were at risk?' he'd said when I told him how they always worried about me.

Once I'd realised I was safe I'd stopped pulling out my hair and he'd been delighted to have helped me.

'Don't worry, I'll be fine,' I tell him now. 'Like you say, it's just a case of bringing your work forward and I won't be alone.'

'I'm pleased Kirsty is coming to stay,' he says. 'She'll be good company.'

I can't help thinking her visit has also eased his guilt at leaving me.

'I'll see you Sunday,' he calls over his shoulder as he walks down the path.

I will be fine. I'm certain. I'll keep busy and the time will pass quickly until Kirsty arrives. I mop the floors, change the bedding in the spare room and begin tackling a basket of ironing. The weather is still cloyingly hot, too hot for ironing, so I only manage twenty minutes' worth. I need some air. This house is nowhere near as cool as Black Hollow. I have a strong desire for an ice lolly but there are none in the freezer so I grab my purse and head out to the local shops. I'm going to treat myself to a fruit sorbet lolly and get a ready-made salad for my dinner. I don't have an appetite for a hot meal.

Stepping outside I'm dismayed to find it's no cooler than it was indoors, even hotter in fact. The heat radiates off the black tarmac of the road and the sun beats down on the top of my head. I can feel the warmth of the pavement through my thin flip-flop soles. Apart from the occasional car going past the street is deserted. The high temperature must be keeping people indoors and the footpaths are too hot for dogs' tender feet, so even the dog walkers are absent. I still remain vigilant. I constantly look over my shoulder and squint to see along the road ahead. Could I live here again? I try to recapture the feelings I had when we first bought the house – my excitement at being on the property ladder and feeling like a grown-up at last. It seems a distant memory now and too much has tainted the initial joy I'd felt. I look back at what should be a shiny image but it's as mottled as an antique mirror.

I approach the mini-supermarket and can't help but notice the piles of rubbish around the bin, the graffiti on the side of the building and the CCTV camera hanging off the wall at a ridiculous angle. No doubt the local kids have used it for target practice. I browse slowly around the store, relishing the cool of the refrigerated goods aisle and lingering by the freezer. I choose an ice cream and items for my meal then pay for them. The assistant at the checkout yawns widely and barely looks at me as she scans the items. She almost throws the change across the counter before picking up her phone again to check the screen. I think about Muriel in Lower Bramcote and my mouth twitches with the beginnings of a smile. This assistant can't even make eye contact and Muriel almost wants to know your bra size. I pause after leaving the shop to unwrap my lolly and throw the paper in the bin.

'Well, well, well. If it ain't the woman with the fucking big gob. I've been waiting for you.'

I turn, alarmed, at the voice close behind me and find myself staring into the leering face of Lewis Rigby. He's leaning against the wall, his muscly arms folded across his chest. Panic flares in my whole body and a hundred decibel warning screams in my head. I turn on my heel and run.

'I'm right behind you, Natasha.' He laughs and I almost stumble. He's found out my name! I curl my toes, trying to keep a grip on my flip-flops, and run as fast as I can. I'm reminded of my recurring nightmare where I'm trying and failing to outrun Dean Rigby but this time adrenaline is coursing through me, giving me more speed than I thought possible. My shopping bashes against my leg. My lolly drips orange syrup and splatters my white blouse, but I don't care. I clutch the bag and the wooden lolly stick in sheer terror and I can't let them go. I can hear his feet thumping the pavement behind me but he's breathing a little heavier now. He's carrying a lot more weight than me and this solid heat is like wading through treacle.

'You can run, but you can't hide,' he shouts. 'I know where you live. And I know where your parents live.'

His words reverberate through me but I keep on running. Sweat pools under my arms and across my stomach. My lolly falls from the stick and I throw it into the gutter.

'I know where your boyfriends' parents are too,' he gasps. 'I'm coming to get you soon. It's payback time.' His voice is growing fainter so I dare to glance over my shoulder. He's standing in the middle of the street with his hands on his knees, trying to draw breath.

I run all the way home then unlock my door with shaking fingers. He knows where I live. Oh Jesus! Does he really know where our parents are or is he lying? Has he got my phone? I've got some addresses in my notes app and all my contacts are in there. This is my worst nightmare. I should call the police but what can they do? Put an injunction on him to keep him away? That won't stop him. He and his family have no regard for the law.

I run upstairs and quickly rinse my hands under the tap to wash off the sticky residue. The cold water across my wrists cools my blood but I'm still shaking. I'm damp all over with a fine layer of sweat. My chest is tight from running and fear, and I feel sick. He's coming to get me. I lean over the sink and retch but nothing comes up. Has he got a car nearby? Will he be here soon? *Get out. Get out!* I splash water onto my hot face then rush to the bedroom and grab a holdall, slinging clothes in it randomly. I sweep my toiletries and make-up into another bag then hurry around the house shutting windows. I snatch up my keys, purse and phone, then dash out to the car, looking left and right along the street. There's no sign of Lewis Rigby but his mocking face is so fresh in my mind that I'm behind the wheel and tearing off down the road within a minute.

I don't hesitate to think about where I'm going. There's no way I can stay at Reuben's parents' house any more or even my mum and dad's. I can't risk making them a target. Has he really found out where they live? Does he know about Black Hollow? He didn't mention it. Had he run out of breath and was unable to say anything more or is it the one place I can hide from him? Because why would he hang around this neighbourhood if he thought I was living somewhere else? No, I think it's too far away for him to target and the goings on there are too subtle for the likes of him.

I still don't relish the thought of being at the Hall on my own, though. I drive out of Luton, cursing every red light and constantly checking my rear-view mirror, until I'm in the countryside. I need to be sure Lewis Rigby can't find me before I stop the car. I want to ring Reuben but he'll be boarding his flight now. I'll have to wait until I get to the coach house. I pull up in a lay-by and check the doors are locked then call Kirsty instead. There's no reply so I leave a message on her voicemail. 'Change of plan, sorry.' I'm surprised my voice is so steady when I still feel jittery. 'Don't come to Luton tomorrow. I'm heading back to Black Hollow. Give me a call when you get this and I'll explain. Maybe you can get a train to Swindon and I'll pick you up from there instead.'

By the time I reach the Cotswolds my shoulders ache from gripping the wheel and my eyes are tired from constantly checking if I'm being followed. I'm pulling into Lower Bramcote just as Kirsty rings. I park outside Bob's house and answer it.

'What's going on, Tasha? I thought we'd agreed we'd stay in Luton?'

'Can you come to the Cotswolds?'

'Hmm… I'm not sure I fancy being in the middle of nowhere.'

'I can't stay in Luton, Kirsty.' My nervousness is back and I'm sure she can hear the tremor in my voice.

'What's happened?'

'Rigby found me. He was waiting outside our local shop. He chased me along the street.'

'Bloody hell. That must have been terrifying. Have you told Reuben?'

'I'm going to call him as soon as he's landed in Budapest. I've just arrived at Lower Bramcote. Can you come here?'

'Of course I will. I'll stay a few days to keep you company. I'd like to see the place anyway.'

I'm pathetically grateful to her and arrange to collect her from Swindon tomorrow lunchtime as Kirsty doesn't own a car when there's good public transport in London.

I seem to wait ages for Bob to answer the door and find myself looking behind and scanning the lane frequently. I know Lewis Rigby isn't here but I can't relax. Bob has a new key safe on the wall but I don't know the code. I'll ask him for it so he doesn't have to get up for the door next time. I hear Bonnie barking excitedly and her claws scrabbling on the hallway floor. Eventually the door opens a crack and he peers out. He's leaning against the wall with one crutch under his arm and the other resting against him. His face breaks into a wide beam of happiness when he sees me.

'Tasha! My dear girl.'

'Hello Bob.'

Bonnie is desperately trying to squeeze past him to get to me and she's almost unbalancing him. He's trying to keep her in but I know she won't go far. I push the door open and take his free arm.

'It's so good to see you,' he says and I'm humbled when I notice his eyes are moist with emotion. 'Are you here for good?'

'I'm not sure yet but I hope so.' An Olympic winning tug-of-war team couldn't drag me back to Luton – not with that monster lurking in the streets. I desperately need Reuben to understand that staying there is no longer an option. There must be some way I can make Black Hollow more attractive to Reuben. Perhaps we could invite lots of guests – family and friends for weekends – to reduce his sense of isolation.

Bonnie has shot through the doorway and is jumping up, her sharp claws scraping painfully on my bare legs. 'How are you coping with Bonnie?' I push her gently away but she's too excited to calm down.

'Roger took her out today,' Bob says. 'I'm getting my cast off this week so I should be able to take her out for short walks soon.'

I have a cup of tea with Bob and feel some of the tension easing in my neck. Sitting in his pretty garden with nothing but bees humming and a blackbird singing, thoughts of the Rigbys and Luton begin to recede into the distance.

'Could you possibly take me and Bonnie to visit Jim on Saturday?' Bob asks, lowering his cup carefully onto his saucer.

'My friend Kirsty is arriving tomorrow and staying for a few days,' I tell him. 'Can we go another time?'

'Oh.' He looks crestfallen and I feel a pang of guilt. 'Only it's Jim's birthday on Saturday so I thought it would be a lovely surprise for him. We could call his sister and let her know we're coming. What if your friend came with us?'

'Maybe. I'll ask her but she probably won't mind if I leave her alone for a few hours.'

Bob grasps my hands in his and gently squeezes them. 'Thank you, thank you,' he says. 'You don't know how much this means to us.'

* * *

As I pull up outside Black Hollow I look about for signs of life but the builders must have packed up for the day. They're probably exhausted working in this thirty-degree heat. Everyone thought the weather would cool down after the storm but it hasn't made any difference, although the forecast says it will be almost chilly by the weekend. I look across the grounds towards the stream and see the crime scene tape around the area has been taken down. They must have gathered as much information as they could from the site but even though I know the skeleton will have been removed I'm going to avoid the place for now. The image of a bleach-boned hand protruding through the soil, as though it was trying to grasp the air, is still vivid in my mind. Was it my mother's hand? The hand that should have cuddled and soothed me, fed me and bathed me?

I swallow a sudden lump in my throat and turn away. I need to call Reuben to tell him where I am. I go to the coach house and pick up the landline phone.

'Hi, cherub. That's good timing. I'm in the taxi on my way to the hotel. Everything all right?'

I try to swallow again the tide of emotion that closes my throat. I'm so glad to hear his voice. 'No. I'm back in the Cotswolds. I can't stay in Luton.' I hear Reuben sigh heavily and the relief I felt a moment ago is replaced by a flash of anger.

'Has something happened? I thought Kirsty said she'd prefer to stay in Luton.'

'Rigby was outside the Co-op. He chased me.'

'What! Jesus. Are you okay? Did you call the police?'

'I outran him then drove straight here. He said he knows where our parents live. I was petrified. I'm worried he'll find out I'm here. I haven't called the police yet. I wanted to tell you first and there probably isn't much they can do anyway.'

'I'm so sorry I left you there on your own. I doubt he'll discover your whereabouts now. You should be safe but definitely call the police. When is Kirsty getting there?'

'I'm picking her up from Swindon tomorrow morning.'

'Will you be all right tonight?'

'Yes, I'll be fine,' I say, realising I should use this incident to reiterate my need to be away from Luton. I can't tell him I'm frightened here too.

'Lock all the doors and windows and get an early night. You're a brave woman, Tash. I'm proud of you and I love you. Call me in the morning and we'll talk about where we go from here.'

I phone the police next and tell them I was chased by Lewis Rigby and explain the background. They tell me they will look into it and check the CCTV at the shop.

'The camera is broken,' I tell them.

'That might be a decoy. Lots of shop owners do that but have another camera or two hidden. We'll let you know the outcome.'

* * *

Back at the Hall I stand on a chair and bang nails in the wall to pin a sheet over the window in the dining room. I check all the windows are fastened and slide the heavy bolts across the doors then once I'm ready for bed I shove the chest of drawers over the doorway. I'm taking no chances and there's no way I'm getting up for anything tonight. I'm too scared to turn the lights off but it's too bright to sleep so I drape a black sock across my eyes like an eye mask to block out the light. If I wake up I won't have to fumble to turn the lights on. I lie down and fall into an uneasy sleep.

But I'm not in my warm bed. I'm back in the library and can sense an evil presence. The room is filled with menace which sucks the air from my lungs. It crawls across my skin in tiny shivers and twists my insides. It's blacker than the darkest corner but all I see is red, because for me, red is the colour of fear and fear is my whole world now.

I want to move, to escape, to scream, but I'm trapped; not by ropes or chains, but by the red flames of fear that consume me.

It's getting closer.

The air thickens and I feel the weight of its presence pushing me back into the wall.

I can smell it. A dark, animal scent. A predator stalking his prey ready to rip me apart – but not yet. He's enjoying tormenting me first, though if he's going to kill me, I hope it's quick.

A rustle of fabric, a foot shuffling on the dusty floor.

Terror grabs me by the throat and squeezes. I don't want to die. My bladder weakens and a trickle of urine runs down my thigh. My heart and limbs are paralysed and I'm sliding down the wall – fragile and defenceless.

Can he see me? I can't see him but I know he's there.

Silence.

Is he there?

I sit up with a start and the sock falls from my eyes to reveal the bright room. A nightmare. A horrible nightmare with no Reuben to stroke my hair gently and soothe me. I lie bathed in sweat and tentatively feel the bottom sheet. It's damp with sweat but that's all. Thank God. I couldn't bear to think I'd started wetting the bed in terror too.

Chapter 50

'Oh my God, Tasha. This place is amazing! You never said it was a mansion.' Kirsty turns slowly on the driveway sweeping her gaze across the building and grounds, her bottom jaw hanging loose. 'You've even got a bloody lake!'

I smile at her wide-eyed expression. I'd played down my description of the Hall because I didn't want her to think I was gloating but I can't help the immense swell of pride in my chest.

'I don't think I could live here, though,' she adds.

The swell shrinks to a small ripple. 'Help me get this indoors then I'll show you around,' I say, puffing with exertion. Kirsty has brought an enormous suitcase with her and it's nearly pulling my arm out of its socket. I can't begin to imagine what she has in it. But then she always took heaps of stuff on our holidays so I shouldn't be surprised. She'd plan outfits for each evening with matching bags, shoes and jewellery while I'd squeeze everything into hand luggage. I hope she hasn't brought dressy outfits this time. I don't think the regulars at The Dog House will notice if she's colour coordinated but I have to make allowances for Kirsty. Working in the fashion industry means she is always conscious of people's clothes and accessories and she likes to make a statement.

We drag the case into the hall then wander from room to room, pausing often for Kirsty to admire a piece of old furniture or a view from a window. When we encounter the plumbers lifting a giant roll-top bath into position in the master bedroom en suite I see her stand straighter and flick her dark hair back. She loves flirting and is a sucker for a man with muscles.

'Morning, ladies.' Adrian lowers his end of the bath and wipes his brow on his arm.

Kirsty looks at me and raises her eyebrows. I know what she's thinking. I frown and give a small shake of my head. Adrian may be fit but he's married with two young children.

'Hi Adrian, Hi Pat, Kirsty is having the grand tour.' I bustle her out of the room again and she clutches my arm.

'Do many of your builders look like him? No wonder you don't mind staying here on your own. Perhaps it won't be so boring after all.' She giggles and flutters her ridiculously long eyelashes at me.

I'm not going to tell her I don't like it here on my own and I already miss Reuben.

'Is it spooky in here at night? I mean, you're miles from anyone. Do you get lonely?' she asks.

'I prefer it when Reuben's here but I've made a few friends locally and William is at the end of the drive.' I don't mention I've been petrified at times and William is seriously disabled. He's as vulnerable as me, if not more so. I don't want to scare her away and besides, I still don't know if the strange happenings are part of my overactive imagination or God forbid – paranoia. I lead her up the attic stairs.

'It's bloody creepy though,' she continues. 'All these dark corners and portraits staring at you. Look, their eyes follow you about the room.' She shivers dramatically then peers out of an attic window. 'There's not a house or a living soul in sight. What does Reuben think of it? I can't imagine him living here somehow.'

Neither can he, I think sadly. Perhaps Kirsty knows him better than I do. 'He likes the house but he misses his friends and family when he's here.'

Reuben and I had a long chat this morning. He now fully accepts that I can't live in Luton and has said perhaps we can find a compromise where we're both happy. I'm not sure what but at least the rift between us is getting smaller.

I lead the way downstairs to the dining room – now my makeshift bedroom. 'I have to stay in here while the coach house dries out. It shouldn't take much longer but they need to replace the flooring and redecorate. I thought we could share the same bed if that's okay with you.'

Kirsty stares at the king-sized bed. 'Whatever,' she says, but her shoulders relax as she realises she won't be in a room upstairs on her own. 'As long as you don't snore!' She pushes my arm and laughs. 'Hey, can we go out somewhere tonight? How far is the nearest town? We can get a taxi if you fancy a drink.'

I've been expecting this suggestion but not quite so soon. Kirsty loves going to busy bars and clubs and enjoys meeting people. I'm happier curled into an armchair with a book. We're like salt and vinegar, completely different but we complement each other. It all stems back to when we were at school together and Kirsty rounded on some kids who were teasing me for spending my lunchbreaks in the library. She'd visited the library with me the next day and we've been firm friends ever since. When I asked her why she'd done that she'd said it was because she fancied my brother. When I told her I didn't have a brother we'd both found the situation ridiculously funny. We've been close friends ever since.

'I'm a bit knackered. Can we go to the local pub instead? We can go into town on Saturday. It might be livelier then.'

'Okay, it's a deal.' Kirsty sighs and rummages in her bag for her phone. My heart sinks. I haven't told her there's no signal. She peers at the screen then walks to the window and holds it closer to her face to see how many bars she's got. 'Where's the best place to stand to get a signal?' she asks.

'Erm… a mile or so down the lane.'

She looks at me agape. 'You're kidding.'

I don't react.

'You're not kidding.' Kirsty rolls her eyes. 'Do you even have a landline?'

'In the coach house. We've applied to the phone companies to put a mast on the land but they need to assess how many people are in the area and whether it's commercially worthwhile.'

'In that case there's no way I want you to ever leave me on my own here after dark.'

'I wouldn't do that to you.' I don't want to be here on my own in the dark either. I wonder if Kirsty will witness any strange goings on or whether my mind won't play tricks on me with her present. 'We've plugged a Wi-Fi extender into the kitchen so you can get the internet. I've been working from there.' I hope she doesn't get bored here and want to go back to London. No. She's too good a friend to do that to me, especially after my encounter with Lewis Rigby.

She nods. 'Okay, cool. At least I can go on Facebook and Twitter.'

Since moving here I've been tempted to get involved in social media myself, even though I've avoided it for years, so that I can at least connect with other people. But I've been too petrified that it might help the Rigbys to find me. Kirsty unpacks her case, tossing a moulded pillow onto the bed. It makes a loud thump.

'Bloody hell, Kirsty.' I pick it up and examine it. 'No wonder your suitcase weighed a ton. I've never felt such a heavy pillow.'

'It's a memory foam neck pillow. It goes everywhere with me. I can't sleep without it.'

I find space in the sideboard for her clothes and she hangs dresses on the curtain rail. At least two of them are what I'd call 'going out' dresses. It feels so good to have her here. We'll have such a laugh together. I'll be able to sleep better tonight too.

Before I drive to the pub I stop by William's place to introduce Kirsty to him. They shake hands politely.

'It's great meeting you, Kirsty,' William says. 'I'm pleased Tasha has got some company. Black Hollow can be a lonely place.'

I wonder for the first time if William is lonely. He doesn't seem to have any friends but I suppose it's difficult to socialise when you're stuck in a wheelchair and places are inaccessible.

'He seems friendly,' Kirsty says as we get back in the car.

'He's lovely,' I say.

The pub's quiet when we arrive but a few locals drift in and stand at the bar.

'Okay, how many out of ten for the guy in the padded body warmer.' Kirsty gives me a wicked grin and I know she's about to dissect and analyse the attractiveness of the men. Julian and Roger make their usual appearance and Kirsty leans over whispering, 'He's peng!' flashing her gaze over at Julian.

'Peng? What sort of word is that?'

'God Tasha, you need to get out more. You know… fit, handsome.'

Julian doesn't appeal to me one little bit but I join in our old game. I feel relaxed and happy for the first time in ages and more like my old self. I hope Kirsty stays at least a week.

Chapter 51

'Promise me you'll be back by eight.' Kirsty flops onto the bed, her arms above her head. 'I know I've been here three nights now and should be used to it but it starts getting shadowy and dark indoors by then.'

I move around our bedroom picking up her clothes and folding them into a neat pile. 'I promise. Jim's sister, Doris, won't want us visiting for long. She'll be worried about her cats being scared away by Bonnie. They hide up the lane when the dog is in the house.' I'm looking forward to seeing Jim's face when we walk in with his dog. 'We won't be late and as it's Saturday the traffic will be lighter.'

Kirsty could have come with us but she said she has a friend in the area today and he's going to call in. I'm not sure whether I believe her. Kirsty changes her men as often as she changes her handbag but how has she organised it with no phone signal? She might have done it through Facebook but I worry she's meeting up with Adrian. I'd feel partly responsible if she damaged his marriage. I've noticed her chatting and laughing with him a few times and when I approach them he looks sheepish and rushes off. I can't decide if he's feeling guilty about spending time with her or knows he should be working.

I give her a brief hug before I leave. 'It's so great having you here, Kirsty. I hope you can stay a few more days.' I worry she'll get bored and clear off home like she did once before when a group of us hired a remote cottage in Norfolk for a week.

'I'll probably stay until Tuesday,' she says and squeezes me back.

Yay! Three more days, and Reuben will be back on Wednesday. Surely by then I should feel able to stay on my own for one night without worrying about strange noises and things that go bump in the night. The past few nights have been uneventful which rather confirms that it's anxiety that's been making me jump at nothing.

Kirsty sits up abruptly. 'Hey, if you go near any food shops can you get some iced doughnuts and maybe some pizzas? I'm craving junk food after all the healthy stuff you make me eat.'

I laugh. It's been too hot to eat anything but salads and fresh fruit. 'I will as long as you promise not to up sticks and bugger off like you did in Norfolk.'

Kirsty laughs. 'I promise, but only if you promise to get back before dark. See you later.'

As I leave the room I notice the box of old photographs. Kirsty and I spent a companionable hour last night going through them. I wanted to look at pictures of my mother again now that Bob has confirmed it is her and it was good to have someone to talk to. I'd stared at Sally's face for ages.

'You look like her,' Kirsty had said. 'Your hair's different but you have the same eyes and heart-shaped face.'

I'd felt strangely warmed by this, as though a connection with my past had been securely tied. I'm going to call the police on Monday to see if they have any more news on identifying the body. I'm convinced it's my mother now and I even got a bit tearful last night. Kirsty was great, though. She'd hugged me and told me to wait until we found out who it was.

'The skeleton might belong to a soldier from the civil war for all we know!' she'd said.

* * *

The air is a lot cooler when I step outside. It seems the heatwave has skulked out the back way rather than making a dramatic exit through the front door with a crash. I'm glad. I hate thunderstorms now. I'm a few minutes early for Bob. Bonnie dances figure of eights around my legs as Bob walks slowly but steadily to the car. He's had his cast removed and resting has improved his knee so he's feeling quite sprightly.

'I'm so looking forward to this, Tasha. Jim will be thrilled to see Bonnie.'

'And you,' I add.

The journey is straightforward although I can feel tension building in my arms and shoulders as we cross the county boundary into Bedfordshire. I know I'll be at least fifteen miles away from Luton but the fear won't go away. Aspley Guise turns out to be a pretty little village, with its square of quaint, gabled houses and quiet lanes steeped in history.

'A lot of people who worked at Bletchley Park were stationed here,' Bob says. 'Some houses were requisitioned as headquarters for senior war officials.' Bob and Jim were children during the Second World War and they love to talk about it. 'Jim and Doris were evacuated to Aspley Guise and they had a wonderful time here. That's why Doris wanted to come back and live here.'

Bonnie is ecstatic when she sees Jim and his face lights up like a Christmas tree. She climbs onto his lap and not even food will persuade her to get off again. Jim and Bob settle down for a game of dominoes so I head to the shops in Woburn Sands to get some treats for Kirsty.

When I get back I'm surprised to find Doris preparing us a meal.

'You will stay, won't you? Jim is so enjoying himself it's a shame to cut the visit short on his birthday.'

I glance at my watch. It's already 5pm and it's at least a two-hour drive. I promised Kirsty I wouldn't leave her alone in the dark but I can't drag Bob and Jim's dog away so soon, especially as Doris has made such an effort. I look at Jim's happy face. 'That would be lovely,' I say.

The meal takes a lot longer than I'd anticipated. I check the time again and silently will Bob to eat faster. As Doris rinses the plates in the kitchen I tell Bob we need to go soon, and get up to help Doris, but before I get there she appears in the doorway, her face illuminated by candlelight. A simple sponge cake is adorned with numerous candles stuck in blue icing words – 'Happy

Birthday Jim.' I sit down again and we all sing. At this rate it will be dark before we get home. The cake is cut and eaten with frustrating slowness. Jim is tearful when he says goodbye to his dog and I can see pain and guilt flicker across Doris's face.

'Thank you for bringing them,' she says quietly after I've helped Bob into the car and strapped a reluctant Bonnie into her harness. 'I feel bad but I've already given up my independence to look after Jim. I couldn't give up my cats as well. They're the love of my life. If only Bonnie didn't chase them...'

I touch her arm and thank her for dinner, promising to visit again some time. I'm worried about Kirsty now. I can't even call her to tell her I'm running late.

It's dark by the time I return to Black Hollow and I'm dismayed to see no lamplight coming from the windows. I'm certain the heavy curtains don't block it out that well. I get a torch from my glovebox and enter the deserted hallway with trepidation.

'Kirsty?'

Silence.

I push open the dining room door. There's no sign of her. I hurriedly switch on some lamps and feel a small measure of relief as the room becomes bathed in a warm glow. I look around and suck in my breath. Kirsty's belongings have gone. The piles of clothes I'd folded this morning, the tumble of shoes by the door and the scattering of make-up across the sideboard – all gone. I sit down heavily on the bed, my limbs weighed down with disappointment. Has she gone off in a strop because I was late home? But how did she leave? She couldn't have dragged that bloody great suitcase along the drive? Did she use the coach house phone to call a taxi? Or did she go off with the man she was meeting? Kirsty is a dear friend and a lovely person but she does have the occasional mood swing. Maybe she's sulking because I wasn't home before dark. I go straight to the coach house and call her mobile but there's no reply so I leave a voicemail. I'll have to try again first thing tomorrow.

I get ready for bed quickly – I'll wait until morning to have a shower – and check the bolts on the doors, then drag the chest of drawers across the doorway. I'll sleep with the lights on. I lie down in the wide bed and stretch my arm out to the empty space, then sit up in surprise.

Kirsty's favourite pillow is still here. The one she never goes anywhere without. She really must have been in a temper when she went if she's left this behind.

I try to sleep but the fox is screaming in the woods again, making the hairs on my arms stand up. I'll never get used to that terrible sound.

Chapter 52

I doze fitfully, alert to any sound. Did I hear footsteps outside? Is Kirsty back? I tense and strain my ears, waiting. There's a tapping sound on the window. Is it a loose tendril of wisteria blowing in the wind? This time it's a knocking sound. My heart thumps and I hold my breath. Surely Kirsty would knock on the front door. She wouldn't want to frighten me like this. Or is she playing a trick on me? I slip out of bed and pull on my dressing gown. I turn off the lamps so I can see outside then pad silently over to the window. *It's fine, Tasha. There's nothing to be scared of.* It's probably Kirsty pratting about. She'll be standing there with her legs crossed laughing hysterically. I draw the curtain cautiously to one side then scream in horror.

A man has his face up to the glass and he's grinning at me. I drop the curtain and step back but his features are branded on my retinas and I can still see his shaven head, thick neck and small, hard eyes. His teeth are yellow and uneven and he has a gold earring in his left ear. Who is he?

I can hear him laughing now. Is this the same laugh I heard a couple of weeks ago on the night of the storm? It doesn't sound like it. I'm petrified. My heart races and I feel light-headed. What shall I do? Hide in the cupboard? No, he knows I'm here. He's rattling the handle on the French doors now. I can't breathe. What if he tries to break one of the small panes of glass? At least there's no key in the door to tempt him. The rattling stops and time crawls by as I wrap my arms around my shins and wait for further sounds. Hopefully, he's given up and gone.

A sudden, heavy pounding on the front door reverberates through the hall and I whimper in fear. I don't know what to do.

I can't stay here. I leap up, throw on a robe and shove my feet in my shoes then grab my torch and rush to the kitchen. I shine it around the room looking for the knife block. There are five slots but only four knives. Damn. Where has the big one gone? I pull the next biggest knife from the block and grab a small pot of white pepper from the worktop, then go through the scullery to the back door. Dare I attempt a sprint across the courtyard to the coach house so I can call the police? It's only a few yards away and the trespasser is right around the front of the building. I hesitate. I'm too scared to go forward but I'm just as scared of staying here.

I slide the bolt back quietly and turn the key. It makes a small click. I can't hear the front door from here but hopefully he's still there, waiting for me. I open the door and shine my torch around. Nothing.

Go, Tasha! Run. I pull the door closed, then run on tiptoes across the yard to the coach house. I fumble with the keys as I daren't let go of the knife. Shit, shit, shit! At last I find the right one and get it into the lock. Thank God. I'm about to push the door open when an arm wraps itself across my windpipe, stifling my scream. My knife clatters to the ground.

I pull at his arm with both hands to free my throat so I can breathe; my mind shattering into fragments in my panic. 'Help me!' I want to cry, but there's no one to help even if I could get the words out.

'Where's Simon?' a rough voice whispers in my ear.

Simon? I'm torn between relief that it isn't me he wants and terror that Simon might be close. Not that I'm free from terror now. Far from it.

I aim my heel at his shin but he pulls me sideways and laughs.

'I like a bit of fight in a woman,' he murmurs into my ear.

Dear God no. 'Please don't hurt me,' I manage to rasp. 'I've never seen Simon. He's in prison.'

'Not anymore, he isn't. He told me he was coming here. He owes me and this place must be worth a bleedin' fortune. Who the hell are you? His fancy piece?'

The man loosens his grip but not enough for me to get away. He turns me around then pins me roughly against the wall, his forearm pressed across my chest and ready to slide up to my throat at a whim.

'He's my uncle but I've never met him.' My speech is fast and high-pitched. 'I inherited this place a few months ago.' I stare at his empty eyes, no compassion or emotion in them apart from a spark of anger.

'He told me he was coming into big money. I did a good piece of work for him and now he owes me. He'll be back and when you see him tell him Gripper wants payment for the Kensington job.'

Kensington? That was where… Pain shoots through my knee as he pushes me to the ground. My fingers connect with something – my knife! – but by the time I've stumbled to my feet he's gone. I rush into the coach house and slam and lock the door. I press William's number into the phone with shaking fingers.

'William, someone's been here looking for Simon. He said Simon owes him money. He… he grabbed me by the throat. I couldn't… it was horrible. I couldn't breathe.' I'm starting to cry and my words are getting jumbled.

'Where are you? In the coach house? Where did he go?'

'Yes. I don't know.' I'm sobbing uncontrollably now.

'Wait there. I'm on my way.' The phone line goes dead.

I sit on the damp floor with my back against the wall, pulling out hairs to soothe myself, my mind replaying what just happened. When I get to the moment when I took the knife from the block I suddenly recall the empty slot. This man didn't threaten me with a knife and the door was locked so he couldn't get in. If he didn't take it, where is it?

Chapter 53

'Tasha. It's William. Open the door.'

I scramble up, wobbling slightly on my numb feet. Pain throbs through my knee as I put my weight on it. I open the door but of course William can't come inside because he can't get the wheelchair over the step. I stagger forward and collapse into his arms, sobs wrenching out of my chest. With his strong arms around me I almost feel safe again.

'Tell me what he looked like and exactly what he said,' William asks when I'm a little calmer.

I pull away from him and wipe my wet eyes with my fingertips then tell him as much as I can remember. I sniff and he pulls a handkerchief from his pocket. His face is expressionless in the dark.

'Did he go past your house?' I ask. 'How do you think he got here? I didn't hear a car.'

'I looked out for him after you called but there was no sign of him. He might have cut through the woods and left his car further along the lane. Where's your friend, Kirsty? I thought she was staying for a few more days.'

'She went off in a huff because–' My God, what if she hadn't gone off at all? What if she'd been taken off? Maybe someone snatched her before she finished packing. Simon or the horrible man who just attacked me. No, that's stupid. She'd taken her things with her.

Yet she'd left her precious pillow behind.

That was only because she was in a mood. Wasn't it? My voice is verging on a wail and I fight to control my emotions. 'She's gone without saying goodbye. I'm worried about her.'

'Phone her.'

'I tried a short while ago but it went to voicemail.' I try again at William's suggestion but there's still no reply.

'She's probably asleep.'

That's true.

'Try her in the morning.'

I will. The suggestion reminds me that it's the middle of the night.

'I don't think that man will be back tonight,' William says. 'It sounds like he wants his message delivered and he's got to allow time for that. Even if you can't actually deliver it because Simon isn't here.'

What if he is here though? That would explain the clothes and the food.

William yawns and I suddenly realise I'm keeping him up. Should I ask him if I can stay at his place? No, he only has one bedroom and his sofa is far too small to sleep on.

'Thanks for coming William. Will you come to the door with me then go round to the lawn in front of the French windows? I'll wave to you when I'm in my room.'

'Of course,' he says.

A few minutes later I stand at the window and wave. I've put all the lamps back on but with the curtains behind me I can see his outline in the moonlight. He waves back then turns his chair and trundles off.

I put jeans, a loose sweatshirt and trainers on. William is probably right when he says the man won't be back but I feel too vulnerable in my nightwear. I'd rather sleep fully clothed in case I need to run away. I lie awake with the television on and the volume turned down low to give the illusion of company but every muscle in my body is tense. The light-hearted sitcom and canned laughter help a little to lessen the threatening atmosphere in the house.

As I stare vacantly at the screen I try to work out what's niggling at the back of my mind. There was something Gripper said that made a connection in my brain. What was it?

Kensington.

He said he'd done a job in Kensington. That's where my father was bludgeoned to death. God, had Simon hired that man to murder my father? Is Gripper someone he knew in prison? But why kill my dad? Was it to get his hands on the inheritance? If that's the case then I must also be a threat to Simon. I don't think my anxiety has made me paranoid at all. I think Simon is out to get me. I've read books where the predator decides to play with the victim and torment them before killing them. Is that what Simon is doing?

I'm barricaded in but still don't feel safe. I keep the knife inches from my hand and the white pepper I found in the kitchen tucked into my front hoodie pocket. I daren't sleep. I'll stay awake all night and as soon as daylight comes I'll be out of here. But where will I go? I've run out of options. I'll have to go back to the B&B while I wait for Reuben to come back. I wonder why I didn't call the police from the coach house and suppose I was too panicked to think of it. I'll call them in the morning. That man killed my father and I want him locked up. Simon too.

I can't imagine falling asleep – I don't envisage ever being able to sleep again – but I can't take the risk so I sit upright in the armchair, holding my knife and pot of pepper while inane American sitcoms play across the television. I don't find them funny at the best of times but now I stare woodenly at the screen and turn everything over in my mind. I left Luton to find a safe haven but I'm in more danger here.

A tinkling of broken glass from the direction of the kitchen has me leaping out of the chair as though it's on fire. Shit! Simon's coming for me. I check the pepper is securely in my pocket then push the chest of drawers away from the door. I need to go through the drawing room if he's in the kitchen. I grab my torch and car keys and run through the dark room and into the hall. Which way? Which way? I start towards the front door then change my mind. He might have done this to lure me outside. He might be waiting for me.

I'll hide instead.

I run up the stairs and along the landing to the box room. I pull open the huge cupboard and climb inside then pull the door shut. I grab a musty suit from its hanger and put it over my head. It'll take him ages to search the house and find me here.

'Hello, Tasha.' A slow, creepy whisper comes from right next to me. Fuck! He's already in the cupboard. Or are there two of them? It's not the same whisper as Gripper's. My heart stops beating and the hairs lift on my skin. How did he get in here? I throw the jacket off, lean sideways and shove my knife in his direction. I hear a grunt of pain. I burst out of the cupboard and run across the landing then down the stairs. He's stumbling along behind me. Maybe I stabbed him in the leg. I fumble with the front door locks then throw the door wide, snatch my keys from the hook on the frame and rush outside towards my car.

I stop in horror. My car's on fire. Bright orange flames are curling themselves into a ball, circling the interior. I don't have the keys for the old Renault parked near to it and there isn't time to get them. As I attempt to run past the blazing car a window explodes and glass scatters at my feet. I dodge round it and keep going as the flames escape through the opening.

I don't want to die. I don't want to die. I start along the driveway. I'll go to William's house. I should have asked to stay there, to sit up all night on his sofa. He'd keep me safe. But Simon could be gaining on me and I'm too visible in the fire light. I'll have to go into the woods where I can hide first.

I switch off my torch and race across the lawns, grateful when the moon disappears behind a thick cloud. I burst into the ferns and undergrowth but try not to trample them. I can't risk leaving a trail for him to follow. I was frightened of these woods but now they shield and protect me. I'm shaking all over and my breath comes in ragged gasps though I'm scared to breathe in case he hears me. The moon breaks through the clouds and faint blue light filters through the trees to give me a brief view of the way ahead. I stumble on, stubbing my toe painfully on a fallen branch and snagging my jeans on bramble thorns. The moonlight disappears again but my eyes are adjusting and I can make out shapes in front of me – a dip in the ground, a huge oak tree.

I stop to listen. Nothing.

No sound of anyone crashing through the woods, but a noise to my left freezes the blood in my veins. It's a whimper. I wonder if there's an injured animal lying there but then the whimper comes again. It's not an animal, it's a human.

Chapter 54

I stand rooted to the spot, afraid to move. Whoever it is they're in pain. Is it Simon with the stab wound in his leg? Or did he hurt William and dump him in the woods before he came for me?

I tread cautiously towards the sound, straining to see in the dark. The moon shows its face again and slants beams of light through the trees. There. I can see a mound near the undergrowth rolling slightly from side to side. I edge forward, scared that I'm walking into a trap.

The human form moans again and this time I recognise who it is. *Kirsty.* Oh my God! What's she doing here? I rush forward, stumbling over a tree root and righting myself before I fall on her. Her arms are tied behind her back. I kneel down and, taking her shoulder, roll her gently towards me. Her arm is wet.

'Kirsty, it's me,' I whisper.

She moans louder this time.

'Sshh. We have to be quiet or he'll find us.' My voice is barely audible but she nods. She has a black band of fabric tied around her eyes and a gag in her mouth. Shall I cut it with the knife? No, I might hurt her. I fumble with the knot, my fingers clumsy with panic and my mind racing. How long has she been here? Is she badly injured? Did he rape her? At last the fabric loosens around her face and I manage to remove the gag. She takes in a huge gasp of air and I lean down to whisper in her ear.

'Stay quiet. I'll untie you then we'll get out of here.' I sound calm but inside I'm in turmoil. Next, I work on the blindfold. This is difficult as her hair is caught in it but I untangle the silky strands and get it off without hurting her too much. Finally, I untie her wrists and feet, constantly looking up and listening, fully alert to any clue that Simon has found us. I can't see or hear any sign of him. Hopefully he'll have gone along the driveway thinking I've gone that way. Kirsty rubs her wrists and one ankle then nurses the other with both hands. She's sobbing softly. I wrap my arms gently around her and hold her. She's shivering.

'Are you injured?' I whisper. 'Can you walk?'

'I'm bleeding,' she whispers. 'He stabbed me.'

Shit. 'Where?'

'My arm. I was trying to protect myself. I've lost a lot of blood. I think I've broken my ankle as well.'

What will we do now? I think fast, then get on all fours facing the tree trunk. 'Can you climb on my back?'

She struggles towards me, her swollen ankle lifted from the ground. I feel her weight land on me and brace myself as she wraps her arms around me, one gripping more firmly than the other. She moans with pain.

'Hold on to me,' I whisper. I walk my hands, one over the other, up the trunk of the tree, pausing now and then and exhaling slowly with the effort of taking her weight. Once we're upright I wrap my arms around her legs and pull her in tighter. I stagger, then take a tentative step forward. I can do this. I'm going to save us. My knee is aching from my earlier fall. We've only gone a few yards when my legs wobble and my back screams in protest. How far is it to William's place?

I can't see much and I can no longer put my hands out in front of me. My toe hits a log and we sway precariously as I try to sidestep it.

'You're strangling me,' I whisper to Kirsty as her grip tightens around my neck. I can feel a trickle of blood running down my chest from her arm. I need to bandage it but I have to move her in case he comes back for her. I'm desperate to ask her what happened but I need to keep moving, to put some distance between us and the man who is after us. Is it Simon? It must be. Who else can it be? Julian. What if it's Julian? I stagger on, every muscle radiating pain throughout my body. 'Did you see who took you?' I ask eventually, panting with effort.

Kirsty's breath is warm and damp on my ear. 'No, he grabbed me from behind as I crossed the yard. He put a knife to my throat and told me he'd kill me if I tried to escape. I was so frightened.'

I feel her tears wetting my cheek. 'It's okay now. We'll be safe soon.' As I say this my foot disappears down a rabbit hole and we tip over sideways into leaf mould and soil. Despite the soft ground my left shoulder hits it hard and Kirsty grunts as the air is knocked from her lungs. She rolls off me with a whimper of pain. I don't think I can do this. She's too heavy for me. I'm not strong enough. I can't leave her behind though so I'll have to try once more.

'Shall I drag you to that tree? You need to get on my back again.'

I pull her under the arms but she whimpers in pain.

'Stop. Leave me here and go for help. Cover me with the leaves and I'll wait for you. Call me when it's safe and I'll call back. He won't find me and if he wanted to kill me he'd have done it earlier. It'll be quicker this way.'

She's right. It will be quicker. I'll call the police from William's place. Before I leave her, I take off my hoodie and T-shirt then put my hoodie back on. I need the pocket to conceal my weapons. I bind the T-shirt around her arm and tell her to press on it to stem the bleeding, then I cover her body with the leaves and lean down to kiss her cold cheek before placing a few bigger leaves on her face. The smell of damp undergrowth and last year's decomposing autumn is strong. 'I'll be as quick as I can. Stay quiet until you're sure it's me. If I call the word 'peng' you'll know it's safe to come out.'

Kirsty gives a weak giggle. 'Thank you for saving me, you're a true friend.'

I haven't saved her yet but I am a true friend, as she is to me. I feel terrible leaving her in agony and in the dark all alone. I should have known she wouldn't desert me. I should have raised the alarm when she disappeared.

I struggle on, completely lost, stumbling forward and catching glimpses of the moon which I try to keep over my right shoulder. I've heard tales of people going round in circles when they're lost. The woods suddenly seem vast and I feel like I've been trying to find my way out for ages. It's incredible that I heard Kirsty but then she was on a direct path from the house. Maybe whoever put her there didn't intend leaving her for long. I pause. Is that a glimmer of light through the trees up ahead? I push forward again but I'm impeded by a wall of brambles which scratch painfully at my bare hands and face and tether me by my clothes. I'll have to find a way around them. I go sideways, frustrated that I can see where I need to be but I'm unable to get there, when suddenly the trees thin out and I'm at the edge of the woods near the driveway and the small bridge. Thank God, thank God.

I look around before hurrying along the rutted track. Lights glow behind the diamond-paned glass of William's coach house, warm and inviting with the promise of safety. I run around the back of the building. William is still up and must be watching television. I can hear him laughing at something. I knock on the door, my heart beating with anxiety. I need to get help for Kirsty as quickly as possible.

William comes to the door and looks surprised to see me. I feel tearful with relief.

'Tasha! Is everything all right? You look terrible. What's happened?'

I squeeze past his chair and into his lounge. 'Shut the door, quickly. There's someone after me.'

He pokes his head out of the door and looks from left to right then backs up his wheelchair and presses the button to shut the door. I run into the lounge then turn to him.

'Where's your phone? I need to call the police.'

He doesn't reply. He has a strange expression on his face as though he's not in control of his features. Is he having a stroke? Is he as frightened as me? He puts his hand behind his back and pulls something out. I realise he's holding my missing kitchen knife. 'Where did you–' My words shrivel and die as his face contorts. My confusion turns to horror as William gets to his feet and rocks my world out of orbit.

Chapter 55

'Hello Tasha.' His voice is different – harsh, mocking and cruel. Is it the one I heard in the cupboard? A shiver runs through me. I don't understand and my brain can't register what I'm seeing and hearing. I stand and stare, trying to make sense of it. This can't be true. William wouldn't hurt me.

'Wondering how I got inside the cupboard?' he asks me, and I nod, shock numbing my brain of all rational thought.

I look at his legs and see a cut in the grey fabric of his jogging bottoms with a circle of blood around the hole. It is him. I stabbed him.

'Andrew and I used to have great fun tricking visitors with the secret staircase.' He chuckles.

'Secret staircase?' I echo, my voice sounding hollow and far away.

'It's hidden behind the bookcase in the small office near the kitchen. I came in the scullery and went straight up the stairs. It comes out behind the wardrobe you hid in. It was built for the servants to use years ago to take bathwater and coal upstairs but we put the cupboard there and took the back off it.' He looks pleased with himself. 'I thought you might try to hide and I was going to listen where you went. I couldn't believe my luck when you hid in there with me. Saved me looking for you – although that would have been part of the fun.'

'You can walk?' I ask. A stupid question as he's taken two steps towards me, my kitchen knife still pointed at my chest. I'm reminded of my recurring nightmare on the railway bridge, and my knees weaken.

'Yep, and run and play football. "*Ooh, poor little William*," he chants in a mocking high-pitched voice, "*how awful for you to be disabled. Let me know if I can help.*" Where do you think I've been disappearing to all these times, eh? I had to go out of the area so I could walk about and run. In fact, when this is over I might even climb Kilimanjaro. I've always fancied doing that. Yes.' He pauses as though deep in thought. 'It's been hard being confined to the wheelchair but hey, the payoff was worth it.' He gets closer and I walk slowly backwards until the sofa is pressing into my calves.

'But why?' I'm so stunned I can't form whole sentences. Nothing adds up and my mind races around for an explanation.

'Why pretend? So I can be William, my dear girl. The wonderful William who was loved by everyone – almost as much as my nauseating brother Andrew was.'

Simon, Jesus, he's Simon. 'But where's the real William?'

'Taking a long dip in the lake. You'll be joining him soon. And your pal, Kirsty. She's just waiting to be collected for the pool party. She'll be along later.' He laughs at his own joke.

'But Bob recognised you as William.' *He wants to kill me. Think. Think.*

'I haven't seen him for thirty years and you told him I was William so why would he question it? We always did look similar as boys. People used to think William was Andrew's brother. They spent all their time together and shut me out. Do you realise how lonely this place can be?' He gives me a penetrating look. 'Yes, of course you do.'

How can I overcome him? He's so much stronger than me. I've got a knife but his is bigger. Can I move quicker than him? Can I keep him talking? 'Is all this about my inheritance?'

'*My* fucking inheritance!' Simon flushes red and his eyes bulge with anger. 'I'm a more direct descendant than you are. Your frigging father came to see me in prison, feeling benevolent and offering forgiveness after his cancer diagnosis. Trying to tie up loose ends, he said. I didn't want his forgiveness. I just wanted my share of the inheritance. But no, it all went to him, old golden bollocks, and he had a foolish longing to do the old place up – restore it to its former glory. Pah! It was never glorious to me. He even told me a local property developer had offered good money for it. Just rubbing salt in the wound like he always did, the smug bastard.'

'What makes you think you'd inherit if I died? Surely it would go to Reuben.'

'Not unless you'd married him or written him into your will. He said you didn't want to bring the wedding forward but when he told me you'd promised to sort out your will I thought it was time to act.'

I need another question. Think Tasha! 'Was Gripper at the same prison as you?' I don't need to ask him if he had my father killed. I already know the answer. *Is there something I can throw at him?* I look around the room but it's sparsely furnished.

'Cell mate. He'll cut me into pieces if I don't pay him. He isn't called Gripper for nothing. I just need you out of the way so I can challenge the will. A spacious, modern house and a yacht. That's all I want. Oh, and perhaps a few exotic holidays and a gambling fund.' A cold smile crosses his face.

Now I can't drag my eyes from the knife glinting in his hand. 'I'll share everything with you,' I say. *Just let me out of here. Let me get help for Kirsty. Who needs money when they're dead?*

'Like hell you will. Anyway, I don't want to share it, I want all of it. I wanted to find the money that was hidden too. I knew the old man had a secret stash somewhere. The sofa was a bloody stupid place to hide it though. Fucking mice.' He puts his hand down the side of an armchair and pulls out a length of rope. 'I knew you'd come here. It's been tremendous fun tormenting you but it's gone on long enough. Now Gripper's looking for me I need you gone. Put your hands out.'

Not a chance! I hunch my shoulders and thrust my hands into my pockets. I'm surprised when I feel the plastic pepper pot. I forgot that I'd shoved it in there as I ran through the kitchen. I need to keep Simon talking a bit longer. I need to loosen this lid as the holes in the top of the pot won't release enough pepper.

Don't let him see your hand move, I tell myself. *Another question, I need another question.* 'Why did you sleep in your old bedroom?' I ask. 'Why not the coach house?' I'm carefully twisting the lid from the pot with my fingertips in miniscule movements that he won't be able to detect.

'When you've slept in a cell that's only six feet by eight feet for nearly twenty years, the last thing you want is a poky coach house. I can't wait to get out of here either. I only stayed here because I had to as part of my cover story.' He looks around the room. 'I need space now.'

'How come the locals didn't know you'd stolen William's identity?' The lid comes off with a barely audible pop but I cough to cover it anyway.

'William found me staying at the Hall. Felt sorry for me which was a novelty for him. He was sick of people pitying him. That's why he avoided the village, which suited me. I had to make sure you didn't employ the same builders, though.'

I have the pot of pepper in the palm of my hand. I inch my arm back slowly so he won't notice. 'And did you put a rat on the coach house doorstep?'

'I did!' He smiles at the memory.

So I wasn't going mad. I feel a wave of relief but it's short-lived.

'Reuben told me about the Rigbys and the mice on your doorstep in Luton when he watched the football here. He said you were running away from trouble. I wanted you to think they'd found you.' He chuckles softly. 'I thought the cat was a nice touch too. Did it give you a fright?'

He's really proud of himself, this evil man. He's killed my father and the real William, abducted Kirsty and made my life hell for months, making me think I was losing my mind. I feel anger building in my chest and welcome it. Anything is better than fear. The pot is at the edge of my pocket and I'm ready for him.

'You tampered with the scaffolding.' I picture him watching it collapsing and try to recall his exact expression after it had happened. Had I mistaken excitement for amazement?

'Shame Michael was back so soon. I was hoping to disrupt the building work longer than that.'

'You total low life! No wonder your mother didn't love you.' My anger has risen like bile in my throat and I'm desperate to hurt him. *Come on, I'm ready for you now.* His face is contorting into strange shapes as he struggles with his conflicting emotions.

'I liked you, when you were William,' I continue. 'Perhaps you should have taken on another persona years ago. Maybe everyone wouldn't have detested you so much then. You're pathetic when you're yourself, a worthless specimen of the human race.'

Simon's mouth grimaces with rage. He lunges forward with the knife but I'm too quick for him. I step to the side, at the same time as throwing the contents of the pepper pot right into his face.

'Aaaargh! You bitch.' He clutches his face then frantically tries to rub his eyes clean with the bottom of his T-shirt.

I circle around behind him then shove him hard before pushing his chair away from the front door and jabbing at the button to open it. He falls onto the sofa then tries to clamber up again, one hand cupped over his eyes. I'm about to run through the door when I stop and go back to him.

He claws at the air as he hears me approach. Can I do this? I think of my father and William and of Kirsty hiding in the woods then I plunge my small knife deep into his other leg and pull it out again. He yells in pain. I should stab him in the heart or at least in the gut but I can't bring myself to do it. It would make me no better than a Rigby. I just need to stop him coming after me. I don't want to kill him – just disable him. I feel hysteria bubbling up in me at the irony and I almost laugh.

I race out of the gatehouse and onto the driveway. I could run back to Black Hollow for the old Renault but I can't face going back in the Hall for the keys. I'm not even sure where they are as I haven't driven that car since Reuben gave me the Ford Focus. I can still see an orange glow in the distance. I turn to the lane and begin to run down the road. It's difficult in the dark and I almost fall a couple of times as I get too close to the verge. It's over a mile to Lower Bramcote but it's the only civilisation around so I have to keep going. I need to get help for Kirsty before she loses too much blood.

I haven't got very far when I hear an engine starting. Oh no. He must have washed the pepper from his eyes and made it to the car. I should have stabbed him through the heart. I look behind me and see headlights through the trees. He's coming after me.

Chapter 56

I tumble over the verge and fall into a clump of stinging nettles growing in the ditch at the base of the hedgerow. The jagged leaves embed their poisonous hairs into my face, neck and hands but I daren't move. Prickling pain burns my skin. I see the lane grow brighter through my closed eyelids. Will he see me? Is he slowing down? I hear wheels catch soil and stones at the edges of the road then the car rushes past, sucking the air with it. I breathe a huge sigh of relief.

I wait until the sound is some distance away then sit up. I take out my little torch and quickly look at the base of the hedge for a gap big enough to crawl through. I cut the light instantly. There. I might be able to manage that space between two thick stems. I pull my sleeve over my hand and crush the stingers away with my forearm then crawl commando-style on my front with my hood up. It's a tight squeeze but I make it through and find myself in a corn field. Tall leaves wrapped around thick cobs of corn march in silent rows across to the horizon. I almost cry with relief. He won't find me in here. It's nearly as tall as I am. I run along the edge of the crop for several yards then slip sideways into the corn, trying not to leave any evidence of my route.

Once I'm in deeper I straighten up and run as fast as I'm able in the direction of the village, trying to push the corn cobs aside as I go. This cuts the corner off. The cobs bash into my chest like miniature baseball bats and my hands and face are burning from the stings but I keep going. I hear the car coming back down the lane and slowing to a crawl. I bite my lip and tense my stomach to trap the scream that's trying to escape. Can he see my silhouette through a gap in the hedge? I duck down and wait, breathing heavily. He cruises past slowly then on to the coach house. Blood pounds in my ears. What if he goes back for Kirsty? No, it's me he wants.

I start running again, a stitch like a knife under my ribs. I reach the other side of the field and make my way along the perimeter until I see an opening through the hedge to the next field. This one has a low-growing crop that I can't identify. I'm more exposed here and running is treacherous over the rough terrain. I can't risk spraining an ankle and my knee is throbbing. I can see village lights on the other side. Shall I cut across and risk him spotting me or shall I go around the edge?

I take the sensible, coward's route and hope it hasn't cost precious minutes of Kirsty's life. I strain my eyes to look ahead. Gardens. Thank God. I'm at the back of fences and lawns. One has a gate to the field so I carefully lift the latch and creep through and along the path. If my estimation is correct these should belong to the row of cottages before Bob's. I consider shouting and banging on doors to wake people up but they might be too scared to open the door and Simon might be back soon. I can't take that risk.

I make my way around the end cottage to the front then sprint along the pavement to Bob's cottage, my ears fine-tuned to the sounds behind me. I tear up his path then press the new code into the key safe and remove the key. I hear Bonnie stirring. She gives a sharp bark behind the door.

'Bonnie, it's me, sshhh.' I don't want her to scare Bob into thinking he's got a burglar. My hands are shaking so hard I drop the key with a clatter and Bonnie barks again. I scrabble for it with both hands. There it is. I let myself in, shut the door quietly then lean back on it and slide down to the floor with relief. Bonnie jumps on me and licks my face, delighted with my midnight visit.

'Bonnie?' I hear an anxious voice drifting down from the bedroom upstairs.

'Bob, it's me, Tasha. Sorry to wake you. Can I use the phone? It's an emergency.'

'What's happened?' he calls. I can hear him moving about and his bedroom light clicks on, illuminating the landing upstairs.

'I'll explain soon. Where's your phone?'

'Right by you in the hall.'

I look around and spot a dark green, dial-fronted phone sitting on a small table. How have I not noticed this before? I thought telephones like this could only be found in museums these days. I place my shaking finger in the plastic circle over the nine and pull the dial round. It purrs back to the beginning with agonising slowness.

* * *

The police take ages to arrive. I've checked Bob's doors and windows are secure and made him a hot drink. He's sitting at the table, his eyes round with shock as I pace about the kitchen and tell him what's been happening.

'Do you think it was Simon who pushed me over?' he asks and I stop abruptly, my mouth open with surprise. I hadn't even considered this.

'It probably was. He didn't want you telling me anything more about him. He didn't want his cover blown. It must have been such a shock for him when I said you were there. No wonder he didn't want to stop and talk to you.' I glance at my watch again. *Please, please get here soon!* I can't stop thinking about Kirsty shivering under the pile of leaves, terrified at being alone in the woods with a killer on the loose, her blood seeping from the gash in her arm.

I see a flashing blue light on the wall near the front door and rush out of the kitchen. Bob calls after me.

'They'll catch him again, you'll see.'

There's only one policewoman at the door. She registers my surprise.

'I'm PC Chapman. The others have gone straight to the coach house,' she says. 'I've come to fetch you. Can you show us where you left your friend? If she's bleeding heavily we can't afford to waste any time.'

'I'll wait up for you, Tasha.' Bob stands in the hall in his stripy cotton pyjamas looking small and defenceless, his back bent and his hand on Bonnie's collar.

I'm about to tell him to go back to bed as I hurry out of the door but what's the point? He won't be able to sleep. 'Keep the doors locked, Bob,' I say. 'Hang on! I need to put the key back in the key safe.' I rush out into the cool, dark night and put the key away so I can get back in later. Curtains in neighbouring houses are twitching as I get in the car. The blue light must have woken them.

My skin still tingles and aches from the nettle stings and I'm shocked at how painful a harmless looking plant can be. My back twinges from lifting Kirsty as I climb into the police car but my discomfort is nothing compared to hers. She must be in agony with her broken ankle. Alarm grips my stomach – even worse, she might bleed to death.

'We've been given the information from your initial call but tell me anything else you can think of that might help,' PC Chapmen says.

I describe the events in the woods again and she nods. A policeman approaches the car as we park along the driveway to Black Hollow Hall. 'No sign of Simon Harrington,' he says.

My heart lurches with fear. Where is he? Has he gone for Kirsty? Two other uniformed men are nearby, both holding large flashlights. PC Chapman gets out of the car and I follow suit. She hands me a flashlight. An ambulance is waiting on the verge, facing the gates for a swift departure. The crew hover nearby then are told to sit in their cab with the doors locked until the police return.

'Where did you exit the woods, Tasha? Can you retrace your footsteps?' one of the men asks me.

I look along the edge of the trees, trying to spot something that will trigger a memory.

'Wait.' I run along the driveway. 'I came out of the woods there. Just over the stone bridge. I remember thinking if I'd gone any further I'd have been in the stream.'

We enter the dark, silent woods. It's started to drizzle and water drips from the trees and runs down my neck like Kirsty's blood and tears. How will we ever find her? The police officers walk two in front and two behind me, shining light onto the ground.

'Here,' one of them says. Broken stems show where ferns have been trampled underfoot. I look ahead and see the gorse thicket.

'That way,' I say, pointing to the left. 'I had to go around the thorny patch.' It's fairly easy to see where I'd rushed through the undergrowth initially but then we reach an area of pine needles and sandy soil. The others stand still while I turn around and try to visualise my earlier pathway. 'I think I remember bumping into that fallen tree… or maybe it was a different one.' My voice tails off with uncertainty.

Simon will surely have fled the scene and the police are here so I'm safe. 'Kirsty?' I call. My voice carries through the still night. Finding my friend is all that matters now. 'Kirsty?'

A sudden gunshot cracks the air in two and echoes around the trees. Almost simultaneously a thud sounds by my ear and my face is showered with splinters of bark. Rough hands grab me and pull me to the ground. I lie there winded and frozen with fear, my heart knocking against my ribs. I've been shot at. He's still after me and now he's got a gun.

Chapter 57

'Assistance needed. Suspect has firearms. He's shooting at us.' PC Chapman's voice quavers as she talks into her two-way radio. She's as shocked as I am. They all switch off their torches and we're plunged into blackness. We crawl on our forearms into a clump of ferns and brambles that pull at our clothes and pierce our skin. Our heavy breaths mingle in our shared fear and I feel blood pulsing through my temples.

'Is the main house that way?' a constable asks me in a whisper. 'Where the shots came from?'

'I think so. I found Kirsty in that direction. He must be looking for her.' Is he using her to get to me or is he out to harm any women he comes across?

'How far did you move her?'

'I'm not sure. I carried her for several minutes before we fell.'

'He'll have a job to find her then. You've probably saved her life.'

If she survives losing so much blood, I think. *If any of us survive!* My stomach knots with fear but also tightens with anger.

'One of us will get you back out of the woods to safety, Natasha. This is too dangerous.'

'No! You need me. Kirsty needs me,' I whisper urgently. 'I promised I'd come back for her.'

I won't let him win.

A huge oak tree looms into my vision several feet away as the moon makes an appearance through the tree tops. 'I think she's over that way, the other side of that tree. We can crawl so he won't see us.' I don't wait. I crawl out of the thicket towards the oak tree on my hands and knees and hear the police team following close behind me. Another shot rings out but not as loud this time. It must be further away. What's going on? Is Kirsty trying to escape the woods? A dip in the ground and a clearing suddenly look very familiar and I have to stop myself standing up and rushing forward.

'Peng,' I call softly. I see PC Chapman turn to me. She probably thinks I'm going nuts. 'It's our password,' I explain. There's no reply so I call again and listen.

A barely audible voice carries on the light breeze. 'Peng.'

My heart bursts with joy. She's alive! I feel my throat closing with emotion and tears spring to my eyes. The police run with heads down and knees bent to the source of the voice and I'm close behind them. The leaves move and Kirsty's arm and face are revealed. She sees me and reaches for me. I wrap her in my arms and rock her gently as her body convulses with sobs.

'Maybe we should wait here for the firearms team,' a young policeman says.

PC Chapman takes Kirsty's pulse. 'No, we need to get her to the ambulance straight away. Her pulse is weak and he might come looking for her.'

It seems to take ages to get Kirsty to the ambulance. It's too risky for someone to stand and carry her so she has to lie across the broad back of a policeman who crawls and shuffles his way across the woodland floor, muttering in pain occasionally as he puts his hand on something sharp. I crawl alongside them. I don't want to leave her side. When we finally get to the edge of the woods we all run to the vehicle. The ambulance crew rush to open the doors and Kirsty is carried inside. There isn't time to load her onto a stretcher. Simon might still be lurking somewhere with his shotgun. I climb in behind her and soon we're zipping along the narrow lanes and on to the nearest hospital. I clutch Kirsty's hand like a lifeline. I try to focus on her so that I don't need to think about the terrible happenings of this long, dark night but I'm worried Simon will follow us to the hospital. He's clearly a nutjob and doesn't understand the game is up.

We reach the hospital and Kirsty is taken away for treatment. I sit in a side room following a brief check-up but my mind is still on high alert. Everything plays on a loop in my brain like a video clip on repeat. PC Chapman sits beside me, guarding me. I should feel reassured but she'd be no match for an armed madman. Her radio crackles and she presses a button and listens to it. The armed response team have found Simon at the edge of the woods near the house. I leap up from my chair and stare at her.

'He has a severe head wound and he's been shot in the back by his own gun,' the disembodied voice continues.

I have a strong urge to laugh. I think I'm a bit unhinged. 'Is he dead?' I ask.

PC Chapman shakes her head. 'No. They'll bring him here for emergency treatment.'

I feel as though I have no substance and I'm floating like a helium balloon. He's coming here but he's injured. Am I safe? I must be. He's too injured to come after me and he'll be guarded by the police. I sit down again. *Shot? By who?* Everything suddenly clicks into place. I tug PC Chapman's sleeve and she looks at me quickly then looks away again, still deep in conversation with the caller.

'Gripper must have got him,' I say.

She stops talking. 'Gripper?'

She asks the caller to hold while I explain then she relays the information. Now they're looking for Gripper. I don't think he'll come after me though, and he's unlikely to get far.

A young nurse with a tight, bouncy pony tail and warm brown eyes approaches me and I stand up.

'Natasha? Your friend Kirsty is being admitted overnight for observations. She's had a blood transfusion and stitches but we still need to plaster her ankle. You can come and see her quickly before she goes to the ward then I expect you'll want to go home to bed.'

Home? Where is home? I feel as though I'm in a rowing boat in the middle of a storm. Cast adrift with no oars and no land in sight. Where is a safe harbour?

'Are you all right?' The nurse looks at me with a worried frown.

'Yes.' I give myself a mental shake. 'Which way?' I follow her brisk, trim form along a cream-painted corridor then into a large room with curtained-off cubicles. She sweeps aside the green fabric to reveal a bed and a chair. Kirsty is lying with the sheet and thin cotton blanket up to her chin. Her eyes are closed and her face is deathly pale but as she hears me approach her eyes fly open and she gives me a weak smile.

'Tasha!' She lifts her hand towards me and I rush forward to grasp hold of it and perch on the edge of her bed.

'I'm so relieved you're okay,' I say. 'I've been so worried about you.'

'I'm only okay because you moved me. He came looking for me, didn't he? You're so brave, Tasha. The bravest person I know.'

'I only did what anyone else would have done.' I don't feel brave at all. I think this might knock my confidence even further. *How can I trust anyone again when I'm so bad at judging characters? How will I feel safe in the dark?*

'A lot of people would have put their own safety first. Where will you go now? Not back to Black Hollow Hall, surely.'

'Definitely not. I don't ever want to stay there again. I might offer it to Julian after all. He's right about it being too isolated as a single dwelling. If it's divided into apartments the new occupants will have neighbours.'

'Won't you be sad to see it carved up? After all, it's part of your family history.'

'I've only met one member of the family and he's an evil bastard. I doubt they were all like that but they were certainly dysfunctional. I'm sorry not to ever meet my real parents but I feel no emotional tie to Black Hollow Hall now. I keep thinking about those bones lying in the grounds all those years. I should have asked Simon about them. I still don't know if they're my mother's remains.' The fear and horror of the night is pressing in on me and now the adrenaline has gone I feel suddenly weak. My eyes prickle and I blink away the tears then I straighten my shoulders and swallow. 'But I'm going to look forward now.'

I stand up and tug my sweatshirt down. 'Bob's waiting for me. I'm going to ask if I can sleep on his sofa for a few hours. I'll come and get you when you're well enough to be discharged. I can use the old Renault – if you can fit in it with your cast on – then maybe we can stay in a B&B while I wait for Reuben to come back from Budapest and we decide on the future.' To heck with the expense.

She puts her head back and closes her eyes again. She looks exhausted. 'Sounds like a plan. The Renault will be fine. I can put the seat back and it won't be a full leg cast. I might go and stay with my parents for a while until I feel better. Will you go back for my pillow?'

'What, now?'

'No,' she chuckles softly. 'I'll manage for one night. I'll need all my stuff as well. The police took my clothing for forensics and these hospital nighties aren't great for my street cred.'

I smile at her but my heart sinks as I realise we don't know where her clothes are. What did Simon do with her belongings?

'I'll go back to the house in daylight when the workmen are there and sort everything out.'

After hugging Kirsty goodnight I wait outside the A&E reception area for a taxi. Even though it's 3am there are still people milling about. A young man wearing a fake leather jacket and tatty trainers lurches towards me. I smell the alcohol on him from five metres away. He has a fresh bandage on his hand.

'Hello darling. Fancy kissing this better for me?'

I step away from him and wait nearer the entrance.

'Snooty bitch,' he mutters under his breath. He sways towards me again then grasps my sleeve with his good hand.

'I need a tenner for a taxi.' He breathes fumes over me and I try to back away but he won't let go.

I don't know where it comes from but I feel an overwhelming sense of self-preservation. I've had enough of being pushed around and pursued by others. I won't let it happen again. I pull myself up to full height and shove him hard in the chest. He staggers back in surprise and drops his hands to his sides.

I walk away then turn back to him. 'Fuck off, creep!' I say.

His mouth goes slack and his eyebrows shoot up then he shrugs and looks away. 'Whatever,' he says and shuffles back indoors.

As I walk to the waiting taxi I hold my head high and smile. Kirsty would be so proud of me. I am Natasha Hargreaves and I'm not going to be intimidated by low-life thugs anymore.

Chapter 58

'Are you sure you don't want me to come with you?' Reuben asks.

'Definitely.'

'I imagine those places can be quite scary,' he persists.

'I'll be fine.' I need answers and I'm determined to do this on my own.

'Can I come over later? I thought perhaps I could stay for the weekend and come back to Luton on Monday.'

'I don't know when I'll be back and I'm taking Bob and Bonnie to visit Jim tomorrow. I thought you were going out with your mates?'

'I'd rather see you, Tash.'

'Sorry, I've made plans. Maybe you can come over next weekend. I'll call you when I get back and let you know how the visit went.' As I hang up I feel a twinge of guilt at the abrupt way I've spoken to Reuben but I still haven't fully forgiven him for letting me down and abandoning me when I needed him. All those months of fear, justifiable fear too, that he dismissed as paranoia. He almost had me believing it. If he'd been more supportive about the Rigbys I'd have told him about the happenings at the Hall and he might have protected me better. He left me to cope on my own, so now I am. I don't need him.

I grab my jacket and keys then leave the small cottage and hurry down the path. I'll nip in to see Bob before I go. As I shut the gate I admire the display of late yellow roses framing the pale-green front door. I like this little cottage. I've only been here eight weeks but I'm settled and far enough away from the Rigbys to feel relatively safe. I'm grateful to Julian for telling me about this rental place and thankful that the solicitor agreed the rent could be paid from the renovation funds. I can manage the project from here and don't have to stay on my own in the coach house.

I walk along the road and within minutes I'm at Bob's front door. I can hear Bonnie's excited bark as soon as I open the gate. She must recognise my footsteps.

'Do you want me to come with you?' Bob asks. 'I could wait in the car with Bonnie.'

'It could take ages and I need to do this on my own, but it's sweet of you to offer.' I give him a quick kiss on the cheek and he squeezes my arm. 'I'll come and tell you all about it later,' I say.

I slip behind the wheel of my new Volkswagon Polo and set my sat nav to Milton Keynes. As I drive along the country lanes I wonder what lies ahead. I'm still surprised that I received a reply to my letter but then we both have something the other wants.

Two hours later I pull into the car park and cut the engine. I lean my head back and close my eyes, trying to relax the tight muscles in my neck and shoulders. *Right! You can do this, Tasha.* I follow the signs to the Woodhill visitors centre and sign in, then join the queue for security. A woman behind me has a hacking cough and I resist the urge to cover my nose and mouth with my hand. Up ahead I see a guard walking up and down the line of people with a large Alsatian. The woman behind me starts to moan.

'I don't feel well,' she says. 'I think I might faint.'

She rushes off, her thin arm thrusting open the door to the ladies' cloakroom. A female security guard runs after her. I look around in puzzlement.

'Carrying drugs,' the large man in front of me says. 'She wasn't expecting the dogs here today.' He looks me up and down and I cringe at his direct gaze. 'I hope you're clean. If the sniffer dog sits next to you, you're in trouble. First time here?'

I nod. I feel vulnerable in this alien world of criminals and relatives of criminals but then I realise to my shame that I'm one of them. Maybe Reuben was right and I should have let him come with me. It's all very well being independent but it's hard at times.

I reach the desk where I have to remove my jewellery and hand over my handbag for storage until I leave. I give the guard the items of clothing I was asked to bring and involuntarily flinch as I see the Pink Floyd tour T-shirt. I follow the directions through to a large, open room furnished with tables and chairs that are bolted to the floor.

The edge of the hard chair digs into the back of my legs as I sit and wait for the prisoners to emerge from the holding bay. There are numerous officers around the room watching people as they prepare to meet their loved ones who have been incarcerated at Her Majesty's pleasure. The first few prisoners file through wearing brightly-coloured tabards and weave their way across the room towards their relatives and girlfriends. Some are grinning, while others look away as soon as eye contact is made. I watch a man briefly hug a woman and kiss their small baby on the forehead.

I wait as time stretches away. The chair opposite me remains empty. Where is he? When he replied to my letter he promised to see me in exchange for money. Is this another cruel attempt to torment me? I wrap a hair around my finger and pluck it out as I stare at the door, willing him to appear. A man pushes a wheelchair through and I look over his shoulder to see if Simon is behind him then look back at the man in the wheelchair. He has short hair and is clean shaven but his eyes are familiar. A cold wave of shock travels from my head to my feet as I suddenly realise it's Simon and for a bizarre moment I think it has all been a bad dream and it's really William. The wheelchair gets closer and the officer manoeuvres it to the side of the table. I edge away but I see the security guards watching. Surely Simon won't try to attack me now?

'Hello Tasha.'

I flinch as I recall the last time he said that but thankfully he's speaking normally. The officer steps back and stands a few feet away.

'Surprised to see me in a wheelchair?' Simon asks.

I nod. Surely he's not still pretending to be disabled? I look down at his feet then stare in horror as I realise his legs end below the calf. He has no feet. What's happened to him?

'You did this to me, you bitch!' He whispers the last two words so that only I can hear them.

'Me? But weren't you attacked by Gripper?'

'A flesh wound and concussion. No, you did this. The knife wound in my leg got infected and I got sepsis. I'll be in a wheelchair for the rest of my life. I hope you're pleased with yourself.'

I don't know what to think. Am I pleased? Is this karma? I feel a weight of sadness descend on me at the wasted lives and futility of greed. I swallow. 'I'm here to ask you about my mother, Sally.'

'Have you transferred the money?'

'Some, yes.'

'How much?'

'Fifty pounds.'

'Is that it?' His voice rises in pitch and I see several pairs of eyes swivel in our direction. He looks from left to right and lowers it again. 'I need more. I need it for the canteen – we have to buy our own toiletries and extra food items.'

'You'll get more if you give me information.' I'm beginning to feel in control now. I can get up and walk out of here at any time. Simon can't even walk. 'Please, just tell me – was that my mother I found in the grounds of Black Hollow Hall?' The police haven't been able to identify the remains but if it is my mother's skeleton, I'd like to give her a proper burial.

Simon opens his mouth then hesitates. His voice softens. 'I didn't mean to kill her. I loved Sally. I was trying to stop her running away after you were taken off her. I grabbed her and she tried to scream so I put my hand over her mouth.' He shakes his head roughly. 'I tried to give her the kiss of life. It was all your fucking father's fault. He took everything that was mine, even my mother. We were a happy family until he came along.'

I stare at him, tears springing to my eyes. Poor Sally. My poor mother – how terrible to die so young and in such a violent way. Simon watches my face and waits for me to say something but I can't speak for a minute. I need to absorb what he's said. The weight of sadness I feel gets heavier and sits in my chest like an ominous growth. I'll never meet her now. 'But why did you want to hurt me? Surely if you loved Sally you wouldn't harm her child?'

'But you're not just Sally's, are you? You're fifty per cent fucking Andrew.' He straightens his back. 'Anyway, is that it? Have you got what you came for?'

'I'll need you to write a full confession for the police so that I can arrange her funeral as next of kin.'

'In for a penny in for a pound,' he says flippantly. 'One more crime isn't going to make much difference, is it?' His mouth is a tight line as he looks around the hall at the prisoners and police officers.

'One last question. Did you hide the locket up the chimney?'

Simon looks at his hands in his lap then back at me. 'It broke when I grabbed her. I had to get rid of it but I couldn't bring myself to throw it away. I used to look at it from time to time. I've spent a lifetime regretting what I did to Sally.'

He has some compassion in him then. I stand up and look down at him but can't muster up any pity or understanding for him. 'I'll transfer another £200 to your account as agreed then I want nothing more to do with you.' I turn and walk away. I can feel his eyes on me but I don't look back.

* * *

'What will you do now?' Bob asks me as we sit in his kitchen sipping hot tea. He knows I've been waiting for answers and needed time to think everything through before making any decisions.

'I'm going to organise a decent funeral for my mother then I'm going to get Black Hollow Hall valued for a possible sale to Julian.'

'I can't believe you're going to give up on the old place, Tasha, after all you've been through. Are you going to let go of your dreams so easily? What about all your plans for a family business?'

'I… I don't feel comfortable there anymore. It has too many bad memories.'

'Then replace them with good memories,' Bob says. 'The house isn't to blame. It's the people who are in it that are important and it had so much potential, you said so yourself. And what about Reuben? Have you forgiven him?'

'I'm not sure that I can yet. He put his job before my safety and peace of mind. I need to think about what's good for me now. I still have feelings for him though, so I'm going to take things slowly for a while. Give him a chance to prove himself. There's another four months tenancy on my little cottage and the counselling has helped with the nightmares so I'm better at coping on my own.'

'Well, I'm glad to have you nearby and I've got some ideas I'd like to share with you.' Bob smiles at me and gets up. 'I've got a nice bit of shortbread too.'

As he peers into a cupboard my phone rings and Reuben's name is displayed. I excuse myself and walk into the hall. Bonnie trails behind me with her lead in her mouth.

'I was going to call you soon,' I say. 'I'm with Bob now.' I bury my fingers into Bonnie's soft fur and she leans against my leg.

'I've just seen the local news, Tash, and had to call you straight away.' He's speaking fast and sounds excited. 'Lewis Rigby has been charged with grievous bodily harm with intent and he's been refused bail. He's off the streets and he'll be put away for at least five years.'

I feel weightless and I'm too shocked to speak.

'Tash? Did you hear me? You're safe now.'

'I am, aren't I?' I'm laughing and crying at the same time. It's over. It's finally over. I can register myself at a new address without fear of Lewis Rigby tracking me down. 'I'm not coming back to Luton though.'

Chapter 59

Ten months later.

I stare down at the outline of a body drawn in chalk on the stone-flagged floor of the hall. The yellow crime scene tape flutters around it in the draft from the front door where Reuben and his father are carrying in boxes of wine. 'That's brilliant!' I say to the man in police uniform who stands next to it ticking things off on his clipboard.

He smiles. 'Wait until you see what else we've got in store for your guests.' He bends down and fishes items out of a box at his feet then waves a pair of handcuffs at me.

I laugh and make my way through the sitting room to the library which has been requisitioned as the incident room. Display boards with photos, family trees, letters and newspaper clippings are dotted around the room and a table is scattered with documents and background information. Everything is ready for our first murder mystery weekend. We have eight paying guests plus two whom I refuse to charge. Mum and Dad have done a brilliant job of persuading their numerous friends from the cruise ship to stay for the weekend. All the guest rooms will be occupied and I've had a busy week adding the finishing touches with fresh flowers and luxury toiletries.

I retrace my steps and walk through the drawing room, admiring the restored sofas and soft furnishings. I need to check the dining room. I stand and catch my breath. The huge table is covered in pristine white cloths and laden with shining silver cutlery and crystal glasses. Two huge candelabras hold white candles aloft and silver bowls display fat pink roses. It looks stunning.

'How's Mum coping in the kitchen?' Reuben asks as he lines the red wine up on the sideboard and begins to uncork it.

'I'm on my way there to find out but I'm sure she'll have everything in order,' I say. 'She's in her element catering for a large group of people.'

'I know. She always cooks for twenty even when there are only six of us.' Reuben laughs.

In the kitchen Margaret is taking a large tray of freshly baked rolls from the AGA. They smell delicious and my stomach rumbles. She beams at me and wipes her red face on her upper arm. The kitchen must be ten degrees warmer than the rest of the house.

'How are you getting on? Do you need a hand?'

'All under control. Lily's a great help.' She beams at a thin girl that we've employed from the village to help with the catering. Margaret touches her young assistant on the shoulder, who grows an inch taller, then continues to fill small plates with a trio of smoked fish and salad garnish. Margaret glances at the huge clock on the wall. 'Six o'clock. Dinner's at eight, you say? What time are the guests arriving? Lily will bring out the canapés half an hour before dinner is served.'

Margaret has really done us proud with her catering skills and she loves her new job. Years of cooking for the family and trying new recipes have given her the skills required to provide the catering for our murder mystery weekends and bed and breakfast trade. She wants to start with the wedding feasts soon but realises that may be a step too far so we're arranging for an agency chef to work alongside her.

'They'll be here soon. I thought I'd give them time to settle into their rooms before the actors begin their scenes.'

I look around the cosy kitchen at the copper pans, traditional kitchen units and granite worktops and my chest expands with happiness. It's unrecognisable from the dark and dusty place where I was so frightened. In fact, the whole house is unrecognisable – bright, warm and full of love and laughter. Reuben's parents had jumped at the chance to move out of Luton to live in the coach house and his sister, Jessica, and nephew, Alfie, are frequent visitors. Reuben's dad loves the sit-on mower and is managing the grounds and general maintenance really well. Not that the Hall needs much maintenance at the moment as the builders did a brilliant job. I ran out of money before we could resurface the long driveway and rebuild crumbling garden features but we have plenty of ideas for bringing in an income. We have tenants in the gatehouse and regular visitors for bed and breakfast so the place is always busy and full of people.

Bob has even brought his own ideas to our business ventures by organising educational weekends for gardening enthusiasts. I'm astounded by his knowledge and I'm learning a great deal. He might be limited physically but his brain is still as sharp as flint. We've drawn up designs for a new rose garden to be dedicated to my mother and grandmother and we're even creating a maze in the grounds for children to enjoy. Not an inch of the property is wasted. We have a dog agility training course in the meadow which the local dog trainer rents from us, fishermen using the lake and there's paint-balling in the woods. I'm never alone here and it's so wonderful to live my life without fear. I sleep well at night, don't pull my hair anymore and definitely have no symptoms of paranoia.

I step outside into the paved yard and walk around to the front to stand on the lawns and admire the house. It looks incredible and it's hard to believe it's mine. I hope my father would be proud of me and what we've achieved here.

Reuben walks out of the front door and crosses the lawn to stand beside me.

'You've done a brilliant job with everything, Tasha. I'm so proud of you. Black Hollow Hall has probably never looked so beautiful.'

'You've been fantastic organising it all. I just make everything look nice.' I smile at him.

Reuben's experience of setting up festivals has really come into its own here. We have so many events lined up over the next few months, from weddings and corporate team builds to cookery and art weekends. He says this is similar to his old job in lots of ways but it's even more rewarding because it's for ourselves and we don't have to put up with annoying work colleagues.

'I still think we could host a rock concert or a rave,' he says with a teasing grin.

'No way! We'll stick with the classical evening and the jazz night.' I sweep my gaze across the grounds and Reuben senses the change in my mood. He's so much more perceptive these days.

'What's up, Tash?'

'Do you think this murder mystery evening is disrespectful to my mother and grandparents?'

'Not at all. If you were exploiting the fact that terrible things happened here then it would be different. This is just a light-hearted event. You've shown your mother how much you respected her, Tasha. The funeral service was beautiful.'

'It was, wasn't it?' I smile at the memory. The whole village had turned out to pay their last respects when we'd buried my mother's remains next to my father's in the churchyard. It had been a moving but emotional day. The best part for me though, had been meeting Sally's sister Lynn. I now have an auntie and we plan to meet up regularly. She has three children so I've gained cousins too. An instant family and none of them law-breakers.

Deep water diving equipment had been brought in by a team of six divers from the police underwater search unit. It had taken two days to find William and another two weeks for the post-mortem but we'd finally been able to organise a local burial for him as well. I met his frail, elderly mother who was devastated by the loss of her son but grateful to us for sorting out the funeral. The people in the village and surrounding areas have embraced us into their community and promote our business venture at every opportunity.

'We make a great team, Reuben,' I say. 'Shall we make it legal?'

His brow furrows then he turns his head to look directly into my eyes. 'Are you asking me to marry you at last?'

'Yes, I think I am. I'm ready for the future now and I'd like you by my side.'

Reuben lifts me up in the air then kisses me on the mouth. 'Let's go and tell everyone!'

'We can announce it later,' I say. 'The guests will be here soon.' I take his arm and inhale the scent of jasmine and honeysuckle as we cross the threshold of our amazing home and business venture. I've nothing to fear now. I can breathe properly at last.

THE END

Printed in Great
Britain
by Amazon